ALSO BY EMILY SENECAL

Strangers on This Road
Danger in Academia
Enemy at the Wedding
The Heartbroken Brides
Death on the Menu
The Night Ferry
The Missing Tourist
Beneath These Streets
Murder on Santorini
An Empty House
Saints and Enemies
In a House of Strangers
The First Time We Met
The Element of Truth

BOOKS IN THIS SERIES

Dark Web of Deceit

spiders in a dark web

EMILY SENECAL

This novel is set in real places, but this is a work of fiction. Names, characters, businesses, places, events and incidents are either the products of the author's imagination or used in a fictitious manner.

ISBN-13: 978-1793435538

Cover Image © _media_ on Reshot
Cover artwork by ems

To Al, with love

chapter 1

If I'd known it was going to be the last day of life as I knew it, I would have done a few things differently. Woken up early instead of late, giving myself time to get ready instead of rushing around my apartment, hairbrush in hand, throwing on whatever clean clothes I could find. Ordered that chocolate croissant when I picked up my daily coffee. Spent less time sulking in my cubicle and chatted with the few coworkers I didn't dislike. Eaten lunch anywhere other than at my desk.

I would have packed the essentials. Been ready when Marianne called.

But that's all moot at this point. I didn't order the croissant, and I wasn't ready. Her call, the ringing of my phone that afternoon and my eager reach to answer, set off an explosion in my life. Sent it on a wildly new trajectory, without any of the comforting sign posts and landmarks that had led me to where I was when it all started.

I can't regret what happened. Those chaotic weeks threw me in a direction, and landed me in a situation, that would have been unimaginable before. Now I can't imagine life any other way.

It did come with a cost, as most gifts will; a cost apart from disorientation, discomfort and distress. There are things, now, I wish I could forget. Could Lysol wipe out of my memories. Because now that it's over, *I don't want to know what I know.* I don't want to carry it around like a ticking bomb, a grenade with the pin pulled out, always conscious that it could go off and destroy everything I care about.

It might be powerful, this knowledge. I'd still rather not have it.

I couldn't ever regret where I ended up, or consider going back to the way things were. Stumbling through days and weeks and months of low-grade discontent in a job I didn't want, a world that didn't fit, wanting what I didn't have. Not even knowing what I really wanted—until it had tumbled into my hands.

Life was simpler, and far less dangerous. But I wouldn't go back.

■ ■ ■

I slowly turned onto the narrow, dusty lane, deeply rutted with dried puddles, hedged in by thickly growing grass, shrubs and the occasional late-blooming spring wildflower, the wheels of my car thumping unhappily on the unpaved road. In the distance I could see a small grove of towering oaks, strong and vital in spite of their size and age, with a rocky hillside rising immediately behind. This was my destination, the place I'd be indefinitely calling home. My windows were rolled down, allowing a cool, fresh breeze to blow across my face. It mingled with the dust stirred up by my tires.

After about a quarter of a mile of thumps and bumps, I arrived at a rickety wood and wire gate spanning the road, part of a fence of the same materials surrounding the small property. I got out and opened the rusty padlock with the key I'd been sent, pushing the gate open before driving through. Immediately the bright sunlight was severed by the dark, deep shadow of the oaks. Five mammoths who'd grown up or been planted together at the edge of the foothills, their branches stretching unbelievably far from their trunks, mingling peacefully together high above me.

I stopped the car in the center of the grove and got out. I stood in a small yard, as dusty as the road but tidy enough, housing a tiny whitewashed shed and several bulky stacks of unknown items covered by tattered tarps. My eyes drifted around, taking everything in, before I allowed myself to focus on the battered red camper.

I'd been here once as a pre-teen, visiting my father's friend Joe—Uncle Joe, we always called him. I vaguely remembered a hot afternoon spent exploring the grove, scrambling up the rocky slope above, sitting in lawn chairs around a shabby plastic table and eating salami and cheese sandwiches my mother had made that morning before we left home. It wasn't a long drive from San Mateo to Half Moon Bay, but I only remembered making it once. My father and Uncle Joe had laughed at jokes we didn't understand and reminded each other of stories out of the past, but Marianne and I weren't expected to listen. My mother drank a beer and smiled at them, maybe only half-listening. By the time the afternoon light began to wane, we were tired of exploring, and my parents drove us back home.

Now Uncle Joe was dead, and so were my mom and dad, and the camper and small property surrounding it were mine.

A perfect place to hide, Marianne had said, her voice tense. "They won't trace you there, Lo. You'll be safe."

A shiver travelled up my spine in spite of the warm day, and I glanced uneasily behind me.

Nothing. Nothing in sight but rolling hills and sudden, tree-lined gulches and knee-high grasses and dusty roads, the mountains to the east, the ocean to the west. There weren't many houses out here, a few farms; it was mostly preserved open space lightly crossed by power lines. Though the nearest farm's property came right up to my fence, they used the fields as grazing land for cattle and the occasional herd of goats. I'd seen both on my drive in.

There's nobody out there, I told myself, and tried hard to believe it. The anxious knot in my stomach thrummed softly at a low pitch of fear. Taking a deep breath to steady my nerves, clutching the set of unfamiliar keys in my sweaty hand, I closed the car door and went up to the camper.

It was an old one. I didn't know much about campers, but I could tell from the bullet shape that it wasn't made in the past few decades. For that reason it had a certain charm, in spite of the years of dirt and rain spatter on the outside, the scratched and faded red paint peeling off in places to reveal a dull metallic gleam beneath. There was no truck to pull it, but it didn't have any wheels to roll on anyway. It was firmly—I hoped—mounted on some kind of wood frame. One metal rung acted as a step for the door.

I unlocked and opened this, finding the latch a little stiff but manageable, and peered into the dark interior. It was stuffy, but smelled clean—like Pine Sol, like it had been cleaned and then shut up for a long time. Uncle Joe died two years ago, my father last year. As far as I knew, nobody had lived there since Uncle Joe was moved to hospice. Reassured by the homely smell of cleanser, I climbed inside and reached over to pull open the nearest window shade, the roller kind. It snapped out of my hand and flapped loudly upward around its roll, startling my already taut nerves into a jump of fright, my heart beating wildly. Even as I reacted this way, I started laughing—of all the things to be afraid of just now, a window blind was probably the most absurd.

It felt good to laugh—to feel my face expressing something other than worry. I quickly moved around the small space, raising the blinds at all the windows on either side, before taking stock of my sanctuary.

With a sudden rush of nostalgia and familiarity, I remembered this place. I had one of those sharp, clear memories of standing right here as a twelve-year-old, looking around the interior with delighted envy and appreciation. In two intervening decades, I'd completely forgotten this, forgotten how much I'd adored Uncle Joe's camper, forgotten how Marianne and I had played our teenage version of "house" in it—big city apartment—until my mother had driven us outside with reminders that this was Uncle Joe's home, not a playhouse.

It was a darling place, perfectly planned and proportioned, every convenient cupboard and drawer and seat fitting together with no wasted space, yet there was a smooth and luxurious aesthetic created by the curved, light wood that covered every surface but the counter and seats. I walked around touching things, as I had as a child. I knew that the couch slid out with satisfying clicks to form a double bed, revealing a secret cubby behind the back where blankets, sheets and pillows hid during the day, with shelves that could be used for holding nighttime water cups, books and reading glasses.

The bathroom at one end had a stainless steel toilet under a tiny steel corner sink, a white fiberglass shower wedged beside them. A small kitchenette, the counters covered in gleaming white Formica, had a sink, a stove with two burners, and a perfectly-fitted—and relatively modern—steel and glass fridge tucked beneath a counter. Cupboards stood ready to serve as a pantry, while others were fitted with clothing rods and shelves for shoes. Drawers were lined with clean white rubber mats.

Every surface shone. It was beautifully clean, and absolutely empty, no sign of its previous owner remained. Not a paperback left on the bookshelves, not a spice in the small cabinet above the stove fitted with spice racks. I remembered it being clean when we'd played here, but also lived in, cozy, with shelves full of worn books and towels hanging in the bathroom. Whoever had cleared the camper out when Uncle Joe was ill, or after his death, they'd done a thorough job of it.

Unlike the dingy outside, the stainless steel, light wood and white interior of the trailer was as bright and contemporary as an urban studio. I didn't know when Uncle Joe had bought it, or if he'd remodeled it himself, or how long he'd owned the land. The exterior, yard and all, gave an impression of decay, even poverty. Uncle Joe hadn't been wealthy, but between social security and an annuity, ending with his death, he'd apparently had enough to live on comfortably. He'd owned a battered pickup, as well, which he'd donated to a local shelter before he died. It was easy to see that outward appearances hadn't mattered to him, but comfort, and a beautiful home, had.

Though we'd only come as a family to visit Uncle Joe one time that I remembered, he'd been a regular visitor at our house, arriving once or twice a year with a net bag full of produce, a twelve-pack of Sierra Nevada beer and a delighted grin. Like the camper, his somewhat shabby, grizzled appearance, worn clothing and thickly bearded face disguised what was inside: a kind, intellectual soul. Marianne and I mostly went our own way when my parents entertained, but we liked Uncle Joe and enjoyed chatting with him over my mom's barbequed chicken with mashed potatoes, his favorite meal. He never asked us questions about schoolwork or teased us about boys, but instead wanted to know what books we were reading, what places we wanted to travel to, what we liked to imagine.

He'd been a nice man. My dad had gone downhill quickly after his old friend's death, only surviving him by seven months.

I tried the kitchen tap without any success, then realized that the power wasn't on and that it was needed, according to the pages of instructions that came with the keys, to run the pump to the well, which was visible as a squat metal tank behind the camper. Fortunately the instructions included how to turn the pump on, along with the pilot for the hot water heater and circuit breakers.

One of the saving graces of this place, in my mind and especially now that I planned to stay here, was that it was connected to the natural gas and electrical grids. Local gas and power lines crossed the property near enough to connect, while the well and filtration system provided clean water. I even had cell service, though it wasn't strong—only one bar showed on the cheap burner phone Marianne had handed me the last time I saw her.

I sat down at the booth-style table, feeling suddenly limp, exhausted and hopeless, the phone slack in my hand.

Where was Marianne? Was she all right? *Why hadn't she called?*

It had been three days. Three long, tiring days of driving from city to city, sleeping in my car in the corner of parking lots because it wasn't safe to register at hotels, buying gas and gas station food with the wad of cash she'd given me along with the phone, nervously checking the other customers, other cars, as if I knew who I was looking for.

As if I knew who might be coming for me.

It should only have taken about eight hours to drive here from LA, where I'd spent the last five years, but Marianne had insisted that I go north all the way to Sacramento first. I spent a few hours in a Wal-Mart parking lot in West Sacramento, panicked and cramped in my back seat, trying desperately to trust the world enough to close my eyes. The sun hadn't come up when I was already heading back south down I-80 and west through Napa, then circling back down to San Francisco and the South Bay for another restless night at an office building near SFO. Finally, today, sliding quietly through Pacifica and winding down Cabrillo Highway, past the city of Half Moon Bay, to the turnoff leading to Uncle Joe's.

I'd thought about stopping for supplies in Half Moon Bay, knowing I'd need much more than I had with me, but had wanted to make sure of my surroundings first. If the camper had turned out to be uninhabitable, it wouldn't have made sense to roll up with a trunk full of groceries. Now, it seemed, I'd need much more than food—towels and sheets, all the basic pantry items down to salt and pepper, hand soap and toilet paper.

All I had with me were some of my clothes and a few personal items I'd tossed frantically into a bag while Marianne stood by the door demanding we go *now*. My apartment—ugly and airless and featureless as it was—had at least been stocked with all the essentials. Marianne had given me a few thousand dollars in cash, which would last awhile. But how long was a while?

How long would I have to do this?

What had Marianne gotten herself into? What had she gotten *me* into?

All at once, the weight of everything seemed to fall on me heavily, to the point that I could barely breathe. Tears spilled down my cheeks, but I wasn't exactly crying. It was just too much. The fear—the strain—the confusion and questions and unknowns—the suddenness of my departure, leaving everything familiar all at once—my home, my job, my friends—disappearing from all of them, without any idea when I'd be able to go back.

If I'd be able to go back.

Which was silly. Ridiculous. Because how could I not go back? How could that be it? I'd have to give notice to end my lease, at least—cancel my utilities and Internet, pack up my belongings, sell or give away my IKEA furniture, change my contact address on all my accounts. I told my supervisor I had a family emergency back east—I don't know why I said that—and that I'd be gone at least a week. I'd have to quit, at some point, if only to salvage my chances of ever being hired again.

Marianne had said not to worry about any of it. She'd take care of it, she said—in the very same voice she'd used when we were kids and we broke something accidentally, or a challenging task needed to be done. "I'll take *care* of it, Lo. Don't *worry* about it."

But I always did worry. Worry that we'd get in trouble, worry that the spider would bite before it could be killed, that the knot would fail on the homemade swing.

And no matter how much I worried, I never let her fix or face or attempt whatever it was alone.

Those childish troubles and trials seemed so far off and empty now. Now, when Marianne herself was out there somewhere, vulnerable, unreachable, and involved in something dangerous.

Now, when I was desperately afraid for both our lives—and I didn't even understand why.

■ ■ ■

The Safeway in Half Moon Bay was busy with late afternoon shoppers, but I found the crowds comforting. I wasn't in a rush; what did I have to go back to? I took my time selecting what I needed, working off a mental list, circling back around the unfamiliar store until my cart was full. In the stationary aisle, I picked up a few paperbacks and magazines, knowing I'd go insane from boredom reading only the few ebooks already loaded on my tablet, until I was able to buy more. I'd already spent an hour in in a discount home goods store which I'd happened to pass on the way, stocking up on everything I'd need for the camper, so this would be my last stop before heading out of town again. Fortunately everything was on or visible from the main road, since I didn't have my phone to help me search or navigate and my refuge came without the convenience of wifi.

I had to show my ID for the wine and vodka, but figured it was safe enough—not that I really knew what was safe and what wasn't. Marianne had told me not to use any credit cards or register my name with any hotels or log into any of my accounts or contact anyone I knew. She'd turned off my phone and pocketed it, she'd given me strict instructions about how to get here and what to do if I saw someone acting suspicious—*run*. And call the one contact number on the burner phone for help— otherwise not to use the phone for any reason and not to pick up if it rang. The number, which I didn't recognize when I looked at it later, was programmed under the initial "M."

That was it. There hadn't been time for anything else. Not even for explanations. If I hadn't seen the fear in her eyes and known her so well, I wouldn't have believed her when she said we were in danger—desperate danger—and I had to trust her and do what she said.

Of course I trusted her, and I did believe her and followed every instruction. But that didn't mean I felt any less confused and conflicted about the whole thing.

If I'd been followed, if I was found, I didn't see how I could have helped it. So I flashed my ID at the checker and met her eyes when she verified my identity and started ringing up the booze. I wasn't a heavy drinker and didn't have aspirations about becoming one, but the alcohol would help take the edge off; off the edge of both the fear and the loneliness. I also didn't want to make frequent trips to town, if I could help it, so planned to make this supply of food and drink last a while.

It wasn't security I felt, as I turned out of the parking lot and back on Highway 1, but it was something akin to that, a pale copy of it. Nothing terrible had happened, I was stocked up on supplies, I'd made it safely. The power and plumbing were working. I had hot water and a door to lock myself behind. Nobody knew I was here.

Somewhere in a county office, my name was on a paper stapled to the deed of the property, but the slow grinding of bureaucracy and the timing of their deaths had kept first Uncle Joe's then my dad's estate in probate. The attorneys had been working to untangle the various threads, the property itself held in limbo until everything could be finalized. A few months ago, the attorneys had sent me the keys, along with basic instructions and copies of some of the legal documents, which I'd barely skimmed before shoving them back into the envelope. They'd continued to pay the insurance, the property taxes, and the utilities, which were minimal, out of Uncle Joe's small estate. He'd left just enough to cover the costs until the estate was settled, while my father's estate was covering the legal fees associated with the probate.

I couldn't sell the property or transfer ownership, I couldn't build on it or remove anything of value from it, but I could occupy it. I could hide here, for a while. Marianne was the only person I'd ever told that it had come to me.

The groceries were unloaded and about half of them put away when I heard the sound of a car coming down the lane. I hadn't really understood how quiet it was out here—just birdsong and the occasional distant sound of a vehicle or tractor or airplane, and, closer, the low hum of the pump and water heater. No voices arguing from the street below, no throb of traffic on a nearby street broken by squeals of breaks or blares of horns or screams of sirens, no heavy aircraft passing overhead and shrieking children passing by on their way to and from school. LA was noise itself—thick with noise and sticky with grime and asphalt. My small second-story apartment was full of it, echoed with it twenty-four hours a day.

Here, I could hear a car approaching from a mile away.

I dropped the bag I'd been holding and dashed to the door, my heart racing with sudden panic. There was nowhere to hide in the camper. There would be nowhere to hide outside, nowhere to run to where I couldn't be seen.

I'd thought this was a refuge, but now I saw the truth. It was a trap, a place to be cornered and treed. My car was out front. The gate wasn't even locked.

Only then, after days of resisting, did I let my thoughts stray to the dull metal object that lay in the bottom of my duffel bag on the floor of the clothes cupboard. It was loaded, Marianne had told me when she shoved it into the bag. I hadn't checked. I hadn't touched it. I'd never held a gun, much less fired one.

"Last resort," was what she'd said. But a last resort for what, or for whom, I hadn't wanted to consider.

Even as I allowed myself to think of it, I knew I wasn't going to use it. I stood motionless, my breath coming in shallow gasps, staring out the small, dirty window in the door with wide, dry eyes. I could see it now—a dark sedan, coming slowly down the rutted lane, closer and closer, partially obscured by the dust it was raising even at a low speed. It had a roof rack of some kind on the top of it, or lights—

And then I saw that it was a police car.

My panic faded as quickly as it had come, collapsing in a sodden sense of relief that didn't last as my anxiety grew again—a different kind of anxiety. This was still a problem. Maybe it wasn't assassins—or whoever I'd lain awake imagining and dreading in the cold, dark, lonely hours the past few nights. But it wasn't good. I watched numbly as the police car drew up in front of the closed but unlocked gate and a man stepped out, watched him looking over the property with a calm, assessing air. He wore sunglasses and a light brown uniform with the standard belt and badge, but was otherwise blank—just the shape of a man, no features, nothing that I could take in.

I was going to have to step outside and talk to him. My hand shook on the door latch, Marianne's voice, unnaturally harsh and loud, echoing in my head.

"No police, Lo. Do not go anywhere near the police."

"But—but why? If you're in trouble they can help protect you—"

"They can't. They just can't, OK? They can't help either of us. And if you go to them they'll arrest you."

A shocked silence as I watched her throw clothing into my duffel bag and zip it closed.

"What?" I finally demanded. "What are you saying? Are you— what did you do?"

Her mouth clamped tightly shut. "You don't need to know. But trust me, Lo. The police won't help—not the FBI or local cops or anybody. They can't. Stay away from them. Just—just please hide. Hide as long as you can—for me. I'll try to make it right."

And then she'd gone.

And a cop was walking up to the front door of my hiding place.

chapter 2

"Hello?" He called out. "Anyone home?"

With a deep breath that didn't help at all, I swung open the heavy door and stepped outside.

"Hi," I said, my voice pitched just a shade too high.

He'd been standing next to my car, and took a few casual steps toward me, removing his sunglasses as he did so. It was really too dark under the shadow of the trees for shaded lenses. We stared at each other for a moment, and then he introduced himself.

"I'm Deputy Tom Marquardt," he said. "Are you staying here?"

"Yes, I am. Hello. I'm Lola—Bright," I reached out my hand awkwardly, and he stepped forward to shake it, a brief cool shake. I had to give my name; it was too risky to do anything else. It was on my car registration if he ran the plates on my Acura, not to mention on my driver's license. I didn't know how to believe Marianne when she said the police would arrest me if I went to them, but I trusted her enough to at least obey her command to avoid them. She hadn't said what to do if the police *came to me*.

"Nice to meet you, Lola. Are you a relative of Joe's?" the deputy asked.

"Sort of. He was a family friend. I inherited this property last year, but it's the first time I've visited."

"Oh, I see." He smiled, relaxing slightly; watching him as carefully as I was, I noticed. "We heard it was caught up in some kind of probate mess."

I nodded, forcing my lips to curve into the semblance of a smile. Now that I could make out his features, I saw that he was around my age—maybe in his late twenties or early thirties, tanned, with hair bleached light by the sun and the sort of weathered look that even younger people get when they spend a lot of time outside. From a dating perspective, he wasn't unattractive—if I'd seen his picture I'd have clicked on his profile, swiped right instead of left. I couldn't help the analysis, even if I wasn't thinking of the deputy in those terms. Five years on the LA dating scene had taught me to make lightning-fast first impressions of men and adjust myself according to what I saw.

Tom Marquardt was a surfer at heart, this was just his day job. He had surfer hair, surfer skin, a surfer's body. I had the sense that he was inclined to be friendly and open-minded, but could be tough if necessary. And had we connected online and gone on a first date in LA, he wouldn't have called me for a second one.

"One of the neighbors saw the car turn in earlier and called it in," he explained easily. "Not that they were trying to make trouble or anything, but nobody's been out here for a while and they were concerned it might be a trespasser. We had a few squatters hanging around this past winter so people have been watching out."

"That's good of them," I said mechanically, hoping none of the people watching out were especially inquisitive or neighborly, and feeling the hope wither as quickly as it had bloomed. Of course they would be either inquisitive or neighborly, or both. Uncle Joe had lived here for decades, he'd made friends in the area. He was a loner, but not a misanthropic one.

"Are you planning to stay long?"

"I'm not sure," I said honestly. "I needed a break from LA—my job ended, and it seemed like a good chance to come check out the property and—and take a vacation, you know. It's so beautiful here."

"Are you originally from LA?" he asked.

"No—the South Bay. I moved down there a few years ago."

"Like it?"

"Not really," I admitted. "I'm thinking of moving back up north."

He smiled again. It was a nice smile, showing nice teeth, but I was too keyed up to really appreciate it.

"I don't blame you. Other than the waves, there's not much about SoCal that appeals to me."

I knew it: surfer.

Suddenly it felt a little uncomfortable to be standing around in the yard. Was he going to stay? Should I ask him in for a—water, or coffee? Or a cocktail; did they drink on duty in places like this?

"Did you want to come in?" I asked, feeling like it was better to just tear off the Band-Aid than let the pressure mount, pulling my thoughts firmly away from the lethal object in the duffel bag. "I'm in the middle of unloading some groceries, but you're welcome to…"

"Thanks for asking, but I should get back. One last thing—do you happen to know anyone in the area?" I must have looked at him a little blankly, because he quickly added, "I mean, do you have friends or family nearby, or have you met any of your neighbors?"

"No," I said. "I've only been here one other time, years ago. Why do you ask?"

He cleared his throat.

"Well, it's just that—not that there's anything to concern you, but there are some people in town who aren't as… uh, respectable, as you might want."

"Respectable," I repeated.

He fiddled with his sunglasses, seeming slightly embarrassed.

"We've been asked—I mean, we've been keeping an eye on them, and it was suggested that we drop a hint to any visitors about the—the situation. It's not that big a deal, but better to be safe than sorry, right?"

"Yeah—I mean, of course. So they live around here, or…?"

"They—it's just some people who run a bar down the road. Nothing you need to worry about, but if you go there, just keep your guard up."

Just what I needed—more things to be afraid of.

"What are they under suspicion of?"

"I'm not at liberty to say." The talking point slipped awkwardly out of his mouth. "I wouldn't have mentioned it, except they told—it was suggested that we make people aware of the situation. Plus," this with more frankness than his rehearsed phrases, "it's one of the only bars around here that isn't an overpriced grill, so almost everyone ends up going there anyway."

"I'll be careful," I assured him. "I'm not really that into going out."

This was the truth. The last thing I wanted was to spend time in some local dive bar, alone or making new friends, much less one where the owners—or managers, or whoever—were being watched by the police.

"OK. Well, if you do feel like a break from nature, a bunch of us play trivia there on Friday nights. You'd be welcome to join us."

"Oh—um, thanks. I'll think about it."

"It's just down the highway a little ways, the Hideout."

Ironic on so many levels, I thought, but didn't say aloud.

"OK. Thanks," I said again.

With another smile and a wave, he headed back to his car, me slowly following as far as the gate. When he'd driven back down the lane and was completely out of sight, I clicked the padlock into place, and went back inside.

■ ■ ■

Deputy Tom's visit had given me a lot to think—and worry— about. My mind buzzed unhappily with new information as I finished putting away what I'd bought, automatically finding the most efficient place for each item before moving to the next.

When the food items were done, I moved onto the housewares: bottle opener, can opener, pot and pan, kettle and mug, minimum cutlery, plates and glasses, paring knife, cutting board, dish towel, pillow, blanket, sheets and towels—which were at least new if not freshly washed. Finally the toiletries, which the grocery store had fortunately sold. Toothpaste, shampoo and conditioner, hand soap, face wash, and household supplies: toilet cleaner and brush, all-purpose cleaning spray, paper towels, dish soap, toilet paper.

After two hours, it was dusk, and my tiny home was complete. Three books and two magazines sat on the bookshelf. The bed was made and folded away, ready to be pulled out tonight. I turned on one of the low lamps above the couch and was glad to see it work, since I hadn't bought any light bulbs. My limited items of clothing had been hung up and folded, my toothbrush sat in a little steel toothbrush holder above the bathroom sink.

Satisfied with my work, if not with my thoughts, I stepped outside and walked to the edge of the trees. The sun was sinking low directly ahead of me, casting its last orange beams onto the camper, warming my skin.

So peaceful. Peaceful and lovely. I found myself wishing that I'd come here before—with my dad when Joe was alive, or even after both of them were gone and the place had come to me. I wished I'd been able to enjoy it without gnawing anxiety and guilt and fear, staying here for a quiet rest as Deputy Tom believed, having a relaxing getaway from the stresses of daily life. I could imagine what that would feel like—how glad I'd be to have this place to come to, how much pleasure I'd take in being out here on my own without this heavy weight of dread. How much fun it would be to plan a walk by the ocean or in the hills tomorrow, to nest in the camper I'd coveted and adored all those years ago.

But I hadn't taken that chance. And for now, anyway, none of that was possible.

I turned my back on the sunset and went inside, pouring myself a large tumbler of red wine and forcing a few crackers and slices of cheese down with it. I hadn't had any kind of appetite for days now; it was the best I could do. The wine tasted good, though, and I drank it thirstily.

If I'd been dieting, this would have been a lucky break, but I wasn't dieting. I'd always had a tendency to be on the skinny side—but not the kind of skinny with big boobs and a sexy butt. The other kind of thin, the adolescent boy figure. Women who feel they have too many curves might resent someone like me, but it wasn't better to be flat and angled. I still had cellulite on my thighs, just not the bust that went with it. I could wear those much-coveted smaller sizes in clothes, but they didn't show off anything interesting. I might have pulled off my straight figure with a few extra inches, but I was average height. The only things I felt I had going for me were my mouth and cheekbones—high, elegant cheekbones and a wide mouth that balanced them out. Men who reached out on dating apps usually complimented one or the other. "Great cheeks." "Beautiful smile."

Nobody ever complimented my body, which, given the context, was just as well, really. And nobody ever said that I looked like a Lola—it implied a far more sexy and exotic kind of woman than I. My hair was a naturally dirty blond, worn long because it tended to curl wildly when it was short, my eyes so dark a blue they looked brown, my skin medium fair—not a likely combination given my genetic makeup. My mom, in happy ignorance of my future figure and coloring, had adored Barry Manilow's "Copa Cabana" and named her only child after the song. She'd belted it in the car at the top of her lungs, always out of tune, usually with the windows down. If I'd had a brother, he almost certainly would have had been called Rico.

Two tumblers of wine and seven chapters of a predictable historical romance were enough to send me to sleep. The last wearying days had tired me out enough to sleep soundly, though I woke several times during the night, hearing the hooting of an owl in the distance, the soft thrum of a car that faded almost as soon as I identified it and before I had time to react. The camper felt solid and relatively safe—the door was locked, the windows latched and too small to climb through, the thick metal around me like my own private bomb shelter. I couldn't stand a siege for very long, but I was somewhat protected. Right now that was really all I could hope for.

Waking up slowly in the dim light of morning to the sound of wildly joyful birdsong, I felt stronger and less exhausted, as if both my mind and body had gotten sufficient rest. I wrapped up in a sweater—even snug inside the camper I could tell the outside air was crisp—and made myself a cup of instant coffee and half-and-half, sipping it at the tiny booth and looking out the window. The mountains stood tall against the light from the east, so that the property would be in shadow long after sunrise, even after the sky itself was pale blue. A soft mist drifted across a gully, which lay some distance to the south, thick with brush and trees. Birds of various kinds hopped and flew cheerfully around the yard and the grassland beyond it.

Today I'd explore the property, look through what else was here. Find a cover for the car. Maybe a lawn chair so I could sit outside.

And tomorrow—what would I do tomorrow? Or the next day? Or the next?

How many days would I have to stay here? How many trips would I make to Safeway? How many hours would I spend waiting to hear something—anything—from Marianne?

What if I never heard from her? What then?

I stared bleakly into my coffee cup, unable to give myself any answers. All I could do was get through the next few minutes, the next hour. All I could do was hope.

■ ■ ■

After three days, I was more restless than I would have believed possible. It was almost enough to cancel out the fear, which was still there, but much less believable now, away from Marianne's frightened eyes, nothing having happened to increase my unease. Nobody had come by to check on or bother me, not one nosy neighbor or Good Samaritan with a casserole. No suspicious cars had slunk by the lane, no curious "hikers" had lingered on the nearby hillside—nobody I saw, anyway. It was almost enough to make me doubt.

That is, until the phone rang.

I'd been outside in the yard, which now held a small metal table and chair set from under one of the tarps and some other odds and ends that made the place feel more homey. In the shed I'd found a battered but useable cruiser bicycle, complete with wicker basket, along with an air pump and gear grease, both on a set of dusty shelves holding a variety of tools and cleaners, paint cans and wasp traps. I'd spent an industrious hour polishing and oiling and pumping so that it would be ready to use—if I felt brave enough to go anywhere.

In between reading, doing crosswords fortuitously pre-loaded on my tablet and sorting through the yard and shed, I'd kept the camper spotlessly clean and washed my car using a bucket of hot water from the shower and a hose. There was only so much to do, and only so many books to read, before I'd exhausted every task and devoured every page.

Even as I shrank gratefully into the sense of security I felt in my new home, I was also growing antsy. Maybe if I'd had places I was required to go, obligations and appointments, I would have appreciated the quiet seclusion more. But it was hard to stay in the circle of oak trees. Hard to be wary and watchful all the time in this self-imposed exile.

It was the phone call that decided it. Even as it raised all my hackles and revived my fear at full strength, it also spurred me into action.

I almost didn't register what was happening at the first low trilling noise. I'd decided to paint the rusting metal bistro set, and had begun to sand it down before applying a coat of the red enamel paint I'd found in the shed. It wasn't until the third ring that I realized what the noise was, throwing myself into the camper and grasping for the small black phone with desperation as soon as I understood—and then stopping, my breath coming fast.

"Don't pick up the phone if it rings," Marianne had said.

"How will you reach me to let me know you're safe?"

"I'll be fine. I'll be in touch, I promise. You have to lie low a while, that's all. The phone's only for emergencies—I won't contact you that way. Don't keep it on."

I'd kept it on. I couldn't help myself. It was my only connection to her. I'd even bought a cheap power cord at Safeway to keep it charged.

And now it was ringing.

And it probably wasn't Marianne.

Which meant it was someone else.

Someone trying to reach me—to find me. Someone out there with this number, a number that only one person had. The phone stopped ringing, leaving me in a sudden silence. I looked at the caller ID. It said "Restricted."

With shaking fingers I turned it off and put it down. I couldn't imagine who might be holding that other phone. It was the first time in my life I'd wished for the sane disruption of a robocall, but how likely was that on a burner number? If the caller wasn't Marianne—*oh God, how I wished it was her!*—but she'd said she wouldn't call. Which meant she wouldn't.

We grew up together, as close as sisters. Her parents left her with mine when they lived overseas, beginning when Marianne was two and I was a newborn. She was my hero, my babysitter, my confidante, my playmate. Our mothers were half-siblings, years apart in age, never close. Now and then Marianne's parents would come back for a short visit and she would stay with them, or they'd take her with them to South Africa or Indonesia or Greenland. They were some kind of global activists first, parents last. Their work, whatever it was, always took precedence. To my parents and me, and to Marianne herself, we were her family and ours was her home.

If she said she wouldn't call me, she wouldn't.

I didn't know what she'd gotten involved in. I didn't know what she'd done or why she was in such trouble. I didn't even resent that somehow that trouble had thrown clinging tendrils over me. Marianne wouldn't have deliberately endangered or hurt me, I was sure of that. Whatever had happened, it had been an accident—some unlucky chance.

I wasn't as sure that she was totally innocent herself, as guilty and disloyal as I felt thinking it. She'd said she was sorry with tears in her eyes, but she hadn't explained—or, more ominously, denied—that there was a reason behind the need to run.

Six years ago, she'd gotten involved with some very strange people. She was living on the East Coast, urging me to visit. When I did go, I found that her lifestyle was beyond anything I could understand or relate to. A dozen people, women and men of varying ages, lived in a filthy warehouse loft together in Newark, all ostensibly dating each other as a group. It was some kind of modern commune. I hadn't liked any of them. I'd resented and felt uneasy about the way they looked at me, the possessive, abusive way they'd treated my cousin. They ranted about the false authority of God and the government while smoking pot and meth and who knows what else.

I still didn't know why Marianne had lived with them. She was intelligent, poised and educated—she could have done so many different things with her life. I left after barely ten minutes, and later told her I hated the way she was living. She'd glared at me— then laughed with a frightening bitter ring to it and hugged me. "Silly Lo," she'd said. "Of course it's awful. But it's an adventure, don't you think?"

Less than a year later she'd emailed to say she was living in an apartment in Manhattan and working at a travel agency. She came out to the funeral when my mom died of cancer, and again when my dad died of complications from a stroke four years later, holding me tightly as I sobbed into her neck. Even if she'd done something truly awful, and even if that awful thing—whatever it might be—ruined both our lives, I would always love her, always stand by her. My playmate, sister and best friend.

All my grandparents died before I was born. My father was an only child, my mother had only the one half-sister, who I'd barely met. Whatever extended family might exist, they were too distant and unknown to count.

Marianne was all I had left.

I stood there staring at the phone, my mind reaching out to her, willing her to be OK. I couldn't process what this meant for me. Was I in more danger, or less? I couldn't know. But I knew now that the threat was as real as she'd told me it was. I'd trusted her, while only half believing it was true. Even as I ran, scared and anxious, even as I hid, I'd only half-believed.

With the ringing of that burner phone, I believed.

Someone was looking for me. They might even have found me. The question now was: what was I going to do about it?

chapter 3

I put down the phone, locked the camper and rode the bike down the bumpy roads and across the freeway to the ocean.

It was a beautiful, breezy day, white clouds skidding across the wide blue sky. The beach wasn't crowded when I got there around two, even though it was probably seventy degrees and warm for this part of the coast. A school bus driving by clued me in that it was a weekday—Friday, I realized. It had been Friday when I left LA. That was a strange thought. Only a week had passed, but it felt as if a year severed the two eras, there was such a gaping void between then and now.

Clusters of beachgoers sat or played volleyball, while those who were alone read, looked out at the ocean, jogged or walked their dogs along the shore. I pushed the bike onto the sand and sat, spending a long time watching. It felt good to be surrounded by people, even if I didn't know anyone. There was something comforting in being near others without feeling crowded, everyone within their own bubble of activity or inactivity.

The phone call had shaken me. It had frightened me into even more intense worry about Marianne, and reminded me why I'd rushed headlong away from my life. But it had also freed me, in some strange way.

I couldn't go on living like this. Whether I stayed here for a day or a year, I couldn't continue under this strain. It wasn't a matter of taking risks—I didn't want to *die*, or even be arrested. I was still confused, still longed for answers and an end to this exile. But as far as I could tell, one wasn't coming. At least not right this second. I'd done everything Marianne told me to do, protected myself as best as I could. I was at my limit, the edge of my resources, in the best safehouse I was capable of finding.

Until I decided what to do next, or until something or someone decided it for me, I wouldn't go on the same way, cowering under the covers. That wasn't how I wanted to spend my last hours or days, if they were going to be my last. I'd do everything I could to enjoy this time. Maybe it was a gift—a karmic reward, a cosmic blessing before the end. Maybe it wasn't. But either way, I wasn't going to waste it.

I leaned back with my head resting on the wicker of my basket, dreamily regarding a huge brown dog as it leapt joyfully into the waves after a stick. It dashed madly back up to its owner, barking hysterically until the stick was thrown again. Again, and again, it never tired of the game, always as thrilled to chase the stick, always as excited to bring it back for another round.

They moved slowly down the beach. Throw, run, splash, catch, return, bark, throw. When they were about even to where I lay, the dog looked over and spotted something—a fat seagull who'd for some time been standing not far from my bike on the sand, eyeing me hopefully in case I happened to drop a sandwich or something equally tasty. Never mind that I hadn't brought any food with me.

With an ecstatic growl the brown dog abandoned its toy and came racing up the beach toward the gull, scattering sand with every touch of its large paws. The gull, no fool as gulls go, spread its wings and flew off. The dog, without slowing down, changed direction and ran full tilt toward me, skidding to a stop and barking furiously just feet away.

Before I had a chance to do more than pull my feet in closer and struggle to sit up, the owner had arrived, grabbing the dog by the collar.

"*Down*, Oss," he commanded. "*Sit.*"

The dog, loath to give up this new game, gave one last ringing bark before obeying.

"Sorry about that," the man said.

"It's OK…" I started to stay, squinting up into the sun to see his face.

Something jolted in my stomach. It was a familiar sensation from the past few days, except that this wasn't anxiety.

It was attraction. More than attraction.

Recognition.

"I think he took exception to your bike," the man was saying. "Sorry again."

With desperate effort, I pulled myself together and scrambled awkwardly to my feet.

"It's fine," I said.

My heart beat strangely inside my chest cavity, thumping wildly around. I tried to meet his level gaze, but found I was too nervous to do more than glance quickly at him and away.

"He's not as fierce as he seems," the man said, and somehow I caught a glimpse of years of this: years of this large loud dog leaping at people and his owner following to do damage control.

"He seems sweet," I said, my voice sounding high and unnatural as it reached my ears.

I looked down at the dog and gave him my hand to sniff. Oss, if I'd heard his name right, was sitting placidly on the sand beside us, tongue lolling, looking as cheerfully satisfied as only a dog can. He licked my hand in a friendly way and waited for something to happen. So did I.

"Thanks for understanding." The man didn't quite, but almost, smiled, nodded, called Oss to heel, slowly walked back down to the abandoned stick, resumed their walk.

I stared after him, wondering what had just happened. Was I going crazy? I'd never seen him before—not to recognize, anyway. He wasn't in line in front of me in Safeway. I wasn't in school with him years ago. I was sure we'd never met.

I just—*knew* him. It was the oddest feeling. My body tingled as I tried to identify what exactly had just come to pass. I'd looked up and—there he was. Like I'd been expecting him.

Except I hadn't. I'd been thinking about nothing in particular, taking a break from worrying about Marianne. I wasn't even daydreaming about romance novel heroes or surfer deputies who weren't my type. Romance—and men—were the furthest things from my mind at that moment.

I watched him get smaller and smaller down the beach with the dog beside him. Once or twice it almost seemed like he was looking back at me, but I couldn't be sure.

It felt awful, like a part of me was walking away.

Which was *crazy*.

I must be going crazy. The strain had taken its toll. Maybe I wasn't even here, maybe I was lying on the floor of the camper having a breakdown and imagining the whole thing.

I pinched my arm, using fingernails. It hurt, which didn't tell me much, except that if this was a fantasy it was an elaborate one. I couldn't fathom what any of this meant.

The most bizarrely absurd part was, I didn't even remember exactly what he looked like. I could recall ordinary features, dark hair, some color eyes… brown? Blue? I couldn't picture his face. I could see his hand, holding the dog by the collar. I could see Oss's big dog grin and floppy wet ears. All I knew was that I was drawn to him in a way I'd never been drawn to anything or anyone. Not even my deepest adolescent crush had felt as powerful or real.

Because it really did feel *real*. Real and somehow… right.

Even if it was all in my head.

■ ■ ■

If I'd been restless before the beach, it was nothing to after it. I couldn't stop thinking about the man with the dog. I didn't even wonder, much, who he was. I just thought about him. I listened to his voice in my mind: *I think he took exception to your bike... Thanks for understanding...* I relived that moment of intense pull and recognition over and over again, every time experiencing the same thrill of rightness, the same wave of nervous excitement.

What was I *doing? I'll probably never see him again,* I told myself firmly. Even if I spent every day of the next week at the beach, I might not see him—and what if I did? What if he was there, would I casually stroll up to him and say, "Hi, I'm Lola, are you my soul mate?" It was laughable.

It was also, I realized with a startled jolt, *possible.* I might actually do it. I'd never done anything remotely assertive and gutsy like that in my life. Texting a guy first was a big deal in my world. But insane or not, I had a feeling that if I ever saw the man again—the man whose name and face I didn't know, but who attracted me with a depth I didn't understand—I wouldn't let him walk away a second time.

And that was almost as strange and disconcerting a thought as the idea of a nameless person or people out there searching for me for a reason I didn't know.

I was too wound up to think straight. I'd ridden home before dark, and now that dusk had fallen was pacing around the yard in circles. I forced myself to sit and eat a peanut butter sandwich, then to slowly sip a vodka cranberry, in the hopes that it would calm me down. Unfortunately, the alcohol had the opposite effect, increasing my excitement and flushed anticipation. Anticipation of what, I didn't know. I felt like Tony in "West Side Story." *Something* was coming. Maybe imminent death by persons unknown, maybe something else that I couldn't even name, but it felt exactly like that.

I took a shower and brushed my hair and teeth, as if I could actually contemplate going to bed. It was also only six thirty.

Without making a conscious decision, I found myself putting on a clean shirt and jeans, stepping into low boots—the only one of three pairs of shoes I'd brought that weren't sneakers—tying back my damply curling hair and prettying my face with the few cosmetics that had been in my purse when I left home.

I carefully closed the camper and locked it, taking a flashlight with me, and walked over to unlock and open the gate before getting into my car. With the same calm resolution, I drove out, closed the gate behind me and headed down the road.

The Hideout was easy to find, just off the main freeway as Deputy Tom had said. It was a weathered single-story wooden building, its windows vivid with lights and movement, sitting beside a large gravel parking lot about two-thirds full of cars. I parked and walked purposefully toward the main doors, paying no attention to a cluster of people smoking the requisite twenty feet from the porch. A hand-painted sign hung above the doors, stating the name of the business, with a distinct piracy-on-the-high-seas inspired flair to the lettering.

The entrance opened into a wide vestibule with doorways on either side, a cork board covered in fliers and notices straight ahead. The right door was closed, though it opened as I came in and two women entered from a hallway, passing me and going through the open doorway on the left. I followed them into a low-lit, wood-paneled barroom.

The bar, taking up almost the full length of the L-shaped room, stood along the far wall, across from booths on the near. High tables in the center were about half full of people, and occasionally the sound of pool balls could be heard clacking from the back area of the large, low space, out of sight around a corner. Classic rock played over the sound system, just audible over the hum of voices. The pirate theme hadn't been carried inside in an obvious way, but the walls held a few interesting brass nautical instruments and framed black and white photos of old ships and forts.

I wasn't looking for anyone in particular. I wasn't *doing* anything in particular. I was just there, just moving forward with a kind of blissful, simple purpose and at the same time no expectations. I ordered a vodka tonic and ate from a fresh bowl of pretzels while I waited for it, smiling internally while I compared the Hideout to the trendier spots in LA. Those places wouldn't be caught dead serving free plain pretzels and Bud Light on tap.

Personally, I thought the rustic vibe had a lot going for it. At least it was real. I'd never enjoyed the hot "scene" bars with long lines to order eighteen-dollar craft cocktails and everyone pretending to be someone else. But the scene was the whole point of going, and so we all went, waited and paid.

I handed five dollars to the bartender and finished the pretzels.

"You made it," someone said behind me. Deputy Tom, of course. I turned and saw that he looked younger out of uniform. His casual t-shirt and shorts definitely suited him better.

"Hey," I said. "Yeah, I was getting a little stir crazy."

"Vacations will do that. I'm glad you showed up—the trivia is about to start. You're welcome to join our team."

"Thanks," I said, appreciating the offer. "I might just watch, though."

"Sure," he said, "but come sit with us anyway."

I didn't mind, it was nice of him to include a stranger. I followed happily enough, still feeling intensely *present*, yet pleasantly detached. In spite of the earlier vodka, I wasn't drunk at all, I was wide awake and taking everything in. I didn't seem to care what happened. I wasn't self-conscious or nervous of doing something wrong. That kind of social anxiety was a different breed entirely from the excited nervousness I'd felt all afternoon.

I followed Deputy Tom, as I continued to think of him, to a group of about ten people bunched in and around one of the bigger booths. He found me a chair and I wedged myself between Tom and a woman a few years older than me, I guessed, with short curly hair and wide brown eyes.

"Who's this?" she asked sociably.

"Lola Bright. She's staying at Joe's place—she owns Joe's place, actually," Tom answered for me. "This is Stacy Markowitz, the beating heart of our team."

"Hi," I said.

Stacy smiled and held out her hand.

"We miss Joe around here," she said. "I heard there was some problem with the ownership."

I explained the situation, and explained it a second and then a third time as more people in the group were introduced to me. About half of them had known Uncle Joe, which wasn't too surprising, considering how small the community was. The ages and sexes were mixed, and I learned as the evening went on that this team had formed out of some of the more serious trivia devotees in the community, with their bitterest rivals (a similar-looking kind of group) sitting at the next booth over. A few other teams played throughout the bar, mostly couples who signed up just for fun.

"We lost the last two trivia nights," Deputy Tom informed me in a low voice. "We've all been studying to make sure it doesn't happen again."

"Studying?" I asked, sipping my drink.

"Latest news, celebrity gossip," he said.

"And of course things like obscure rivers, world capitals, years that albums were released," added Stacy.

"A lot of it is just luck," Deputy Tom—*just Tom*, I reminded myself—said, with a rueful smile. "Our luck's been out the last few rounds, but I feel a change in the air."

"Ever the optimist," someone else said.

Tom went to buy another round before the game started, though everyone on the team was sober enough to focus on the essential task at hand. When the trivia questions started appearing on the nearest TV and the game began in earnest, I still chose to observe rather than participate, though found that I couldn't help getting caught up in the excitement of coming up with the right answer before the time ran out. I enjoyed watching the people on our team, as I thought of them, noticing the married couples, the father and two daughters, those on their own like Tom and Stacy.

It was hard to imagine Tom being single and not on a date. Not because I was attracted to him (and even if I had been, I somehow, illogically, considered myself *taken* now), but because he was approachable, respectful and good-looking, not to mention gainfully employed. His type was rare on the dating sites I knew. Guys like him didn't need dating apps in LA. There was a sprinkling of young, unattached women at the bar, but he didn't seem interested in talking to any of them, not even after the game ended with a rousing victory by Tom's team and some heady celebrating commenced.

He'd stepped away from the table—to the bar, or the bathroom, or both—and I was chatting with Stacy about nothing in particular when she asked, "So, are you into Tom?"

I looked at her for a few seconds, wondering what she was talking about.

"Me?" I couldn't help but ask.

"Oh, sorry, you're probably involved with someone already. Or—I shouldn't have assumed."

"It's OK, I don't mind. I'm not actually… involved… with anyone at the moment," I said slowly, though it didn't feel completely accurate.

"You're into guys, though?"

"It would be guys, yeah," I agreed.

"Then why did my question throw you?" she inquired, smiling.

I thought about it, and found myself answering honestly.

"I haven't been interested in anyone for a while," I explained, mentally adding, *at least, not until this afternoon.* "Anyway, Tom's way out of my league."

"*Tom* is?" she said, laughing and giving me a look—a "you've got to be kidding" look.

"Isn't he?" I wondered.

"He doesn't think so. I doubt many of the guys here would."

"Weird," I said. "In LA I'd be considered way down in the minors."

"Oh, LA," she dismissed with the supreme indifference that only a Northern Californian could show for one of the country's biggest and brightest cities. "Everything is skewed there."

She wasn't wrong. Still, it did make for an intriguing twist, and shed a different light on Tom's behavior that evening.

"Should I tell him I'm not interested?" I asked. "I don't want to offend him, he's been really nice."

"I don't think you'll need to. He won't push if you aren't into it. He's more perceptive than you'd think." She eyed me for a minute. "If you don't mind me asking... How old are you?"

"Thirty-two," I said. I would be on my next birthday, which happened to be next week.

"*Why* aren't you interested in him, again?"

It was my turn to laugh.

"Bad taste, I guess. He's just not my type."

"Ah."

"Is he yours?" I returned bluntly, thinking there couldn't be more than seven or eight years between them, if that.

"No. He's cute, but I like them a little more mature," she explained.

Tom, returning with more drinks and pretzels, put an end to that conversation, and the evening went on. There was no reason for me to continue to feel so excited, to tremble with an electric buzz that had nothing to do with the vodka or the company. It just kept building. Now that I'd been clued into Tom's interest, I could kind of see it. He gave me most of his attention, solicitous but not overbearing. He knew he had looks and charm, and was evidently prepared to use both to his advantage, but was also genuine and likeable.

In my old life, someone like Tom showing attraction to someone like me would have caused me to react very differently. I'd have been flattered and immediately attracted in return. As I told Stacy, in my years of experience, I wasn't likely to catch a Tom's eye in that dating scene.

Now, in this new reality, I seemed to see it from far away—almost as if the situation was happening to a friend or on a TV show. The detachment continued. I knew I wasn't going to date Tom, and I think after an hour he knew it, too, though he continued to sit by and talk to me, as well as to Stacy, who I found myself liking a lot.

Eventually I went to the bathroom myself and then bought a round for my new friends, ordering from the same laconic, weathered bartender who'd poured my first drink. While I waited, a guy sitting on the stool beside me turned around with a slightly slurred, "Hi, beaut'ful."

He was paunchy and puffy and plainly quite pleased with his line. It was the same with all the creeps on the apps—call a woman cute, beautiful, gorgeous, she's supposed to melt like putty in your hand. I'd always found it utterly repellent and embarrassing, and this was no exception. Fortunately my newfound poise didn't desert me.

"Hey," I said vaguely, paying for the drinks.

"You new around here?" the guy leered.

I noticed the bartender eyeing him with something close to the dislike I felt, which was reassuring. At least he wasn't the most popular guy in the bar. I hoped he wasn't the mayor or something.

"Not really," I said, and carefully picked up the full pints, leaving my cocktail for the moment.

"What, you too good for lil' conv-conversation?" Mr. Paunch asked angrily.

It was inevitable: oily, exaggerated flattery quickly followed by bitter rancor when the target didn't respond the way he wanted. Next he'd be calling me a cold bitch.

"Not at all. I'm going to take these back to my friends," I said, moving in the direction of the table.

"Hey, bitch, I'm talking to you!" he bellowed, grabbing my arm above the elbow and splashing beer over both of us and a few bystanders, who shifted uneasily away.

I thought crowd sentiment was on my side and was about to tell him to get his hands off me when someone loomed between us, a physical barrier between Mr. Paunch's body and mine. The grip on my arm was immediately released.

"Problem, Phil?" a smooth, authoritative voice asked from above my left shoulder.

Down, Oss... Sorry about that... Thank you for understanding.

A wave of utter, tingling joy went through my body, shaking me with its strength. I stared up at the side of his head—*his* head—barely registering as Phil slunk to a distant barstool muttering and new drinks were ordered on his tab. I felt numb. I felt more alive than I ever had. I couldn't feel my face.

"Thanks," I said.

The bar wasn't especially well lit, but it was bright enough to see the features that had been so indistinct in my memory this afternoon. He stood just two feet away as the alcohol on my arms dripped onto the floor, glaring after Phil.

"Don't worry about it."

He leaned over to catch a towel tossed by the bartender and turned toward me at last, only looking at me when he reached to take the glasses from my rigid hands. He froze.

So did my heart. It stuttered for a moment before racing at full speed. I stared up at him, he down at me.

"You're the woman from the beach," he said slowly, forgetting to take the glasses.

"With the bike," I said helpfully, my voice unsteady.

"Yeah," he said.

His eyes were brown—a deep, warm brown under arching brows. His features were handsome in a blunt way, faint laugh lines under his eyes. Cropped dark hair, wide shoulders, an average build. We took each other in. I *drank* him in.

"How's—how's Oss?" I asked. "Is that his name?"

"Osiris. He doesn't live up to it."

We stared some more.

"Pete," the bartender called, and he turned his head—reluctantly, it seemed—in response. "Here're those beers, and the lady's vodka tonic."

Pete. He didn't look like a Pete. Maybe a Peter.

Peter.

"Let me get those," he said suddenly, waking up and grabbing the half-empty glasses out of my hands at last. Our fingers touched briefly. It felt as if he'd shocked me, my reaction was that powerful. The electricity raced through my body in another overpowering wave.

He turned and put the two glasses down on the bar, turned back to hand me the clean bar towel. I mechanically wiped my wrists and fingers before giving it back to him.

"I'm Peter," he said, holding out his hand.

"Lola," I said, putting mine into it.

Time stopped. It really felt like it could have *stopped*. Eternity swirled around me in a strange, wild cloud of beauty and hope and ecstasy. Except it didn't, of course. We shook hands and let go. I wondered again if I was going crazy.

"I've never seen you here before," he said.

"I just got here a few days ago."

I have no idea how long we could have gone on like that if the bartender hadn't reminded him again that the drinks were waiting. Peter picked up the pints in large, capable hands and gestured for me to take my cocktail.

"I'll carry these," he said.

I nodded and moved in the direction of the booth. As we approached, the group, who had been noisily talking, abruptly fell silent. I indicated that he put the drinks by Tom and Stacy, and he complied, not seeming to notice the dampening effect his presence had on the people around us.

"Deputy," he said politely.

"Pete," Tom said, less politely. "What are you doing here?"

"I work here," Peter said without rancor, but also without any suggestion of apology. I saw Stacy glancing curiously between the two of us.

"I haven't seen you much lately," Tom said, also looking from me to Peter and back.

"There was a small incident at the bar. It's been handled," Peter said.

"What happened?" Tom asked me.

"Nothing very much," I said evenly. "I spilled some beer on myself. Peter was just helping me out."

It gave me a ridiculous thrill to say his name out loud. I turned to him, not wanting him to leave, but not sure how I could walk away from my new friends—who patently didn't want him to stay—without being unforgivably rude. I recognized their odd response to him, though I didn't understand it. I met Peter's straight gaze.

"Really nice to meet you," I said.

"You, too, Lola," he said. We shook hands for the second time—holding for a fraction longer than was necessary. "Hope to see you around."

I smiled and sat down, and he walked toward a door marked "Employees Only" at the back of the room and disappeared.

chapter 4

I felt Tom's accusing stare boring into me, but it was Stacy who spoke first.

"You don't know who that is, do you," she said.

"Peter?" I inquired, sipping my drink. "I guess not."

"He's one of the people I warned you about," Tom told me.

It hadn't really clicked until now, but of course it made sense. Peter was one of the not-so-respectable people who ran the Hideout. It didn't seem to make any difference to how I felt, but then I didn't know the full story. Maybe that would change things.

I doubted it.

"Is he?" I asked. "What's the deal with that, anyway?"

Tom scowled—looking more boyish than ever—and turned away from me to speak to someone across the table, ignoring the beer I'd bought for him. Stacy and I regarded his back for a long moment and exchanged a glance. She took a careful sip from her full IPA.

"What's the deal?" I repeated.

She gave a shrug and leaned toward me.

"Rumor has it that the owners—including your new friend Peter Owen—aren't on the up and up. Tax fraud, dog fighting and drug dealing are the most common tales. If there's more to it, local law enforcement isn't confirming or denying—but they've made it clear that something's going on."

"That's it?" I said.

She grinned.

"You're kind of weird, but I'm into it," she said. "Personally I think it's gotten blown out of proportion. It's this small town thing. Everyone gets sort of myopic about anything that seems different, even though it's not like there isn't real crime and all that." She yawned. "Anyway, everyone's got it down on this place—though you'll notice it hasn't done business any harm. It helps to be one of the few bars that isn't a wedding venue and doesn't water down the drinks."

The trivia team members started to break off or head home after that—I felt a little bad that my appearance with Peter might have ruined the party mood, but he did *own* the place. They shouldn't really be surprised if he showed up now and then. I opted to leave when Stacy did, at about ten thirty. I wanted very badly to stay, and of course to see Peter again—it was all I could do not to run straight at the door he went through and find him— but I didn't want to draw attention to myself any more than I already had.

Beneath all the excited happiness, I felt a calm certainty that we'd see each other soon. I couldn't tell you where any of this came from, it was just there. In my very cells, part of me at some mysterious atomic level. There wasn't any question about it.

He was mine.

Tom thawed out some before I left, but I didn't encourage him more than basic courtesy required. I could tell he was resigned to the fact that, at least for tonight, nothing was going to happen between us. It still surprised me that he was interested at all, but it didn't really matter either way.

"Maybe I'll see you around," he said with a cool copy of his friendly smile.

"I'd like that. Thanks for including me tonight, it was really fun."

"I'm glad." He hesitated, then added, "next week you could always join in."

"Maybe I will."

He considerately walked us to our cars, waiting as Stacy started hers and drove off and I got in and started mine. I lingered while he turned and walked inside, pretending like I was doing something with my purse. And then I switched the engine off, stepped back out and quickly circled the building, following a gravel path around to the left as if I knew where I was going; as if I'd walked it in broad daylight. My passage triggered a motion light under one of the eaves which lit my way until I reached the back, my feet making a soft scrunching noise with every step. A back entrance stood open, a dark figure was silhouetted against the light. I paused, and he spoke.

"Looking for someone?" he asked pleasantly.

"Yes," I said.

We walked slowly toward each other and put out our hands. It seemed natural—and it was the most astonishing thing in the world. I could just see him, though his features were blurred in the soft glow from the open door. I could smell his scent, clean and masculine with a faint hint of beer, though that might have been me. We studied each other, his hands warm and unfamiliar and comforting on mine.

"Where'd you come from, Lola?" he asked.

"San Mateo, originally. Recently LA."

"Are you staying in town?"

"No. I'm in a camper up the hill a little ways. It belonged to a friend of my father's, Joe—"

"Joe Brown," he finished, sounding surprised. "You're the blonde girl living in Joe's camper. You own it, or you will when probate is settled."

"You heard about me."

"Sure, you're big local news." We were silent a moment. "What about me, did your friends say anything?" he asked.

"Only that you and your partners might, or might not, be involved in something less than respectable."

"I see. And what did you think about that?"

"I thought it sounded vague and speculative. Anyway I'm not totally respectable myself. I'm on the run, in a way."

"On the run?"

I nodded. "I left LA in a hurry. My cousin—anyway, it's a long story. But that's why I'm here. I'm hiding out."

"You're—hiding out from who, exactly?"

"I'm not sure. Someone dangerous. The police can't help."

The breeze off the ocean blew stiff and cold, flinging itself against us even sheltered as we were behind the building, but I didn't feel it. We stood together in the near-darkness, breathing and holding hands.

"You trust me," Peter said slowly.

"I really do," I assured him.

"We don't know each other."

"I know. But it doesn't feel like that. It feels like we… like we're old friends."

"Friends," he repeated.

"For lack of a better word."

"Lola," he said, drawing me closer. "I believe that you're in trouble. I want to hear about it. I want to help. But I'm not… I don't know if you should get involved with me. There's some truth to the rumors, you know. It isn't what people think, but it isn't good."

"Have you killed anyone?" I asked, my pulse rocketing at his nearness.

"No," he smiled. "Have you?"

"No."

"Then I guess we're OK."

We moved toward each other—our breaths quickening—he dropped my hands to slip his arms around my waist—and a voice called out loudly from the doorway, startling us apart.

"Pete? Phil's at it again, I think Tom might arrest him pretty soon." The woman speaking couldn't see me. "Maybe we should let him. He's being a real asshole." She sounded tired and annoyed.

"Be right there," he called back.

We waited.

"Yeah. Anytime now," she called impatiently.

"Later?" he murmured. "If you want to…"

"Later," I agreed.

He turned and walked inside, and I went quickly to my car, passing no one in the dark parking lot. I heard belligerent yelling over the low sounds of voices and music before I closed the door and started the engine.

Later.

■ ■ ■

Later turned out to be nearly one in the morning. I'd fallen asleep on the couch, reading and waiting for him. I was in my pajamas and had brushed my teeth. Pajamas, not a negligee.

Whatever this was between Peter and me, this strong sweet intense connection, it didn't seem to require any effort. I didn't have lingerie with me, but even if I had I wouldn't have been wearing it. I felt no need to impress him, to be sexy or coiffed. I wasn't nervous that he'd expect to sleep with me—or that he wouldn't. It didn't feel like a date in any way. I was just impatient for him to get here, because I missed him.

I'd spent all of about five minutes in his company during the course of one afternoon and evening, and I missed him.

I didn't even think—much—about whether or not we'd have sex. It seemed like we would at some point, given the way he made me feel and the fact that I apparently had same effect on him. I didn't question our attraction or where it would lead. If it happened tonight, it would mean that the timing was right tonight. If not, it would happen tomorrow, or the next day, or the next.

Only a few hours earlier my future had seemed blank... full of unknowns... even impossible. Now there was one big known that quieted all my other fears and questions. Peter would be in it. My old and dear friend who I'd never met before today. He'd be there, one way or another. I didn't imagine, that night as I waited for him, how we'd fit into each other lives, or what roles we'd play to each other. Lover, spouse, partner, friend, ex, family. I wasn't daydreaming about the possibilities.

I just rested, quietly happy and content, even as my body tingled with electrified anticipation. After a while, I dozed off, feeling more peaceful than I had for a long time. Not just since Marianne sent me into hiding, but years before that. Maybe since childhood, when life was so much less complicated and my parents were my world.

The sound of a vehicle pulling up by the gate had me halfway to the door before I'd fully regained consciousness. Not for a second did I think that it was anyone but Peter. How could it be? He'd said he would come later, and it was later. I opened the door in time to see him jump back into his truck, which he'd left idling while he opened the gate. He pulled up next to my car, turned off the engine, got out and went to close the gate.

As he turned, I ran up to him, and this time nobody interrupted.

Peter's mouth on mine—his nose against my cheek, breaths mingled, bodies crushed together. It was heady stuff. An infinitely exhilarating and yet infinitely natural experience at the same time. I'd kissed plenty of men in more than a decade of dating and short-term relationships. Kissing had never been like this.

After a few minutes, he came to his senses enough to suggest, breathlessly, that we go inside. Now that I thought about it, it *was* cold out. My feet were bare, and my thin cotton top and pants weren't appropriate eveningwear by the central Pacific Coast.

Keeping our arms tightly around each other, we hurried to the camper and stepped inside. Peter took a moment to look around, though my eyes were fixed on him.

"I never saw the interior before," he said appreciatively. "It's beautiful, isn't it?"

"I love it," I agreed.

We sat down close beside each other on the couch, as if we'd sat that way a hundred times before. Our faces were toward each other, his arm around my back, my knees resting on his thigh, holding hands.

"How long are you planning to stay?"

"My plans are kind of up in the air," I said. "I don't know what's next for me, or how long I can stay here. I don't want to leave, though."

"Why is that?" he asked, smiling.

I smiled back.

"Two guesses."

"Trivia night?"

"Of course."

We laughed together, though the joke was inane at best.

"I kept thinking about you—after the beach," he said. "It was strange…"

"I felt the same. I felt like I knew you."

"Knew you and wanted you."

"That, too."

"Are we delusional?" he asked.

"I have no idea. I kept asking myself the same thing. I guess it doesn't matter as long as we're delusional *together*, right?"

"It would be awkward if one of us didn't feel the same… the same pull."

"Extremely awkward," I agreed. "Unthinkable, actually."

"Did you come to the bar tonight to look for me?"

"Not… consciously. I wanted to see you, of course, more than anything, and I felt like if I just followed my instincts it would work out somehow. But I didn't know you owned the bar. Deputy

Tom came out here earlier in the week to make sure I was legit, and he mentioned trivia night. I followed an impulse and accepted the invitation."

"He looked annoyed to see us together," Peter recalled, seeming to find some satisfaction in the thought. "Nice guy, for the most part."

"He seems nice enough. He said he was obligated to warn me about you—not you specifically, I mean, but the Hideout people, since I didn't know anybody around here."

"Considerate of him, I suppose."

"I was thinking more along the lines of officious and presumptive."

He leaned back slightly, looking intently into my eyes.

"You don't even know the whole story yet, but... Is that how you really feel about it?"

I reached up to touch his face. It wasn't the kind of thing I'd ever done before, I wasn't especially a toucher. But like everything else with Peter, it felt like the right thing to do. He had a few days' growth of beard, a sprinkling of gray in the brown, though I didn't think he was much above thirty-five, if that. Funny to think that I didn't know his age, or his birthday, or his hometown, but still believed that I knew him. Knew his essential makeup, if not the facts, figures and histories that each person collects over a lifetime.

Instead of answering him, I posed my own question.

"How do you feel about my situation—what you know about it?"

He considered, still looking somewhat searchingly into my face. His hand came up to capture mine, and he kissed it lightly.

"Like I want to help. That it couldn't be anything so bad we can't face it. Like I trust you."

I nodded to show I felt the same, and he leaned in with a kind of hungry sweetness to continue where we'd left off outside. His lips moved with warm strength against mine, the pressure increasing as our passion—as mutual as everything else had been—quickly sparked into a blazing hot burn. More sweet hunger. More intensity. More overwhelming, comforting, thrilling intimacy.

Making out wasn't the lead-up to anything. It was more like we were exploring each other, tasting, enjoying, validating our feelings with every deepening kiss and slow movement of our bodies, heat rising wherever we touched.

We kissed a while longer, finally pulling reluctantly apart so Peter could use the bathroom. *No one ever goes to the bathroom in romance novels,* I thought, finding the paperback I'd been reading on the couch and tossing it aside. I opened the bed, because it seemed like the appropriate thing to do. Peter wasn't leaving tonight, I was sure of that.

He came out of the bathroom after a short interval, kicked off his shoes, slid out of his jacket and jeans and joined me on the bed. He didn't comment, but put his arms around me, kissed me in a lingering way, then laughed into my hair as I failed to stifle a yawn.

"We've got a lot to catch up on," he said, and I could tell he was smiling. "But it can wait until tomorrow. I need to go home for Oss in the morning. Want to have breakfast with us?"

"It's a date," I said sleepily.

"Night, Lola," he said.

"Night, Peter," I echoed, slipping softly into sleep.

■ ■ ■

I dreamed about Marianne. She and I were at an amusement park, sort of like the Santa Cruz Boardwalk, being chased by faceless shadows that kept coming and coming no matter how fast we ran or where we hid. Unpleasantly grim. At some point it morphed into being chased here, on the beach—chased by three big dogs. One of them got Marianne, and then Peter was there, laughing and helping us to escape. The dream changed again, and I didn't remember any more after that.

I woke up early, stretching and feeling Peter's shape next to me, thinking about what I remembered of my dreams. He was still asleep, so I spent a few minutes watching him. His breathing came slow and even. I reached out to his chest and felt his heart, beating under his black cotton t-shirt. It was just after sunrise, with just the faintest blue light coming in through the shaded windows, the familiar chorus of birds cheerfully greeting the new day in the oak trees above.

If I hadn't needed to get up, I would have happily stayed there forever, but now that I was fully awake my bladder became more and more insistent. I climbed carefully over Peter's sleeping form and quietly shut the bathroom door behind me, taking as little time as possible before coming back out. He was awake, already pulling on his jeans.

"Sleep well?" he asked.

"Very well," I said, coming over to kiss him. Again, not something I'd ever done before—casually show affection after spending the night with a guy I'd just met. But this wasn't an ordinary first night with someone, much less an ordinary someone. "You?"

"I didn't think I'd be able to sleep, but I actually did. I've had a lot on my mind lately."

"I can relate to that."

It explained something I'd noticed without really noticing: the dark circles under his eyes, the tense set of his mouth. Together we folded the bed away, then he sat at the table to put on his shoes while I slipped into the jeans and shirt I'd worn the night before. I didn't turn modestly away to change, and he didn't ogle me or make any remarks. I was hyper-aware of him sitting just a few feet away while I slipped off my sleeping tee and slipped on my not-very-impressive bra, and swapped my pajama pants for the jeans, and I could tell he was hyper-aware that I was changing.

Even as I felt a shiver of excitement, this also felt completely normal. Not boring, just... expected. Sooner or later, we'd see each other naked. It would be a familiar sight—stimulating and arousing at times, routine at others.

I put on my shoes and swept my tousled hair into a bun before quickly grabbing my jacket, knowing Peter was anxious to get back to Osiris. We were in his truck—a tan Tacoma, well used and well cared for—headed down the lane within five minutes of getting up. A soft mist had gathered in the sky between the ocean and mountains, but I could tell it was going to be a beautiful day.

He turned right once we reached Highway 1, driving north through Half Moon Bay and several miles farther along the coast road, turning off in Linda Mar, a southern neighborhood of Pacifica, tucked into a small valley rising from ocean up into green, tree-covered hills. We didn't say much on the drive, but it was a peaceful silence. I was never at my best until I'd had some caffeine, and Peter, I was coming to realize, had a calm sort of presence that moved easily between volubility and quiet, depending on his mood and the situation.

His apartment was a short drive into the gently rising suburb, taking us through mostly residential streets with single-family homes. We turned down a wide avenue and passed a mini-mall full of shops and businesses, turning again at the corner where the mall ended. After about a block, he parallel parked on the street in front of a two-story apartment building.

It was bland but not unattractive, the kind of place built in the nineteen seventies and continually remodeled over the years. Peter had a lower apartment with a small patio—not much room for a large brown dog to run around. I could see why he didn't want to leave Osiris too long.

Osiris, who really should have been named Bear or Rocky to match his exuberant personality, greeted us with unabashed delight, rearing up to lick my face and leaping around the room, tail wagging wildly. Peter had left the sliding door open about a foot so the dog could use the patio for any emergency business—nobody would break in after seeing him—but he was undoubtedly ready to get out and stretch his long legs.

There wasn't much time to look around. I saw a pleasantly lived-in space, not dirty but not freshly clean, either. It had a cramped slip of a kitchen looking over a narrow living room with couch, coffee table and TV. On the far end of the room, the glass door gave access to the patio. A hallway opened to the right.

A single person kind of apartment. I was reminded of mine in LA; this was actually quite a bit nicer and in a much better location, but even so had the same feel. One plate and glass in the sink for each day dishes weren't done. One set of keys on the counter. One towel on the bathroom rack.

I didn't think there was anything wrong with being single. I'd enjoyed many aspects of it, more in the Bay Area than in LA, which had a fairly brutal dating scene. I didn't look at singlehood like a punishment or something to be endured, as so many of my dates and friends seemed to, until someone moderately bearable showed up to set us free from purgatory.

All the same, I liked the idea of spending my time with someone—the right someone, of course. That was the whole point behind all my dating. Finding someone to share experiences and troubles and expenses, developing a life partnership. It always made sense to pair up eventually, I just hadn't ever met anyone I wanted to pair up with.

Until now, of course, when I seemed to find myself part of a pre-existing pair with a man I hadn't known existed until yesterday.

While I looked around, Peter was pouring out food for Osiris, who ate at record speed, and collecting poop bags and leash onto the counter. Once breakfast had been disposed of, Osiris was, to put it mildly, very excited about the prospect of a walk.

"I don't spend much time here," Peter said, seeing my inquiring glances. "It's too small for Oss, but there aren't a lot of affordable options in the area. He can come to work with me some nights and hang out in the office or run around outside, so that makes it easier."

"My place down south was worse," I told him.

"If that's true, it must have been really crappy. Ready?"

Osiris sat on the seat between us, leaning heavily over me in order to put his head out the window, one large paw on my leg.

"He's not used to anyone else riding with me," Peter said, laughing as he scratched the big furry back. If I'd needed proof of this, Osiris would have confirmed it.

"What kind of dog is he?"

"He's half Lab, the other half is anybody's guess. I adopted him from the shelter when I moved here a couple of years ago."

"Where from?"

"Tucson. I'm originally from Denver, but I've been slowly moving westward for the past fifteen years or so."

"You don't have much further west to go, unless you count Hawaii."

"I wouldn't mind it, but I like it here, too. Do you miss living in Northern California?"

"I think I did, more than I realized. Honestly, I hated LA. I just moved down there to try something new, but the experiment or whatever it was failed."

"You never know until you try. I felt the same about Tucson by the time I left. What made you choose LA?"

"A girlfriend was moving down, so I joined her and roomed with her for the first year I lived there. My mom had just passed—of cancer—and I'd given up my apartment and job to help take care of her." I patted the big furry body on my lap. "It seemed like a good idea at the time."

Peter nodded without saying anything, glancing at me before returning his eyes to the road.

"Where are we going for breakfast?" I asked, not quite ready for the conversation to get too serious.

"There's a little café I like near the harbor at Pillar Point. It's quiet in the morning and has a nice patio for dogs. Sound OK?"

"Sounds perfect."

I assumed that the harbor parking lot would fill up as the day went on, but there were only a few cars in it at seven when we arrived. We first walked Osiris down around the harbor mouth, allowing him to work out some of his energy before we sat down to eat. Peter told me how he bought the bar with his sister and brother-in-law three years ago, at their suggestion. They moved out from Texas and provided half of the capital, while Peter sold his house in Tucson, took out a business loan and put in the final half. He didn't add any editorial commentary about the situation, just filled me in on the background.

In turn, I told him about Uncle Joe leaving his property to my dad, who then passed away while it was still in probate, leaving the current legal tangle. The conversation was light and casual, easy and uncomplicated background to share.

The hard part would come soon enough.

We held hands as we walked, loosely and effortlessly, pausing when Osiris decided he needed to mark or sniff, walking on when he was done. We were holding hands as we approached the café entrance, the dog bounding along beside us. Just as Peter tightened the leash and reached for the handle, the door swung open and we stepped back to allow two people to exit. Both were wearing tan uniforms.

The first was a woman, the second was Deputy Tom Marquardt. In his hands were a to-go coffee cup and a white paper bag. He came to an abrupt stop when he saw us, the door swinging shut behind him, a shocked expression crossing his tanned face.

"Hi, Tom," I said, trying not to feel sheepish.

He continued to stare, his eyes narrowing, mouth closing with a snap.

"Morning, Deputy," Peter said, with the same detached politeness he'd used the previous night. Osiris wagged his tail, sniffing interestedly at Tom's bag.

"Tom?" His companion had stopped a few paces beyond, looking back at him with some surprise. "Everything all right?"

"Morning," Peter said to her, and she gave him a neutral nod before her eyes came to rest on me.

Tom still seemed incapable of speech, causing her to take a concerned step toward us.

"Tom?" she said again, and this time he responded. Turning abruptly, he strode away, quickly passing her, not looking back. Not far from the truck in the parking lot I could see the patrol car. The other deputy hurried to catch up with him, and as we stepped inside we heard her asking him what was going on. We didn't hear his answer.

"I think your bridges are truly burned now," Peter commented, giving me a shamelessly wide grin.

"That's OK," I said candidly, with an equally shameless shrug. "I wasn't attached to them."

chapter 5

We put in our order and went to sit outside, the only occupants of the small enclosed patio. The sun hadn't yet risen high enough to shine over the hills, and I was glad to have a warm coat on and, in a few minutes, a hot mug to wrap my hands around. Osiris lolled happily enough at our feet, keeping a wary eye on the gulls swooping overhead.

"I have a feeling you might be getting a second warning from local law enforcement," Peter said after we'd sat down.

"Only if he catches me at home," I pointed out. "Anyway, you can't get in trouble for dating someone under investigation, can you? If that's what you are."

"No, but you can get noticed."

"He'd already noticed me. Now he just thinks I have terrible taste in men."

"He might not be wrong."

Our coffees were brought out, the young woman giving me a long, measuring stare before offering a special smile and word to Peter. She said something like "you and Osiris are our best customers," and he responded with friendly courtesy before turning back to me. I was amused, but also hoped she wouldn't do anything nasty to my omelet.

As I drank my latte, I realized that in barely a week here, I'd managed to spark the interest of two of the eligible adult men in the area. I wondered why. I felt like I had a healthy perspective on my qualities as a potential partner, and "strong sex appeal" definitely wasn't one of them.

The only reasonable explanation—for Tom's attraction, anyway—was novelty, someone new and unknown and therefore appealing. The dating pool just couldn't be that big in this population; singles must end up seeing people in the South Bay or the city, immediately adding an inconvenient commute into date planning. And, if my experiences in LA were any indication, that market, while larger, probably wasn't any easier to navigate.

As a longtime singleton, I could empathize with the server's interest in Peter and any possible resentment toward me. Maybe she'd had hopes that one day he would ask her out, or maybe they'd even gone out in the past. I could understand how she felt.

That being said, as far as I was concerned, one of the local bachelors was off the market. Indefinitely. The other was all hers.

"So tell me," I said.

"Me first?"

"You first."

He took a sip of coffee and set down his cup, his eyes on the harbor.

"Well, here goes nothing. My brother-in-law, Hal, is on the verge of being arrested for drug trafficking." He glanced at me; seeing no revulsion or alarm, only the natural curiosity I was feeling, he went on. "I don't think my sister knew about it—or maybe didn't want to know. She definitely wasn't in it with him, but I don't know if she'd testify against him. The federal Drug Enforcement Administration's been investigating him for a while—years, maybe. Before we came to California. He was a truck driver in Texas when Delia married him. It's her second marriage, and not a very successful one. She's loyal, though—to a fault. She also has a kid in college, my nephew. He has two more years at Texas A&M. She and her first husband were married and divorced young, and she raised PJ by herself. A few years ago she met Hal."

He paused.

"How long have you known about it?" I prompted gently.

"The drugs? A while. I suspected he was dealing coke out of the bar not long after we opened—more than two years ago. I confronted him about it, but he denied everything and Delia stood up for him. As much as I liked working there, I was already regretting the partnership. By that time, though, I had everything sunk into the place and couldn't get out. I also didn't want to leave Delia alone with that... I think he's probably hit her a few times. I'm sure of it, actually. She won't admit it, but the signs are there. I've told her I'll help her get away from him, but she won't do anything about it."

"Bastard," I said angrily.

"And then some. If I'd known what he was like... Anyway. I did my best to put a stop to the dealing, at least, and it seemed to work. I didn't see any more of it after that. I probably should've turned him in, but... well, I didn't. Not long after that, Hal started disappearing for weeks at a time. It made Delia unhappy but was easier on all of us. We ran the business, he ran around on her."

Our food came out. Hungry as I was after days of the barest snacking, I almost forgot to eat, I was so engrossed in the story.

"About a month ago, Delia and I got a visit from DEA agents who were looking for Hal. She told them she didn't know where he was, but I'm not sure they believed her. They wanted to interview him for an ongoing investigation. They wouldn't say what it was about. The thing is, if it was just small-time dealing the Feds wouldn't have gotten involved. I finally got it out of Delia that she suspected he had ties to some extremely shady people around the border or even across it. My guess would be cartels."

"They haven't found him?"

"Not yet. His phone has no service, which makes me think he's out of the country. We don't know where he went or if he's coming back. I know the DEA's been checking into my sister and me, and I have a feeling we'll be guilty by association, even if we're not charged with anything."

"You think Delia will stand by him?"

"As long as possible. I think he's a double-dealing asshole, but he's got a hold on her. Even if the business wasn't involved, I couldn't leave her alone to deal with all of this. But my name is on the license, which means Delia and I could both be liable if they find that the property was being used to break any federal laws."

"Would it help if you testified about what you saw?"

"I don't know. It might. The problem is that I'll have to admit I knew about the dealing and didn't turn him in. Assuming they have proof of that, I guess. I just hope they're not interested in minor accessory charges at this point, if Hal is in as deep as I suspect he is." He rubbed his face tiredly and looked at me. "Well, that's the situation. I'd understand if it's... not something you want to be involved in."

"It isn't your fault. Or your sister's. I'm really sorry that it's happening, but it doesn't change anything for me."

"I'm glad to hear you say that, even if it is kind of misguided. Is your omelet OK?"

"What? Oh—it's delicious." I forced my mind back to my breakfast, though was still pondering Peter's story.

"When's the last time you had a solid meal?"

I thought back.

"A week ago Tuesday, or maybe Wednesday. The days have kind of run together."

"A perfect segue. Your turn."

■ ■ ■

I took a minute to collect my thoughts, while Peter patiently ate his eggs and toast.

"OK... My cousin... I was almost done with work for the day—just over a week ago—and my cousin—Marianne—called.

She's two years older than me. She's like my sister. Neither of us has any siblings, and we were raised together—her parents lived overseas most of the time, so she lived with us. I hadn't heard from her in a while so I was excited to take the call—but I could tell she sounded strange. Upset. She told me she needed to see me right now, to leave work and meet her at my apartment. She wouldn't say anything else—she hung up before I could ask any questions, and her phone went to voicemail when I called back. It was almost five, so I told my supervisor I had a family emergency and got home as quickly as I could—panicking the whole way.

"When I got to my apartment, Marianne was waiting outside. She didn't even stop to hug me, she just pulled me upstairs and shut the door and told me that we were in danger. Something had happened—she'd done something, she said, and there was no stopping it now. I'd have to get out of town until everything had been cleared up."

"She didn't tell you what had happened, or what it was about?"

"She wouldn't—she just started packing my clothes and saying that she was doing this to protect me. I kept trying to stop her and make her explain, but she only repeated the same things. By that time I was frantic—I didn't know what to do. I tried to call nine-one-one but she took my phone and told me that we couldn't go to the police. They couldn't help and they'd arrest us—arrest me—on the spot. It didn't make sense, but I could tell she was really scared—and that terrified me. She told me not to use credit cards or to register at hotels, she said to drive here, to Uncle Joe's place, and hide out until she could contact me. I was supposed to take a long route here, through Sacramento and Napa and down through the city, taking a couple of days. She handed me almost four thousand dollars in cash and a burner phone, which she said only to use in an emergency. If someone found me or if I felt threatened in any way, to call the number she programmed in—but never to pick up if it rang."

"That's a lot of cash to carry around. She kept your phone?"

"She turned it off and put it in her pocket. And then she put a gun in my bag. It's all—it was kind of a blur. We finished packing and she helped me lock up and walked me to my car. And left."

"What kind of gun?"

"I don't know. I don't know anything about guns. I haven't touched it."

We finished our last bites, not hurrying. Another couple came out onto the patio and sat at a far table.

"What happened after that?" Peter prompted in a lowered voice, and I quietly told him about my panicked nighttime drive north, about spending a few hours resting in random parking lots, exhausted and afraid. Considering and rejecting going to the nearest police station about fifty times. Getting to Uncle Joe's and laying as low as I possibly could.

"I did everything she said, except I kept the burner phone turned on," I admitted. "It rang yesterday—a restricted number—but I didn't answer and turned it off."

Strange to think that was only yesterday. I hadn't met Peter yet. It seemed like years ago, like a dim and far-off memory.

"Do you want another cup of coffee?" he asked out of a short, thoughtful silence.

"Sure, if you're having one."

"Let's get it to go. We can talk more freely on the beach."

I waited with Osiris while Peter ordered our coffees inside, exiting through the patio gate and meeting him on the sidewalk. We drove down to his favorite beach, the one where we'd met, and had no trouble finding parking. It was still early for the majority of beachgoers, even for a gorgeous Saturday. The sun had already burned off most of the mist and shone bright and warm in a cloud-dotted sky. A light breeze from the Pacific pulled at my hair and cooled our skin.

"What do you think Marianne could have gotten into?" he asked as we walked along, taking turns throwing the stick out into the waves.

"I honestly have no idea. Before she showed up in LA, the last time I saw her was at my dad's funeral last year. We've emailed since then, a couple of times, but she didn't say anything about being in trouble."

"She's never been involved in anything... well, shady?"

"No... not exactly. A few years ago she was part of this sort of commune in Newark. She lived with eleven other people in this horrible loft, and they all dated each other and talked about taking down the system—the ninety-nine percent rising to power, that kind of thing. Marianne didn't ever talk that way, or seem to buy into it, but she stayed there for almost a year. I went there once and hated it—it was... it was gross. And the people were awful. I hated the way they treated Marianne, especially this one guy. He was a dick." I made a face at the memory. "I think he was sort of in charge, ordering everyone around. She moved away eventually, she never said why. It seemed like she was done with all of that."

"Did she stay in touch with them?"

"I don't know. Why? Do you think that's something to do with this?"

Peter didn't answer right away. He picked up the stick and threw it as far as he could. We watched as Osiris went bounding into the water to get it.

"I'm not sure," he said. "It just seems like something isn't hanging together."

"Do you think I was wrong to run?" I asked, open to his honest answer.

"No," he said firmly, reaching for my hand. "What else could you do? I think you were right to follow her instructions. But something's off, all the same. The police, for instance. Why would they arrest you? What are you supposed to have done—and why wouldn't you be able to prove you didn't do it?"

"Identity theft? Someone pretending to be me?" I suggested, one of the only ideas I'd had over the past week.

"Maybe, but you'd still be able to prove that you were innocent of most crimes, unless they really wanted to frame you. No, I think it's something else. I think Marianne told you to leave to protect you from someone, just like she said. But I think she told you not to go to the cops to protect *herself*." I took that in, and he continued, "Not to mention you don't have much to tell them that they can act on. They can't put you into protective custody because you're not a witness to or victim of a crime. All you have is this story—which I believe, and they might too, but it doesn't really get you anywhere. You're still left where you are now… waiting for Marianne to give you the all clear."

"If that ever happens. If she's even still OK."

"I'd say there's a good chance of that. She sounds tough and resourceful."

"She is—both," I agreed, appreciating that he wanted to give me hope.

"There's also the little matter of an unregistered firearm— which would probably get you arrested on federal weapons charges, if the authorities caught you with it."

"I didn't even think of that."

"It seems like the first step's getting rid of the gun. It's way more of a liability than a help. I can't help thinking your cousin knows that."

That made sense, in a sort of sick way.

"What about using my credit cards, and all that?"

"Either the people chasing her—or both of you—have the resources to track card numbers, or she didn't want you to spend your own money. Or something we haven't thought of yet. We don't know where the cash came from, but I doubt she'd have given it to you if it was traceable."

"So she doesn't want me to be in danger, which implies that she's in danger and it somehow involved me—but she doesn't want me to report any of this to anybody official," I clarified out loud to myself. "That would fit. It doesn't explain who called the burner phone, or give me any idea what to do next—besides dumping the gun."

"It looks to me like you have three options. Stay here, maybe indefinitely. Go home and pretend like nothing happened. Or— try to figure out what's going on."

I did not see that third choice coming.

"How would I do that?" I asked, surprised.

"Look for links to Marianne. This could be connected to those people she was involved with, that commune. They sound like trouble. It could be a dead end, but it's the only lead we have right now. If they were really anarchists, maybe they took it to a dangerous place, and maybe Marianne was caught up in something extreme. I say we start in Newark and see what we can find."

I stopped, pulling him to a stop alongside me.

"What are you saying?" I asked, confused. "You want to go— track these people down?"

"Not if you don't want to." He put both arms around me and pulled me in close. "It's a reckless idea, I know that. I might be indicted tomorrow—today—if Hal shows up or the DEA makes a move. They might not even let me leave the state. It might be a wild goose chase, or it might get us into a lot of trouble. We could just stay here instead, wait and see and spend time together. We could go back to LA, if that's what you want—I couldn't stay long, but I could go with you. Or we can try to find some answers."

"You'd put your life on hold for me like that? Go tearing across the state or country without knowing what's ahead?"

Peter leaned down and kissed me once, very decisively.

"We never know what's ahead, honey. And I can't think of any better way to spend my time than with you. If you ever want to call this off, I'll respect that. But until then I'm not going anywhere. I'm not going to pretend I'm a hero, or a saint—I'm not. I'm as... as flawed and scarred and screwed up as the next person. Maybe more than some. I just know that I want you."

"Wow," I said, hugging him tightly.

"Too much?"

"No, it's just exactly how I feel about you."

He looked at his watch without letting me go.

"I have three hours until I have to be at the bar."

"Come on," I said, pulling away and heading quickly back toward the truck.

■ ■ ■

Osiris stayed with me for the afternoon when Peter left for work. We walked the two miles back to the beach, his favorite place, now crowded with day-trippers and families. I relaxed or wandered on the sand, he chased gulls and waves and other dogs, startling then delighting small children as they discovered him to be a large, damp, furry playmate.

I watched him dreamily, my mind drifting between memories of that morning in the camper, to the strangely easy exchange of our difficult stories, to the choices that lay before us.

Before me, it seemed, because while Peter was willing to discuss the pros and cons of each option at length, giving his opinions of the positives and negatives, he wanted it to be my decision.

I knew I didn't want to go back to the gray treadmill of life in Los Angeles. Objectively, I could see that there were benefits to living in the greater LA area—arts and culture and weather and style. But none of them appealed to me a hundredth as much as what the greater Bay Area could offer. This was my home—if not Half Moon Bay, then somewhere else up here. It was expensive as hell, but I was starting out with a prize beyond anything I'd ever earned or received: Uncle Joe's property.

Legal tangles aside, it was mine. He had no family to contest his bequest to my father, and I was my father's sole beneficiary. I'd been too stunned and wounded by my dad's death to fully appreciate what these two men had given me, but now I understood that together they had handed me an opportunity to move back to where I really wanted to be, whether I lived on the land or sold it.

That removed returning to LA as an option. Of course I'd need to go back at some point to wind up my month-to-month lease and empty the place, but it didn't need to happen right now. I knew I wasn't going back to live there. I could contact my supervisor and officially quit, with the same family emergency excuse I'd used for my absence. I didn't think they'd care much— I'd been a temp-to-hire from an agency a year ago, one of two dozen low-paid processors cycling through endless amounts of data, another insignificant cog in a corporate wheel.

For the first time, I let myself feel relieved—more than relieved, *overjoyed*—that this empty, unhappy, interminable period in my life had come to an end. I'd been vaguely regretting the loss of it; regretting the choices I'd made, regretting the earthquake that had shaken me loose. But not anymore.

I was here—free and more content than I remembered being in a long, long time. I had options. I had problems, too: Marianne, the danger I might still be in, unknown questions to answer.

But I also had Peter.

The memory of his mouth on my body, his body joined with mine, the feeling of him inside me and around me—smelling him, tasting him, his hands roaming and pushing and stroking my tingling skin... it distracted me from all other thoughts for several long, aching minutes. First times have an awkwardness to them, and ours was no exception in some ways. It was fast, fueled by a kind of desperate fervor, and that helped—because the second time was slow. Slow, and utterly sensual. All awkwardness had been dealt with, everything deep and private had been touched and mingled. The second time we could explore, tease, pause to kiss and speak and gasp with pleasure.

Just remembering the second time had my skin feeling overheated, a delicious prickling just where delicious prickles are most appreciated. I breathed into the sensation, feeling a mixture of gratitude and electrified anticipation...

A loud woof from Osiris, standing nearby over his latest sodden wood trophy, brought my attention sharply back to the present. I got up and threw the stick for him, walking and thinking about the two options left to me.

Stay here and wait it out—at least until I couldn't put off dealing with LA any longer—and then return here to wait some more. Spend time with Peter, drift and do nothing and hope that Marianne was all right and the problem would be solved somewhere else, far away, incomprehensible and detached from me. Whatever the danger was, it hadn't found me yet, and maybe it never would. Peter had unloaded the gun and taken it and the bullets with him, wrapped in old rags from the shed, and was going to throw it off the deepest nearby pier before he went to work, so that problem should already be solved. For the rest, Marianne had gotten herself into this mess, gotten me into it, and had told me in no uncertain terms that she would handle getting us out of it.

There were plenty of pros to this choice. Everything about it was tempting, the landscape and the freedom and the chance to simply drift, with Peter the cherry on top. I'd be able to help, or give any support I could, when Hal came back or the DEA acted, whichever came first. Peter was sure that something very unpleasant would go down, it was just a matter of time, and I believed that he knew what he was talking about.

It was easy to reject his other suggestion as impossible, absurd—reckless, as he'd said. We didn't even know what kind of information we'd be asking for, much less who would know the answers. We had exactly one lead, and I for one had never tried to investigate anything more complicated than Googling someone I was meeting for a first date, just to make sure they weren't sex offenders or serial killers or known members of their friendly neighborhood KKK.

Peter was fairly confident that we could at least find out something more about the commune, since it was unusual enough to have attracted attention in the neighborhood and they weren't exactly hush-hush about it. As I recalled, they'd actually had a social media account—which I stopped following minutes after I started, it was so disturbing in its fanatic hatred of authority, with distinct undercurrents of bigotry and anti-feminism, as those sorts of things so often feature.

But even if we did find the warehouse and learn more about the people involved, there was no telling that it had any connection to the situation Marianne was involved in now. Peter freely admitted as much, saying that the likelihood of coming up with absolutely nothing to show for the effort was dismally high.

Taking all of this into account, the decision should have been simple. Stay here. Stay put, stay safe, wait and see. Enjoy my time with Peter. Get a new phone and a new job and live my life in peace.

I just couldn't seem to decide that.

For whatever reason, maybe the same impulse that had prompted Peter to suggest the scheme in the first place, I found I couldn't let go of it. Maybe it would mean a fruitless, frustrating trip. Maybe we'd find out nothing, or only just enough to make me even more worried about my cousin. Maybe we'd stir up more trouble than it was worth. Maybe Peter wouldn't even be able to leave the state. I had no very clear idea of what we could accomplish in a best-case scenario. The one thing that drew me to the idea was both illogical and unlikely.

The chance to take my power back.

Not to wait and look over my shoulder for the next week, month, year. Years. Not to never hear from Marianne and always worry, always wonder. But to step out and actively seek answers, to rise up to meet the challenge, even if the effort failed.

It was the very longest of long shots. It was the stupid choice to make. And it was what I wanted to do.

chapter 6

Peter and I had arranged for me to bring Osiris down to the bar at five, before the Hideout got busy, so we could join him for the dinner run and eat together. He said he didn't expect me to stay, since he'd be working most of the evening, but I told him I wanted to. What else was I going to do? I could have handled another long evening alone with mindless novels and red wine if Peter wasn't in the picture, or if it wasn't all so new, with every minute counting more than the last, but it was no use pretending that meeting him hadn't dramatically shifted my priorities.

"I'd rather be there than alone at the camper—even with my new best doggie friend," I'd said.

"We can hang out in the back office together. Or—you know what? I haven't been serving much since the rumors started flying, but I'll come out front if you're there," he said. "It's not like it's helped for Delia and me to stay out of sight. It just made everyone act more awkward when we did show up."

"No more hiding," I'd agreed—hours before I'd consciously made my choice.

No more hiding for either of us, not even at the ironically-named Hideout. As a team we could handle whatever came of stepping forward. Deputy Tom already knew we were together, or at least as together as walking to breakfast holding hands implied, and I didn't think he was the type of person to keep that kind of news to himself, which meant that at least some locals wouldn't be surprised to see me hanging around like a bar groupie. There might be stares and whispers, but what did it matter?

I turned into the Hideout parking lot to find Peter waiting outside for me; he got in and directed me up the road to a burger joint which had an order waiting. Osiris was happy to see him, though less happy to give up shotgun and sit in the back. After that point had been settled with a few firm commands, Peter kissed me and told me to turn right exiting the parking lot.

"I got you what Del always gets, a chicken burger—I have no idea if it's good but she said to order it for you."

"That's great, thanks. You told her about me?"

He flashed me a rueful grin.

"Kind of. She gets things out of me," he admitted.

"I'm not upset—I like that you told her. So… *what* did you tell her, exactly?"

"She asked what was up with me, why did I look like I'd just landed alone on Mars and found it populated by horny female sex aliens, and—" he broke off, seeing me overcome with laughter. "That's the kind of thing she says. It disarms you."

"I can see how it would. So you told her…"

"That I'd met an incredible woman and she was coming to the bar tonight—doing the dinner run with me. She recommended the chicken burger and said she was looking forward to meeting you."

We reached the restaurant in five minutes. Peter jumped out, to Osiris's dismay, returning quickly with two large paper bags full of greasy food, to Osiris's delight. I drove back the way we'd come, a straight shot down Highway 1.

"Delia doesn't know you know all the sordid details," Peter warned me as I parked in the gravel lot. "I think she'd be surprised that I'd tell someone I just met about what's happening."

I turned off the engine and released my seat belt.

"I won't say anything."

"I know you won't." He waited a minute, looking at the front of the bar without moving. Osiris whined impatiently from the back seat, and Peter absently reached back to scratch his head. "I didn't tell you everything."

"That's OK," I said after a pause.

He turned back toward me.

"No, it isn't. I told you I wasn't a saint. I got into some trouble in Tucson. A couple of DUIs and possession of a narcotic. Cocaine, actually," he said, with tart resignation. "I... wasn't in a great place after my divorce, so there were a few lost months. I've been clean for years—it was never an addiction. More like a distraction. But I wanted you to know."

His eyes met mine.

"Divorce?" I inquired.

To be honest, that was the most unexpected part of his confession. A good number of people I knew had meddled with cocaine, or had a DUI at some point or other. It wasn't something to be proud of by any means, but it didn't make you a villain. It also wasn't my place to judge his past mistakes. His marital history, however, was something else entirely.

"A long time ago. We were only married three years—not even three, but it hit me hard when we decided to split." His gaze was as straight and open as ever, and in a flash I knew his pain—the loss and strangeness and disappointment he'd felt during that time. I couldn't find the words to express my empathy, or the fact that hearing this changed nothing for me, so I kissed him instead. From the enthusiastic response, I felt confident that he appreciated what I was trying to express.

We might have continued indefinitely if not for Osiris, whining even more loudly behind us, and the cooling burgers on Peter's lap.

"Come on," he said reluctantly, getting out of the car and leading the way into building, the dog bounding between us.

"Hey," a woman greeted us from beside the bar as we walked in. There were a few scattered customers, nothing like the crowds from last night. We walked over to join her, and I saw that she was an older, shorter, feminine copy of Peter with dark, chin-length hair and eyes puffy with tiredness and worry. "You must be Lola."

"This is my sister, Delia," Peter said.

"Hi, Delia," I said, smiling tentatively. "Thanks for suggesting the chicken burger."

"It's the best thing on the menu," Delia said, giving me the once-over I'd expected. "All these guys just go for the beef, they don't even bother to try it."

"Beef is *beef*," Peter protested, putting one of the bags of food on the bar. "There's no substitute for the original."

"Amen, brother," the lanky bartender, Lyle, agreed, rustling around in the bag. He glanced briefly at me as he pulled out his sandwich.

"Hi," I said.

Peter introduced us, and Lyle stepped over to shake my hand.

"What are you doing here, you silly mutt?" Lyle asked Osiris, who'd been sniffing the leg of one of the customers seated at the bar.

"Causing trouble, as usual," the guy said, laughing and patting the dog's big head.

"Let's take him out back," Peter suggested to me, indicating the other bag in his hand and whistling to the dog. With a quick half-smile at Delia, I followed him through the "Employees Only" door into a hallway, which had cramped but tidy storerooms and offices on either side and opened into the back yard. He led the way into one of the offices, barely bigger than the camper, which held a desk, desk chair and very ugly and battered brown love seat that, if the dog hair was any indication, was Osiris's personal property. On the desk were stacks of papers, a lamp, a printer and a laptop.

"This is where the magic happens?" I asked, sitting on the arm of the sofa, since the usual occupant had taken up the rest of it.

"When it's not happening elsewhere," he said equably, but flashed me a look that brought the color and heat to my cheeks. "Down, Oss. Here, eat your dinner." He scooped dog food from a bag in the corner into a big bowl on the floor, and Osiris fell to ravenously.

We sat side by side on the couch munching our burgers, eating with slightly more restraint and much less noise. Again, the silence was companionable, though it was just as companionable when I broke it to ask what time the bar usually got busy on Saturdays, and Peter answered. He added that Fridays were their best night, with Saturdays a close second, filling up with a mix of locals and visitors.

Only once we'd finished and collected our wrappings—Delia had been right that the chicken was delicious, as were the fries— did I bring up our earlier discussions about the immediate future.

"I thought a lot today about what I want to do next," I told him. He pulled me halfway onto his lap and nuzzled my neck, which was as gratifying as it was distracting.

"Mmm?" he inquired.

"I'm still not convinced it's the right choice… and I know it's the—it's the dumbest…" I continued determinedly, growing somewhat breathless, "but I think we should to go to Newark."

After a final kiss on my collarbone, Peter pulled back far enough to look at me.

"I had a feeling you'd opt for that," he said, smiling slightly.

"You did? Mind sharing why?"

"For the same reason I suggested it. So we can at least try to be free of whatever's hanging over you—and maybe find out what it is, and do whatever we can to help your cousin."

"You're a very smart man, do you know that?"

"I know enough to know I'm not that smart. But for whatever reason," his lips moved intriguingly down toward the point of the V-neck I was wearing, "my intuition is excellent when it comes to you."

"I… can't… can't argue," I said, my breath coming in undignified pants that would have done Osiris proud.

Peter sat up straight and pulled me closer, so that we were practically nose-to-nose.

"You really want to go?"

I nodded.

"I really do. In spite of my better judgment."

"Then we'll go tomorrow. We can catch a red-eye to Newark from SFO tomorrow night—I already checked and there are tickets available. We're closed on Mondays, and they can run the place without me for a few days next week. Lyle can take Oss, or Delia will."

"So efficient," I said admiringly, leaning over to start some nuzzling of my own. His neck smelled fantastic—not like cologne or aftershave, exactly, just the smell of clean skin that had filled my senses the previous night and morning.

"I don't think the DEA will have a problem with me going," he continued, and I was glad to hear that his voice wasn't completely steady. "I checked with my ex-wife, she said they'd probably want to have a warrant to stop me from flying—it would be different if we were leaving the country."

"Your ex-wife?" I repeated, curious.

"She's a cop," he said, not misunderstanding my interest. "A detective in Tucson. Happily remarried to a guy she knew in high school. I've been keeping her in the loop on the situation out here, and called earlier to see if she thought it would be OK to book a short trip back east. She thought it would be fine."

"Did she say to tell the local cops you'd be out of town for a few days?"

"I didn't ask."

We became distracted—it was far too easy to be distracted just now—until we were roused by the door leading to the bar opening and closing, and Osiris dashing out of the room to meet whoever was coming into the back hall. We'd just pulled apart when Delia appeared in the doorway, eyeing us speculatively.

"Amanda just called in sick," she said without preamble, sounding annoyed. "That's the second Saturday night she's missed in a row. I'm thinking it's not a coincidence. It's too last-minute to get anyone else to come in to cover her shift."

"I'll cover for her," Peter said, making no move to stand up.

Delia stared at him with pursed lips, then shrugged.

"Might as well," she agreed cynically. "Everybody's talking about us anyway. At least you and Lola are giving them something new to twaddle about."

"Is Yvonne here?"

"Running late, but she'll be here in ten."

"OK. I'll be right out."

"I'll be in my office."

With a weary nod, Delia walked out, and we heard the sound of a closing door.

"She's taking this hard—understandably," Peter said, rising and tossing our food wrappings toward an overflowing trash bin. The bag promptly slid off, and Osiris moved casually toward it. "Oss." Two big brown doggie eyes rolled in his master's direction. "*No.*"

With a sigh that was almost human, Osiris gave up on the scent of grease and threw himself on the couch beside me, his legs pushing until I was forced to stand up to give him room. Peter picked up the bag from the floor.

"Is there anything I can do to help tonight?" I asked, following him out of the office.

"I think we'll be OK. Feel free to relax—enjoy your evening."

"I'll enjoy it just as much clearing a few empty glasses," I said. "And you're short-staffed."

"We'll play it by ear," he said noncommittally, opening the back hallway door for me. "But thank you for the offer."

The number of people in the barroom had more than doubled, and Lyle was now serving several customers. Peter joined him behind the bar, while I sat on an empty stool at the end closest to the back. A TV overhead was showing a rerun of "Flip or Flop," which I could follow even without sound. The other TVs showed baseball and golf.

"What'll you have? On the house, of course," Peter offered, throwing a bar towel over one shoulder and gesturing toward the rows of bottles behind him.

"Vodka tonic, please," I said promptly, and watched as he poured out a generous amount of premium vodka. There was something to be said for dating the owner.

■ ■ ■

By nine, the room was crowded and Peter, Lyle and Yvonne were kept busy pouring, cashing out and clearing up. Twice I made a round of tables and picked up empty glasses, which nobody noticed except Peter. Yvonne, after one hard glance, ignored me. She was a sharp-featured woman about my age, I guessed, wearing an extremely tight, low-cut black dress, serving with a sort of no-nonsense attitude and not much small talk.

I sipped two vodka tonics and three glasses of water, appreciating every glance Peter and I shared, every time he touched my waist or back as he walked by, every word we exchanged in passing. It was fun to observe without feeling self-conscious about sitting alone. I used to go out by myself in my early twenties just to go out, and never minded flying solo, but in recent years, even just waiting a few minutes at a bar for a date or a friend I felt like I was being sized up and judged by every male in the place—and whether they found I was worth approaching or not, it was an embarrassing and oddly sordid experience. I blamed LA, but the same thing probably happened in meat markets everywhere.

I didn't see Tom as the night went on, but Stacy arrived with three girlfriends. She spotted me and came over, leaving the others to order from Peter.

"Hey," she said in a friendly way. "Are you alone?"

"Not exactly," I said, nodding down the bar. One of her friends was leaning unnecessarily far across the bar top to smile coyly at Peter while she ordered, artistically showing off her cleavage. He said something and she laughed a little too loudly at what I guessed was a polite witticism.

As if he could feel my eyes on him, he looked over at me and grinned before starting to mix a cocktail.

"Oh... So that's a thing, huh?"

"Looks like it," I said casually, somehow unable to keep the profound confidence I felt out of my voice.

She smiled with genuine amusement, raising her eyebrows.

"Dang. I'd call you a fast worker, but I don't think that's it, or you would've gone for Tom."

"It was fast, but... unintentional, you know? It just sort of—happened."

"I'm glad. I've always liked Peter—I mean, thought he was a good guy," she clarified quickly. "Like I said, the rumor mill is stupid. I never thought there was much to it. Though Hal is kind of a slime ball, it's not hard to believe he'd be into something shady. One of those sleazy guys who runs around on his wife and always seems to have an angle. He's hit on me in front of my dates—in front of his own *wife*, which is just... guhh. It sucks, because Delia's cool."

"He sounds like a rat," I said.

"The rattiest of rats," Stacy agreed. "He even looks like a rat—thin lips and beady eyes." She made a disgusted face, and I couldn't help laughing. "It's probably an insult to rats to call him one."

"I can't wait to meet him. Do you want a drink?" I asked.

"My friends were ordering one for me. But thanks. You're welcome to join us, if you want."

We both glanced involuntarily down the bar where her friends continued to banter with Peter.

"Thanks... but maybe another time," I said.

Given their obvious interest in him, I doubted I'd be too popular with the others once they knew the situation. Even if curiosity or kindness won out over resentment and they were nice to me, they might pepper me with uncomfortably intimate questions that I didn't want to answer. I didn't mind Stacy knowing, but she'd already proven herself to be a considerate person, while the only thing I knew about her friends was that at least two of them had amorous intentions toward the guy I was dating.

Stacy accepted my refusal without comment, possibly coming to the same conclusions.

"Well, I'm going to mingle—I'll find you again in a bit."

"OK, cool," I said.

She moved off toward the group as they found seats, joining them at a table in the center of the room. They were all in their thirties or forties, clearly ready to have a good time on a Saturday night. Nothing wrong with that, it could easily have been me out with my girlfriends in LA. We'd occasionally meet at a bar or club, especially those of my friends who were single, which was most of them. I'd only gotten to know a few women, nobody I'd consider especially close, but my friends had friends, and often the groups would get fairly big.

A while later, right after Peter had come over to check on me, placing his hand on my back, I stood up to find all three of Stacy's friends staring frankly, and not very appreciatively, in my direction, and knew I'd been right to keep my distance.

My eyes met Stacy's as I crossed the room toward the bathroom, and we both turned away to hid our grins. It was kind of nice to feel I had an ally, or at least a sociable acquaintance, in an otherwise anonymous crowd. The only other face I recognized was Phil the belligerent drunk, who Peter and Lyle kept a firm handle on.

By eleven I was tired, and told Peter I thought I'd head to the camper. He called to Lyle that he'd be right back and walked me toward the back premises.

"Take Oss with you," he suggested. "I'll be up around one."

"Do you want to go to your place instead?"

"Alone?" he asked, surprised—as well he might be.

"No, all of us. You could pick us up."

He smiled and shook his head, opening the "Employees Only" door for me.

"It's fine. Get some sleep. I'll bring up food for Oss's breakfast."

I didn't know how many people saw us leave together, but had a feeling it was noticed, and probably discussed. The thought didn't bother me; it was just more fodder for the local gossips, which I hoped wouldn't cause Peter and Delia any more trouble than they'd already had to face. Though, as Delia pointed out, at least it was a new topic of conversation.

We collected the dog from Peter's office, walking out through the back exit and around to where my car was parked. Delia's office door was still shut when we passed it.

"See you soon," he said. "We can book our flight tomorrow morning."

"Are we being totally impulsive and stupid?" I asked, getting into the car and rolling down the driver's side window before I shut the door.

"Totally," he said, kissing me briefly and waving us off.

chapter 7

The next morning we sat in Peter's living room charging seven hundred dollars' worth of plane tickets and fees to his credit card. I had all the cash we could possibly need, even after my supply shopping, but he said we'd work that out later, better to book our tickets online now and use the cash for expenses on the trip. The flight left SFO at five minutes after ten that evening, with a return flight scheduled for Thursday afternoon. We were really going.

I'd been fast asleep, Osiris snoring next to me, when Peter knocked on the camper door the previous night. The bed barely fit the three of us, though I found it cozy to be wedged together. It would have been extremely easy to slip into a repeat of our earlier activities, but we were both tired with a long day ahead of us—and I at least anticipated a lot of opportunities in the coming days… weeks… months… to enjoy the physical side of our relationship. There was also a large dog in the bed and nowhere else in the camper for him to lie down, except the hardwood floor—which he'd already made clear was *not* going to be acceptable.

I hoped he wouldn't feel too abandoned with Lyle, who had agreed to dog sit for a few days. At least Osiris would have company: Lyle's two huskies were playmates of his, Peter had told me reassuringly.

"Did you get a chance to tell Delia?" I asked idly, perched beside Peter on the couch while he balanced his laptop on his knees.

"Yeah. I said you had urgent business in New York that I wanted to help sort out, though nothing more than that. I told her we'd come back if anything—if there were any new developments with Hal. She seemed OK with it." He smiled quizzically at the memory. "I think she's already resigned to things being different, now that you're in the picture."

"Do you think she feels like we've moved too fast?"

He gave a half-shrug.

"If she did, she wouldn't say so. She's never weighed in on my choices, though she's seen me make some pretty big screw-ups. It goes both ways, though. I've never questioned or judged what she wants to do—as hard as it can be at times. Especially lately."

"Hal sounds like a piece of shit," I agreed.

"He is that. Let's just hope he stays out of prison for another week."

Using one of my cards this time, at my insistence, we found and booked a hotel in Manhattan, getting a midweek rate along with a twenty-percent-off booking special. I knew Marianne had said not to use my accounts for anything, but I couldn't see that it mattered. It was hard to believe it could, and I didn't want Peter to put anything else on his card after paying for the flights. Not to mention how much he was already doing, along with assuring me that he knew the city well and was looking forward to going back.

I'd only been to New York one time, traveling there with several college friends. We'd spent a long weekend seeing the major sights and celebrating our mini-reunion, which made parts of the trip distinctly hazy in my memory.

On one of the days, I'd left the group and gone to Newark to visit Marianne. I don't know why she thought it would be a good idea for me to see her at the loft. I'd been so uncomfortable I hadn't stayed more than a few minutes, and then Mike, a dirty guy with long hair and an aggressiveness I found extremely disturbing, had entered the scene, and I took the train back to my friends.

The hotel we booked wasn't too far from the headquarters of the United Nations, something I'd missed seeing last time due to my ill-fated outing to New Jersey, though I doubted we'd have a chance to go there. Sightseeing wasn't going to be a priority on this trip. I had a hard time imagining what we'd be doing, but at this point I was getting used to only seeing one or two steps ahead. Peter had spent considerably more time in New York, visiting a childhood friend in Queens over the years. He was more familiar with the transit system than I was, already knowing how we'd get around in Newark and which trains we'd take to our hotel.

Transportation and shelter being arranged, we moved onto the next task: finding out anything we could about the commune, as I called it. Peter handed me his computer so I could log into my Facebook and Gmail accounts, waiting patiently as I searched for references from six years ago.

"I can't believe it's been more than a week since I logged into anything," I said, seeing a startling number of new emails—most of them spam—and notifications come up.

For the first time since I left LA, it struck me that I hadn't once checked social media. No Instagram updates, no Twitter feeds. No texts, no emails, no messages from dating apps—which, come to think of it, I'd need to cancel my subscriptions to. I'd been completely disconnected from everyone and everything. All those distractions and interactions that had taken up such a large portion of my time and attention had been whisked away along with my phone, left behind in my apartment. It was like I'd gone cold turkey and hadn't even noticed. Of course I'd been bored and lonely those days at the camper by myself, but I'd vaguely attributed that to the isolation of my situation and no TV. I hadn't read the news or heard the latest celebrity scandal, and it didn't seem to matter at all.

I wondered if any of my friends had texted me, and what they thought when I didn't reply. Probably that I was busy; so often we didn't respond to each other, they'd shrug and assume that I forgot to tell them I was going out of town or got involved with a new guy. In both cases, I realized with dark amusement, they'd be right.

Looking at my various feeds, the endless meaningless posts and stories and photos and videos, I felt even more disconnected. Many of the pictures and words represented people who I cared about, it was just impossible to care about the things they were posting. That made it much easier to focus on the search at hand. Marianne had very little presence on social media. The only account I knew she had was Instagram, and her feed was practically empty. The most recent update was a selfie I'd taken of the two of us, posted by me the day after my dad's funeral, when we ate lunch at a restaurant on the Bay. It was the last time we saw each other before she showed up in LA.

I scrolled back to around the time she would have been living in Newark. It didn't take long with the lack of content, but found nothing that I could tie back to her living situation. Really there was very little there at all. It seemed strange, now, that she'd posted almost nothing over the years, but then it was possible I'd just never noticed. Lots of people kept a low profile online. Peter, for one, said he only looked at Twitter and never tweeted anything himself.

"Nothing here," I told him. "I might have saved the address in my emails, and I'll see if I can't find the Facebook page they started."

Using my own Facebook profile, I scrolled back... and back... and back... until around the time that I remembered Marianne getting involved with the commune, looking at page likes. I was almost ready to give up, feeling I'd gone too far, when I hit "display older posts" and there it was, right on top.

"Holy crap, I think I found them," I told Peter, almost as surprised as gratified. "'Free the People,' that's what they called themselves."

He leaned to look with me as I clicked on the page name, half-expecting it to tell me it no longer existed. But the page was still active, whether or not the commune was. It called itself a social group and didn't list a public owner. There wasn't much on the group feed, no photos or events. A few articles from anarchist kinds of blogs that didn't even own unique domains, with WordPress and BlogSpot in the URLs. Conspiracy theories about politicians being hired by terrorists and Wall Street being secretly run by China were two of the more comprehendible examples. The last one had appeared five years ago.

"Not much here," Peter finally said, after I'd scrolled down and found only the same kind of article reposts, along with a few memes of the type I'd found offensive. Nothing obviously original or tangible. "Hard to believe they'd be able to mobilize, though I guess this could just be a front for something else. What do you remember about the guy who ordered her around?"

I thought back to the sweltering June afternoon when I'd arrived at the warehouse loft.

"I wasn't there for very long," I said, "and for most of the time he was in a back room—having sex with at least a couple other people," I added, making a face.

"Seriously?" he asked, eyebrows raised.

"Yeah. It was—you could hear everything. I mean, to each their own, but... The walls were super thin, just these partitions they'd put up in a big loft space. I'd had to get buzzed into the building, and when I got to the door Marianne was there to meet me. She seemed on edge, invited me inside but kept me in this kitchen area—everything was kind of primitive but they had running water and a fridge. As soon as I heard the—*moans* and... uck—I started to get really uncomfortable. I could tell Marianne wasn't happy about it, but she pretended like nothing was happening—she introduced me to a guy and girl who were cooking a vegan stew, or something like that. They were totally blasé about what was going on—and *totally* stoned. The air was just thick with pot—which wouldn't have been a big deal, but there were needles and other stuff kind of everywhere—and the place was filthy and smelled like… like BO and rot. I couldn't see how Marianne could stand it. Another woman came in and asked me if I believed in God and started ranting about all this senseless garbage—the stoned people kept echoing what she was saying. I got fed up and told Marianne I couldn't stay, and she said she'd come with me and we could get lunch somewhere in the city."

"Was the sex still going on?"

"I think so—I was trying really hard not to listen too closely— but this guy Mike came into the room—fully naked, just this totally hairy foul naked dude showing up and taking a hit off a bong. Marianne was annoyed and told him to put something on and he told her to shut up, he did what he wanted in his own home—and who the fuck was I. He kept looking me up and down." My stomach turned a little at the memory.

"It was all so… disgusting—and embarrassing. Marianne said I was her cousin who was visiting from California and we were going out to lunch, and he walked over and pushed her up against the wall—pushed *hard*—and said I could do whatever I wanted but she wasn't going anywhere, she was needed there. It seemed like she was going to fight back for a second, but then she just seemed to kind of… *deflate*… and told me to leave. She wouldn't look at me. She said she'd call me later and I got the hell out of there."

Peter was silent, something about his tight jaw telling me he wasn't going to comment.

"I didn't hear from her that day. At first I was glad—I was furious with her for inviting me there and—well, just upset about the whole thing. But then it started to make me nervous. I waited until I got back to the hotel after dinner and called her, and she answered on the first ring and said she could meet me for breakfast the next day in the city, she'd text me where, then hung up. She showed up looking tired and acting keyed up—sort of hyper. I kept thinking she might be on drugs, but… I asked her point-blank why she was living in that place. I told her I thought it was appalling and disgusting—and the people even worse."

"Not exactly tactful," Peter observed.

"No, but I wasn't thinking very straight about it. I couldn't believe Marianne had gotten herself involved with such—such *lowlifes*. She seemed angry, but then laughed in a weird way and hugged me and said that it was awful but it was an adventure. She left right after that."

"Did you see her again while she was staying there?'"

"No, she wasn't living with them the next time we saw each other. She came out for my mom's funeral, and then for my dad's, last year. She seemed back to normal—but she didn't talk about herself much. It's hard to tell with her. She won't show what she doesn't want you to see."

"What about her parents? Are they still alive?"

"They're alive, or at least I think they are. Last I heard they were in Africa somewhere. Marrakech, maybe? That's what Marianne said. She was never close to them—they weren't around a lot. I only met them a few times when we were growing up."

"Other than you and your folks, it doesn't sound like she's had too many winners in her life. What about relationships—anyone other than this Mike guy that you know of?"

"Nothing serious. She dated a few guys in high school and college. Just casually, though. If she had a boyfriend—or girlfriend—in the last six years she never told me about it."

"Is a girlfriend possible?"

"Anything is possible. The commune people—the twelve of them—were all supposedly dating each other, after all. She didn't go into details… I mean, from what I heard there were at least two women going at it."

"Mmph," Peter said ambiguously. I was learning how careful he was with his responses, whether this was a learned reaction or innate to his nature, I couldn't tell. "What did she do for work?"

"She worked for a travel agency a few years ago, that was the last job I heard about, come to think of it. Recently, I don't know. She was an English major at Cal and wanted to be a journalist. She worked in San Francisco for a few years, then moved to New York for a graduate program in journalism. It was a really great opportunity, but she quit before getting her degree. I don't know what happened. We weren't in touch as often when she moved away. I remember she worked for a talent agency for a while, too—right before she joined up with Mike and the rest of them. I think she left that job when she moved to Newark. After that horrible visit, I didn't hear from her again until she'd moved to Manhattan. That's when she started at the travel place. The last few times we saw each other she didn't talk about work, she just said it was a job and everything was fine."

I didn't add, now that I thought about it, that during those visits we talked almost entirely about me—what was I going to do when first my mom, then my dad, had gone and left me gradually more rootless and alone, until Marianne was my only close family. She'd already drifted away from me, too, or we'd drifted away from each other. I really hadn't had anybody for such a long time.

Until now.

"Did her parents pay her tuition?"

I forced my mind back to the conversation. "Did they... Oh, yeah, they did. I always got the impression they had a lot of money."

"Mm. Did they set her up with an allowance, or anything like that?"

"I don't know—if they did, she never mentioned it, and my parents never said anything. I know her parents gave mine cash when she was living with us—every year until she was eighteen, though I don't know how much it was. My dad told me he and my mom had saved it in an account for her. I guess her parents might have started sending it to her after she started college."

He nodded, lost in thought, then seemed to recall himself and glanced at his watch.

"It's after ten. We should probably get moving." He squeezed my leg and stood up. "I'm going to shower and start packing—do you mind hanging out a few minutes?"

"Not at all—if it's OK, I'll catch up on a few emails. Don't feel like you need to rush."

"Sounds good," he said, and told Osiris, who seemed to want to follow him into the bathroom, to stay and keep me company. After staring down the hall for a few minutes, listening with ears cocked to the sound of the water running, Osiris finally gave up and came to lie down on my feet.

I quickly composed and sent a letter to my supervisor telling her I needed to quit without notice due to a serious family emergency out of town. I apologized and left it at that. There wasn't much more to say, and it wasn't like I'd ever been counting on her as a future reference.

After that, I found an email address for my property manager and let them know that I'd been called away suddenly on—what else—urgent family business, and would probably need to stay indefinitely. I said I'd come back as soon as possible and would take care of mail forwarding in the meantime, and went ahead and gave notice to end my lease at the end of the following month, allowing for about five weeks to figure things out and empty out the apartment. It meant paying one final month's rent, but at least I'd get that back twofold when they returned my substantial deposit.

Finally, after logging out of all my accounts, I went to the U.S. Postal Service website and filled out a mail forwarding request form. I was still hesitating over what to use as my forwarding address when Peter reappeared. His short, thick hair was still damp and curling slightly, and he was freshly shaved. He carried a bulging navy blue duffel bag, which he set down before starting to collect Osiris's food and belongings together.

"Looks like I may need to do laundry before we go," he said ruefully. "I didn't realize it had gotten so bad, but I didn't do any last week."

"We have plenty of time," I pointed out. "Come to think of it, I don't have any clean clothes, either. I've been washing my underwear in the sink."

"There's a Laundromat not far from the bar, we can swing by the camper and start a few loads on our way. I want to give Oss a good run and then drop him off so he has a chance to settle in before Lyle heads into work. We should try to leave town by about eight."

"OK," I agreed. SFO wasn't far, only about a half an hour away over the mountains, assuming traffic was on the lighter side. But you could never count on that, and it was always better to check in early. "Hey, um… do you mind if I have my mail forwarded here—just temporarily? I don't know if the camper actually has a mailing address, and I'd rather not use the attorneys for anything if I don't have to."

"Of course—do you have it?" He repeated the address as I typed it into the fields, his voice matter-of-fact. I finished entering my PayPal account information—trackers be damned—and hit submit on the request. As I stared at the confirmation screen, a sort of dizzying sense of security washed over me, bringing a strange lump to my throat.

It had been a long time since I'd had somewhere to call home. Not just a place to live, but an actual home. Somewhere I was wanted and missed and loved. My mother's death; my father's move to a small apartment in a senior residence, his sad, slow withdrawal from me—from everyone, except maybe Uncle Joe; Marianne's distant affection… The past five years had been so full of loss and emptiness. I'd tried to escape it by running south, but my time in LA was a distraction, not a solution.

Now, in this moment, I felt a bittersweet mixture of aching sadness and overwhelming joy. Home. Friendship. Love. All that I'd missed so much, all that I'd so pessimistically hoped to find through dating apps, knowing the whole time somehow that it wasn't going to answer—it was here, right now, represented by this man I'd just met, his dog, and his address.

It wasn't that I felt like this was my new home—it was still just Peter's apartment. I had no desire to move in here. No, it was something much bigger than that.

It was Peter. Himself. The way he accepted me into his life. Told me the truth about his past mistakes and present worries. Believed my story and wanted to help solve my problems. The easy affection he showed me, alone and in front of others. The passion of our new intimacy.

It was all new. So incredibly, astonishingly new. So new that I didn't want to name it—that the few times we'd casually referred to ourselves as "dating" and "together" felt almost irreverent, like putting a price tag on an unfinished work of art. Our declarations had been brief and simple and enough—we didn't need to promise more, not yet.

And even without declarations and labels and vows, the thought of him—by my side, holding my hand, giving me his address so that my mail could come here without a second's thought—filled me with the deepest sense of safety, of *home*, than I could remember feeling in a very long time. To this depth, and as an adult, maybe not ever.

I didn't know if he felt the same way, but it didn't really matter. There are always risks involved with trusting anyone. Opening your life, your stories, your heart to another person requires a desperate leap of faith into the unknown. No matter how quickly or slowly you allow that leap to happen, success isn't possible without vulnerability.

Peter and I had seemed to be on the same wavelength since we met on the beach, seemed to be progressing at the same lightning pace, which felt so utterly effortless. That might not last. At any moment, he might hesitate—stumble—back away. And as far as he knew, I might do the same.

It didn't matter. Even if it didn't last out the week, it was worth it. This crazy magical ride was worth it.

I was safe.

■ ■ ■

I'd thought it was going to be a long day, but the hours went by very fast, blurring together as the evening neared. By the time we got to the camper and had collected clothes and linens to wash, it was nearing noon. Peter wanted to go into work for a while, so we took both cars to the Laundromat, Osiris riding with Peter.

He seemed to sense something was going on and, whatever it was, that dogs might just be the losers in the situation. *What were all of his things doing in that bag*—his favorite toy and food and bowl? He kept sniffing at the bag and whining, looking up at Peter with large, accusing brown eyes. While we started our loads of laundry, he waited in the front seat of the truck, sitting very close to his bag just in case anyone was so foolish as to mess with it.

"Our first domestic task," Peter said as we carried our handfuls of quarters over to the wall of washers.

"It's never as sexy as it looks on TV," I said sadly, throwing dirty socks and underwear into the machine.

"Oh, yeah?"

Without warning, he dropped the duffel he was holding and pushed my body—firmly yet not quite forcefully—up against the open washer door, kissing me before I had time to react. When his mouth moved on mine, the clothes in my hands fell to the floor and I wrapped my arms around his neck. Several breathless minutes later, we were interrupted by a muttered "Excuse *me*," from across the room, where an elderly man had been reading a newspaper. We broke apart, laughing self-consciously—at least I was, Peter just seemed to be laughing—and continued to load the washers.

I could feel my cheeks burning, and glanced at the next row over where a round rosy woman was placidly unloading a dryer. She smiled at me, which made me feel better. Whatever anyone might think about the appropriateness of displaying public affection, it wasn't as though we'd been having sex. We'd just had a gracelessly intense make out session. In a public place. In front of strangers.

Though voyeurism of any kind didn't interest me, sex with Peter at the Laundromat—*alone*—would have been an undeniably erotic experience... For a second I allowed myself to imagine it, then quickly pulled my mind back to the task at hand and finished putting my towels and sheets into a second washer. Not the time or place, I told myself sternly.

Peter and Osiris left for a run on the beach while I continued into town and made my way into a chain drugstore, conveniently right off the main highway like almost everything else. In my mad rush to leave home, I hadn't brought any travel toiletries besides my toothbrush, so stocked up on tiny bottles of various useful things as well as granola bars and candy for the plane and hotel room. Not knowing what Peter liked, I got a variety of standards: Snickers, Starburst and Reese's Peanut Butter Cups, among other favorites. If he didn't like any of those, there was something wrong with him. I also bought a few new paperbacks and magazines, knowing they'd be half the price of what the airport would charge for the same reading material.

I drove back to the Laundromat with my purchases, relieved to see that the previous customers—witnesses to our make-out— had been replaced by new people who never even glanced my way. Our loads were done; I changed everything over to the industrial dryers, sitting down on one of the plastic chairs with a newly-purchased book to distract me while I waited. It was a cheap edition of a Robin Cook suspense, "Coma," which I'd vaguely remembered seeing a movie of years ago on TV. It was an unexpectedly compelling story, and suddenly the dryer was giving a low buzz and the laundry was done.

I took our duffels back to the camper, spending the next few hours sorting and folding clothes, remaking the bed, packing, washing the few dishes and checking the fridge for perishables. Trash had to be taken down to a dumpster in the city, so I collected everything I'd thrown away since I arrived and took a load down. I hesitated over Peter's clothes, mingled as they were with mine, but rather than fold them, which seemed sort of presumptuous—what if he didn't like folded clothes? Or had his own special way of folding?—I shook everything out and tucked it neatly back into his bag.

Before I knew it, the clock read five fifteen, causing me to pick up the pace; Peter and I were meeting at the bar at six. We planned to leave his truck in the parking lot and take my car to SFO, parking at a nearby BART station which cost about a third as much as airport parking. I quickly showered and got ready, checking one more time to see that I had everything I needed, tidying up behind myself so the camper would be spotless when we got back, heading out the door at exactly five fifty-one.

I parked beside the truck at the far corner of the lot, close to the back entrance, and went around that way rather than through the front door, bringing Peter's duffel with me so he could sort and pack what he needed. As soon as I stepped into the hallway, Osiris appeared from Peter's office, running full-tilt at my legs and showing his excitement with loud barks. Peter followed immediately, greeting me with less noise but equal enthusiasm.

"How'd everything go?" he asked, releasing me and taking his bag as he lead the way into his office.

"Fine. The time went faster than I expected. Wasn't this guy going to Lyle's?"

"Change of plans, Lyle will take him home tonight." He didn't explain the reason and I didn't ask. "Are you hungry? We got sandwiches, I ordered a few extras thinking we might want them now and as a snack later."

"I am pretty hungry," I said, looking with interest at the bag of food as my stomach gave an insistent growl. We settled in with two of the subs, the dog watching carefully to make sure that no scraps made it to the floor. "Are you all set to go?" I asked, muffled by a mouthful of bread, tuna salad and pickles.

"Yeah, everything's wrapped up," Peter said, just as inarticulately. He swallowed and reached over to something on his desk, hesitating for a fraction of a second before continuing. "I also got you something… Well, not exactly *got* it, I already had it.

I just turned it back on." He held it out to me—it was an iPhone. I saw that it was slightly scratched and scruffy, not the latest version.

"This is for me?" I asked, putting down my sandwich and wiping my hands on a paper napkin so I could accept it from him.

"It's my old phone. I had them add a second line to my service and activate it for you." His voice was offhand, casual. He didn't want to make a big deal about it, I could tell. I turned it over in my hands and pressed the on button.

"Wow. That's incredibly thoughtful of you," I said, slightly overwhelmed by the gesture in spite of his nonchalance. "Of course I'll cover the costs... Just let me know what I owe you."

"Sure. I won't be charged until next month, so don't worry about it for now."

"Thanks so much, Peter—I really missed having a phone."

"I didn't like not being able to reach you today." I watched the little Apple appear on the screen without speaking, replaying the words in my head. "I mean, it isn't a *tether*, or anything," Peter assured me quickly, as if he'd sensed the direction of my mind. "You're under no obligation—this isn't so I can keep tabs on you or something like that." It was the most flustered I'd seen him. My tiny spark of unease having been quelled, I waited, smiling internally, watching him over-explain. "I just thought you'd want to be able to call people, or use your email—especially since we're going out of town—and I knew your cousin had taken yours. You don't ha—"

I finally couldn't contain myself and laughed, interrupting him.

"I know, you sweet man. I get it—and I'm thrilled to have it."

I leaned over and hugged him tightly to show my gratitude, cradling the precious new device in one careful hand. I wasn't letting this phone out of my sight.

chapter 8

"This is it?" Peter asked, staring up at the brick building beside us.

"I… think so," I said uncertainly, gazing with him and trying hard to match it with the picture in my mind. "It was definitely on this street…"

The problem was, the street didn't look anything like I expected. Gentrification had evidently overtaken this once-industrial neighborhood, which I remembered as being shabby and neglected, flyblown windows giving dim views of closed businesses, empty warehouses with broken panes in the leaded glass. On our walk here from the nearby light rail station, we'd passed two hip, sleek cafés, several trendy restaurants and a number of expensive-looking boutiques, along with large manufacturing buildings converted into high-priced urban apartments. One of these was the building we were looking at.

"I remember the door," I said with more conviction as we approached it. "It's the same door, except it's been painted and cleaned, and all this is new." I gestured at the extremely shiny modern panel that had replaced the old, tarnished buzzers. We looked at it together. It offered a keypad and speaker, nothing else.

"What apartment number was it?"

"Four. I think. There were four floors—and it took up the whole top floor."

"Well, here goes nothing," Peter said, and pressed the number four. We waited. Nothing happened.

"Maybe you need to hit the pound key, or something," I suggested. Peter tried a few combinations of keys, and still nothing happened. I suddenly felt very, very tired.

It was just after eight on Monday morning, probably the worst time possible to show up at a stranger's door. Our trip had gone smoothly so far: light traffic on the way to the airport, a parking spot on the fifth floor of the nearby BART station garage, plenty of time for check-in and security. We ate dinner at a grill in the terminal, only realizing halfway through the mediocre and expensive meal that it was our first time eating dinner out together. Of course, we only met three days ago, so there were a lot of first times to check off, it was just odd to have our first official dinner date be at an airport restaurant.

Our flight left on time, and I actually fell asleep for a few hours, soothed by the glasses of red wine I drank at dinner and on the plane. I woke up with a stiff body and a sour taste in my mouth, feeling exactly like I was awake at three o'clock in the morning, when we landed just after six. I seemed to see and hear everything through a kind of tunnel. Peter was quiet and composed, not the most entertaining traveling companion, but a restful one. He spent most of the time before and during the flight on his iPad, reading what looked like magazines or illustrated books.

He also ate a lot of the candy I'd brought, and we finished the last of the subs.

At the train terminal near the airport, we got a locker for our carry-ons and figured out the best way to get to the neighborhood where Marianne had lived. Light rail seemed like the quickest and most convenient option. I couldn't find the address in any old emails or address books, but did remember the street name, and fortunately it wasn't a very major or long street. After a pricey and delicious artisan breakfast sandwich and strong coffee at the first hip café we passed near the light rail stop, we started walking.

It was a muggy late spring morning, overcast and already warm. I'd taken off my jacket and slung it over my purse, and Peter had tied his sweatshirt around his waist. The clothes I'd brought—two pairs of jeans and a couple of different shirts—might not be light enough if the weather continued this way.

We stood at the door another minute or two without any response, both of us reluctant to leave now that we were here. Probably because I was exhausted, I felt flattened and let down. I'd been fully aware that our chances of success were slim. I'd even expected that we wouldn't have any luck finding someone to talk to, if we found the building at all. But all the same, I was aware of a sinking sensation in my stomach, an impulse to burst into stormy tears.

"We'll come back later," Peter was saying, though I could tell he felt the same sense of disappointment. But really, what else did we think would happen?

"'Scuse me," someone said impatiently behind me.

Without thinking I stepped out of the way, and a twenty-something blonde woman in bright workout gear walking a beautiful Dalmatian passed between us and reached for the keypad, quickly punching in numbers, which opened the door with a discreet buzz.

"Excuse us," Peter said quickly, "could we ask you about a previous tenant?"

She paused in the doorway, visibly torn between annoyance at being stopped and curiosity at his question. It was clever of him to say that immediately—if he'd asked to speak to her without saying why, we'd be staring at a closed door by now. She looked at us for the first time, relaxing noticeably as she took in our ordinary clothes and lack of clipboards or fliers.

"I guess—I'm in kind of a hurry, though."

"We're looking for information about some people who lived here five or six years ago, before it was remodeled," he explained fluidly, "they would have been on the top floor—a large group of people."

We could see we'd caught her interest. She stepped a little further outside, pulling the well-mannered and obedient dog with her, and allowed the door to shut.

"I moved in after that, but I heard about them," she said. "It's the same owner—the same family, anyway. There were, like, ten or twelve of them all in some kind of cult, right?"

"Something like that. Our friend might have lived with them for a while, we're trying to find her," he said.

"Huh. I heard they were really sketchy—drugs and orgies. I mean, it could just be gossip, but I heard about it from the son— he took over managing the place—and he said he'd been inside and seen some weird stuff. I think they were evicted."

"Sounds like the right people," I said, speaking for the first time.

"Could you tell us how to contact the owner?" Peter asked.

"Sure—Napoletti Properties. You should be able to look them up, they're in Jersey City."

"That really helps—thanks so much," I said.

She nodded and typed in her code again. When she'd gone inside, we moved back down the street, my spirits suddenly soaring as high as they had plummeted a few minutes ago. It was irrational, but I couldn't help it. We paused by a bus stop and Peter pulled out his phone.

"Here they are—their address is on West Side Avenue. What do you think—should we call, or try to see someone in person?"

"I feel like they'll be more likely to talk to us if we go in person," I said. "What do you think?"

"I think you're right. Well, next stop: Jersey City."

We walked back the way we'd come.

■ ■ ■

After getting our bags from the terminal, we made our way to Newark Penn Station and caught a train that dropped us off half an hour later at Journal Square. From there it was an easy mile or so walk to the address of Napoletti Properties. We stopped and got coffees to go at Starbucks at the square, sipping them as we walked. I started to feel more awake now that the caffeine was kicking in and my breakfast had digested. I'd felt chatty on the train ride, so Peter had obligingly set aside his tablet and talked with me.

"How old were you when you got married?" I asked.

"Twenty-four. I was too young to know if was the right choice," he said easily. "Kathe is a few years older than I am. I wouldn't say she *pushed* me into it, but it was definitely something she wanted more than I did."

"How long had you been together?"

"Not long—about a year. We met at the University of Arizona and moved in together as soon as I graduated."

"And it lasted three years?"

"More like two and a half. She finished her Master's degree and started at the Police Academy while I drifted around trying to figure myself out. Eventually she got tired of running our lives and her career at the same time and I got tired of being mothered. We just weren't a good match."

I liked it when people could be philosophical about past relationships, no matter how they ended. More often than not, the guys I dated were bitter, rude or dismissive (or, worse, a combination of all three) about past girlfriends, and that kind of negativity had become a definite turnoff. Peter's version of events sounded reasonably fair to both sides; plus I already knew they were still on good terms, to the point that he called her for advice and she willingly gave it. I'd tried to remain cordial with my exes, too—though most of my relationships weren't long enough for us to really establish the same social circles, so we generally didn't make it past the "taking some time apart" phase and just stopped communicating altogether.

"What about you? Any ex-husbands I should know about?" Peter was asking.

"Oh, sure—far too many to remember," I said breezily. "Fortunately they all died in their sleep. So convenient."

"Leaving you a rich widow several times over? Outstanding. I knew my luck was in when I saw you sitting by that bicycle on the beach. Seriously, though… Any live-ins or long-term significant others I can feel hostile and jealous over?"

"Not really. My longest relationship was about two years, in and out of college, but we never lived together. I was finishing up at San Francisco State and he was working on launching a startup, which took most of his time. Eventually we just sort of got too busy to see each other."

"Were you living in the city?"

"In the South Bay—that's where I grew up. I lived with my parents in San Mateo, and then on my own in South San Francisco. After graduation I worked at Cisco for a while in an entry-level position."

"That's a good gig," he commented, impressed. "You didn't want to stay and move up the ranks?"

"When my mom was diagnosed, I moved back home to take care of her," I said. "Everything sort of got… put on hold for a few years. Once she was gone…"

"You moved to LA," he finished.

"Yeah. My dad decided he was going to sell their townhouse and move into senior living apartments, and I just couldn't seem to face staying and seeing everything go at once."

Peter looked out the train window for a minute, holding my hand.

"I lost my mom to cancer, too," he said. "My dad wasn't around much—they split up when I was seven and Delia and I stayed with our mom. Our dad moved to Boise and eventually remarried and had three more kids. They're a nice family. We didn't see a lot of them—it just wasn't convenient. We spent a couple of summer vacations with them, but it's been a while since we all got together."

"How old were you—when your mom passed?"

"Seventeen. Delia was twenty. She became my temporary guardian, just until I turned eighteen. I moved in with her and her boyfriend, and then they moved to Texas and got married and I went to Arizona and worked my way through school. I wanted to study architecture, but that didn't really work out."

"So many things we want don't seem to work out," I said soberly.

"And then other things really surprise you when they do," he said, and we looked at each other and smiled.

For the rest of the trip, I thought about our stories. It seemed interesting—strange… even fateful, somehow—that they met and intersected in so many different and similar ways. Losing our mothers to cancer, losing our fathers to divorce or grief, finishing school but not starting a real career, getting derailed in early adulthood from the things we'd hoped for.

Of course they weren't uncommon themes: death, divorce, disappointment, loss. But then add in that our only real family was an older sister, in his case, an older cousin raised like a sister in mine. Add that our homes had dissolved and we hadn't really been able to create new ones as adults. That our families weren't the kind that had reunions and holiday gatherings.

And that someone close to us—or closely connected to us—had made choices that put us in danger, affected our lives and livelihoods, created problems that we weren't responsible for but now had to face, and attempt to fix.

To that end, coffee cups in hand, we approached the commercial building where Napoletti Properties had their office. It was on the first floor, filling up a light, attractive space with windows looking into the street and the building's central hallway and sleek, pale wood furnishings. Just inside the glass door was a front desk with a good-looking receptionist, who greeted us politely and heard Peter's request without showing any more surprise than a slight raising of the eyebrows.

"Mr. Napoletti currently manages that property. I believe they've owned it for some time," he said. "Let me see if he has a moment to assist you."

He stood and walked toward the back of the office, through a grouping of desks that looked like the account manager area of a bank. Two of the workspaces were occupied by professional young women, one of whom had a couple seated across from her with papers scattered in front of them.

At the very back of the room was a large, walled-in office with more windows. We watched as the receptionist approached the office door and knocked, able to see the man who sat behind the large desk but not hear what was exchanged. After a moment, the receptionist returned and asked us if we would follow him. We soon found ourselves in the back office, shaking hands with Mr. Richard Napoletti—"Junior," he added—and being offered coffee or water before the receptionist slid out and shut the door. We introduced ourselves and sat down in two beautiful Danish modern leather chairs.

"James said you were interested in finding out about some previous tenants at our warehouse building on Commerce."

Richard Napoletti looked to be in his mid-to-late forties, short and broad-chested with a slight paunch and head bald but for the last ring of short dark hair around the base. He wore a well-fitted navy suit, white shirt and tastefully-patterned tie in shades of blue.

"That's right," Peter said. "We talked to a resident this morning who said you'd managed the building for a while, and might be able to tell us something about a group of people who lived there five or six years ago. We're trying to track down a friend who may have stayed with them."

Richard eyed us briefly, but was apparently reassured that we weren't after anything he wasn't willing to give us.

"You're talking about that group of potheads who rented the loft space for a few years," he said. "You know somebody involved with them?"

"Maybe. We think our friend was involved with the group for a short time, though we don't know why."

This safe answer—Peter, I was learning, was good at safe answers—seemed to please our host.

"I don't mind telling you about it," Richard said. "It's a weird story. I'd just taken over from my parents and was looking for investors to rebuild the place—this was five years ago. We were losing money on it every time property values went up. Have you heard Newark referred to as 'the next Brooklyn?'" he inquired. We indicated that we hadn't. "Well, it's got a lot of potential for development. You saw what's happening to that street alone, and there's more like that all over the place. That building is already paying itself off—twenty brand-new units, brand-new facilities and a waiting list. As soon as I took over, I started moving forward with the renovation and had no trouble getting the other renter out—there were only two at that point. A ground floor space was being used as a studio by a kind of artists' collective, the other was this group. My dad had a soft spot for the whole sixties collective thing. That loft, though." He shook his head.

"What a complete nightmare. At first they refused to let me in, I had to start eviction proceedings before they'd even open the door. When I finally got one of them to allow me inside, I couldn't believe it. They'd... well, all I can say is I was glad the whole place was being gutted, because the damage was worse than anything I've seen. They were breaking so many laws and codes, it was all I could do to keep my shit together. Pardon me," he said suddenly, with a glance at me.

"That's OK," I said, realizing that he was apologizing for swearing. "I hear it all the time."

He grinned, looking much more likeable.

"Yeah, anyway. Leaving aside all the drugs, which were enough to give my father another heart attack if he'd seen them, they had a barbeque going—*inside*—the place was filled with smoke. There were about a dozen other fire hazards, unlawful partitions and more occupants than I could count. I didn't really want to know what was going on, but I couldn't help looking around—I mean, that's what I was there for. I'd asked to talk to the lessee, if he was present—the name on the lease was Michael Sorenson. Nobody seemed very sober or inclined to be helpful, but one girl drifted off into the back and eventually this Michael showed up. A mean son of a bitch. He yelled at me to get out, spouted off a bunch of garbage about overthrowing the system and tenants' rights and God knows what else—all I knew was, it didn't sound good for the eviction, since the last thing we needed was a messy legal battle. I was about to stand my ground when I saw something that changed everything, and I got the hell out of there and called the police."

"What was it?" Peter asked coolly, though I was on the edge of my seat. Richard Napoletti told a great story.

"A girl was *tied up* in a back room—on the floor—right next to what looked like some kind of homemade *bomb*." He waited as we stared at him. "Nutso, right? I mean, I thought they were messed up, but didn't imagine they were kidnappers and terrorists. If I'd known… well, at least they didn't get away with it."

"What happened?" I demanded.

"They raided the place and arrested the whole damn nest of 'em. The girl they'd kidnapped was barely eighteen, poor kid. I guess they thought her father was a congressman in New York, though it turned out they got the wrong girl—they meant to grab her school friend. They were going to send her home with a bomb *strapped to her*, if you can believe it. I mean, crazy. Most of them got sent to rehab and turned witness, I think, but the guy in charge, Michael Sorenson, he was charged with a couple of felonies and ended up serving time at Rikers Island. I testified at his trial, though it was probably one of the other people who put him away."

"Do you know if he's still there? At Rikers?" Peter asked.

"Last I heard, yeah. He won't be up for parole for a good long while." He fiddled with a pen on his desk while we took that in. "You thinking of going to talk to him?"

"Maybe," Peter said.

"If he's willing to talk to you, he's probably your best bet. We never had any other names on file, and all the rest of them scattered once the place broke up."

"Thank you," I said, not sure how else to end the interview. "We really appreciate your time."

We all stood and Richard Napoletti moved to open the office door.

"No trouble. You're the second people who've ever asked about that group," he remarked, walking us out. "It's definitely the weirdest thing I've ever experienced in this business."

"Oh? Who else was interested?" Peter asked casually.

"Some older guy—I don't remember his name. Seemed normal enough. It was after I'd decided to renovate but before I'd started the eviction process, come to think of it, so the place was on my mind. He wanted to know who was the tenant of record, said he was looking for his daughter. Later on, once I got in there, I wondered which one of them he was talking about, but I never heard back from him. I just assumed she got back in touch with her family once Sorenson was out of the picture."

"Let's hope so," I said, since Peter seemed too preoccupied to respond. We said goodbye, and left the office.

chapter 9

"Well, we know that Mike was into some really extreme stuff," I said as we started back for the train station, hauling our bags with us.

"Right," Peter agreed, his mind still seeming to be elsewhere.

"Where's Rikers Island, anyway?"

"Queens, I think. The other side of Manhattan."

We walked along in silence for a few minutes. As we neared the train station, I found my stomach gurgling in an empty way.

"I'm getting hungry, are you?"

"Mm? Hungry? Good idea. Let's get some lunch—what about this place?" We were passing a café-bakery, one of several along the busy street. It looked inviting and wasn't too crowded, so we went in and ordered sandwiches and iced tea from the cashier before finding seats in the small dining room.

"What did he say that's got you so thoughtful?" I finally asked, after another short silence.

"Hmm? Oh. About the other man who asked about the loft."

"The one looking for his daughter?"

"Right. Wouldn't that be around the time that Marianne moved out—five years ago?"

"Yeah, it would. I don't know the exact date, though. When she emailed me she was already living in Brooklyn."

"Mmphmm."

I waited, sipping my tea. Our number was called, and I went and got the tray with our sandwiches and sat down. We ate. Peter's eyes stayed unfocused, as if he was doing a complicated math problem. I was reaching for my book when he suddenly spoke.

"I don't see how it could be tied to the loft people," he said. "Whatever your cousin is involved in now. It was too amateur, and it's been too long. But I'm interested in the other man who came asking about them."

"Do you still think it's worth trying to talk to that Mike guy?"

"I think so. He might be able to fill in some gaps about your cousin's life, if nothing else."

"*If* we can talk to him—and if he wants to help us."

"He doesn't sound like he'd be the most… *cooperative* guy, but maybe he's had a change of heart," Peter suggested gravely. "Turned a new leaf."

I snorted a skeptical laugh, and finished my last bite regretfully. It was good—melted cheese and ham on a baguette.

"So what now?"

"I don't think there's a lot more we can do today. We can look into Rikers tonight and how to go about visiting someone there. Our hotel should let us check in, even if our room's not ready, and we can leave our bags if we want to walk around."

"Can we catch a train from here?"

It turned out we could—a PATH train would take us to the World Trade Center, a short walk from there to the 5 train and up to Grand Central Station. We had luck in the early afternoon commuter lull and didn't have to wait long for our trains. In just over an hour we'd made our way to our hotel, a fairly nice DoubleTree with tourists of all nationalities spilling out of the lobby onto the sidewalk and into the adjacent bar. Our room was ready; we got our key cards and made our way upstairs.

First time staying in a hotel room together, I found myself thinking. First time on a plane—a train—a subway. First time splitting expenses and following directions to a place we'd never been. First trip, first overnight away from the camper.

First investigation into criminal activities. First prison visit.

After checking out the room and using the bathroom, I found Peter stretched out on the bed, shoes off, iPad in hand. Who knew he was such an iPad person? Something else I'd learned about him in the last twenty-four hours. I lay down next to him, sliding out of my shoes as well, feeling my body relax for the first time since the night before last.

Peter was quiet. I was quiet.

Without any warning, a wave of sheer, utter panic washed over me. My heart began to pound wildly, my stomach rippled with anxiety, my skin felt hot and clammy. I lay still, feeling the blood rush to my ears, heat rising to my face and neck.

What the hell was I doing here?

Was I really in Manhattan with a stranger—a man I'd only met *three days ago*? Did I really believe we were falling in love—that it could be that easy and auspicious and *magical,* like some goddamn fairy tale? How delusional could I get?

All the strangeness, all the nerves, all the doubts I hadn't felt flooded my brain and body, as if breaking through a dam that had held them back the past three days. I knew *nothing* about this man except—well, that he was nice, and thoughtful, and owned a bar and a dog, and seemed to have a solid reputation in town besides the whole brother-in-law drug trafficker thing... which I really only had his word for, after all. Maybe he was in it with Hal. *Maybe it wasn't Hal they were after, but Peter.*

Oh, *God.*

I didn't know anything about him, not really. Only what he'd told me, only what I'd believed without question. I didn't know his political views—what, if any, religion he believed in—how much debt he had—how many women he'd slept with and ghosted the next day.

What if he was a drug dealer—or a serial rapist? Or an alcoholic or painkiller addict or compulsive gambler? What if he'd lied about everything—well, everything other people hadn't already confirmed? What if he had *ten different venereal diseases*—or AIDS—or something I'd never even heard of? I mean, we'd been safe, but all methods were only about ninety-nine percent effective. That left one percent.

What if my IUD and the condom had both failed and I was pregnant by this almost total stranger?

I had tied myself to this man without knowing who he really was. Handed myself to him like a neatly wrapped victim-package. Trusted him like the most fatuous, dim-witted teen under the thrall of her first desperate crush on some "cool, mysterious" sleazy dude in his twenties.

My heart raced even faster as I fully realized the danger of my position, my damp hands clenching into fists, my dread threatening to choke me as it rose in my throat.

I was stuck in New York with him with nobody to call for help. I'd told him all my secrets. Shown him all my weakest spots.

And now there was no way out.

■ ■ ■

A gentle snore came from the lying, disease-ridden serial-rapist-cult-leader-gambler-addict beside me.

I turned my head slightly to look at him. His iPad was face down on his chest, rising and falling with each breath he took. One of his hands rested on the bed between us, the other was draped across his stomach. The fingers were blunt, the skin deeply tanned, nails short and clean.

I could see the tiny lines under his eyes, the light sprinkle of gray in the hair by his temple. He breathing came quietly and evenly, without a repeat of the snore. His lashes lay dark and thick beneath arched brows, his chin was covered by a light shadow of stubble.

Watching Peter sleep, the panicked fear drained out of me. It vanished almost as quickly as it arose, and left a calm, blank emptiness in its wake. My heart slowed. One by one, all my tight muscles released.

It was true that I knew almost nothing about him. He could have treated women poorly in the past. He might have high debt and low prospects. He could very well have voted for the far right candidates in the last major election.

But it wasn't true that I didn't know him.

Fairy tale magic aside, we shared an undeniably real connection. From the first moment he'd spoken to me I'd felt that odd, sure rush of recognition. And he'd felt something similar. It was strong enough to keep us thinking about each other for hours, strong enough to bring us together and keep us moving closer, unchecked by the usual doubts and conventions.

He'd already proven a lot to me, without me asking him to. Everything he said he was going to do, he'd done. My instinctive trust of him hadn't yet been proven wrong. He'd been unfailingly respectful and considerate and honest. Of course there would be more to the stories of his past mistakes and missteps than the basic outlines he'd given me. We'd barely had time to exchange hometowns, much less our deepest regrets.

Maybe he had been something of a womanizing man-about-town, in Tucson if not in Half Moon Bay. Very few single guys I knew weren't, on some level. Many of those who weren't wished they were, which wasn't any better. He'd said he was clean after some issues with drugs and alcohol, but "clean" could be a relative term. I knew he drank beer and wine. Maybe he still partied now and then, or smoked pot for migraines, or went on periodic binges of one kind or another. I hadn't seen signs of any of it during our two days together, but that didn't mean it didn't happen.

Whatever he'd done, and whatever choices he'd made before we met, weren't my concern. They might show poor judgment, but unless he really had killed or raped or swindled someone, or done anything unspeakably evil or corrupt, his past wasn't my business.

Besides, who was I to judge? I'd gone on at least a hundred dates in LA—two or three a month for five years adds up to a lot. I'd slept with several guys I barely knew. I hadn't been a saint, either.

I hadn't gone in for hard partying or heavy drugs, I had too many muddled middle-class American inhibitions from my half-Chilean, half-Dutch mother and mixed-race father, both of whom had tumbled through the seventies and eighties as intense computer nerds, before that was really even a thing. I'd tried ecstasy once with a guy and locked myself in the bathroom for the rest of the night, throwing up in the toilet and moaning on the floor in turns. Strangely enough, we never went out again. I got sleepy when I drank too much, got panic attacks from pot, and had never been interested in or tempted to try anything white and powdery that went up your nose or into your veins.

I wasn't any better a person than anyone who liked those things—it wasn't morality that kept me relatively clean. Probably a cocktail of luck, common sense and the knowledge that my mom would have absolutely hated it and, after she died, that she wasn't around to hate anything anymore. That thought always sobered and centered me. Morality did keep me from committing crimes, of course—and I placed a high value on common decency. But unless I knew for sure that Peter had crossed an indefensible line, I couldn't assume he had.

Of course there was so much about him to learn, besides just the biographical facts. A lot of it I could probably relate to, and some of it might be hard to understand. The same would be true for him. Sure, it was impulsive and maybe irresponsible to leave town with a man I'd just met without thinking twice about the consequences. Looking past the intense attraction and connection, though, was it really so different from going on a weekend trip with a guy I'd been dating for a few weeks? That wouldn't be unheard of. Would I know that hypothetical guy any better than Peter, having gone out with him, say, five or six times, slept with him once or twice, spent a total of maybe twenty waking hours with him?

No, I wouldn't.

In terms of days, and in terms of depth, we'd moved fast. Very fast.

But that didn't mean we weren't right.

With a soft, contented sigh which released any last fragments of lingering tension all the way down to my toes, I curled up beside my lying, disease-ridden serial-rapist-cult-leader-gambler-addict and went to sleep.

■ ■ ■

I woke up after about an hour, not exactly refreshed and rested but at least feeling up to a few more hours of daylight. Peter was still asleep. I slipped over to the window and looked out at the view below; the day was slightly overcast, diffusing the sun rather than hiding it, and humid, a warm eighty-two degrees, according to the weather app on my phone. It was so nice to have a phone again to check things like the weather. Even if nobody had the number and I hadn't taken the time to set up my email or anything else on it, I could call anyone I wanted. I could look things up online.

If I hadn't already gotten over my extreme little bout of cold feet, and if I'd thought of it earlier, the fact that Peter had added a stranger to his phone plan would have helped reassure me. After all, he was the one on the financial hook for that. He hadn't done it as some kind of control measure, not unless he'd somehow managed to turn on a parental tracking option that I didn't know about. And that, I knew instinctively, wasn't in his character. He wanted to be in touch with me—to know I was OK—to know I could get help from him *or anyone else* if I needed it. It was a gift, not a shackle.

Clasping this symbol of Peter's trust in one hand, I watched people and cars passing. Getting here had been something of a blur. Other than a vague thrill at walking through Grand Central Station again, looking up at the high, fanciful painted ceilings and graceful architecture of a different time, I hadn't experienced much excitement about being in Manhattan. Nothing about this had felt vacation-like, with our unusual reason for coming so entirely front and center since we'd landed.

Now that I had a moment to sit quietly and watch New Yorkers and tourists mingling on the street, walking and biking and driving to their next destination, I felt the first stirrings of anticipation. This was a very cool city to spend a few days in, investigations aside. There was so much to see—historical sights and celebrated artwork and Broadway shows, so much to eat, so many neighborhoods to explore and people to watch. I'd barely made it to the most major attractions on my first trip, just enough to appreciate that you could probably live in New York for a lifetime and not see it all.

I hadn't come here with any expectations—about what we might find out or what we might do. But we were here. Even if we just circled the block and came back, we'd see something of the city, find something to notice and value. And we'd go out for meals, if we did nothing else.

"How long have I been asleep?" Peter asked groggily from behind me, sitting up as I turned and came back to the bed.

"Over an hour. How do you feel?"

He yawned and reached for me, pulling me in for a hug and falling back with me onto the bed.

"Better," he said.

Sometime later, after we'd showered—one, rather long, shower—and put on clean clothes, Peter suggested we make a game plan for the next step in our search for answers.

"I did some research on visiting inmates," he said, pulling up a webpage on his iPad. "Rikers is closed Mondays and Tuesdays, but Sorenson will be eligible for visitors on Wednesday, at least according to their schedule. They split it up by last names, A to L or M to Z on different days. That doesn't necessarily mean we'll be able to see him, but at least we know it's possible. Visitor registrations start at one."

"Is there a way to make sure he's really at Rikers?"

"There's somebody named Michael Sorenson there—the webpage lets you look up inmates by name or case number and see where they are. I checked a couple of spellings of Sorenson, he was the only one."

"That's... convenient," I said, startled by how simple it was to find out. I'd imagined we'd have to go through some difficult and time-consuming rigmarole. Costumes and back stories might be required. It goes to show how very ignorant I was about incarceration in general.

"They're specific about what you can wear and bring with you, if you want to take a look at the list later. Seems straightforward enough. We'll be able to go in together, if we get in at all. There's a direct shuttle that leaves from Harlem at twelve fifteen, I say we plan to take it. We can catch the 4 train down the street, it'll take us straight there."

"That's... yeah, that's great." Again, I was surprised at the effortlessness of the arrangements. There was even a *shuttle*. "So I guess Wednesday's settled. We can't do much more until then. What do you want to do this afternoon?"

"What sounds good to you?"

I considered the various options. Museums and sights would be crowded at this time of day. I wasn't quite hungry yet, though I would be in another hour or two. There was really only one place that I wanted to go, if Peter agreed.

"How about the park?"

Central Park had been one of my favorite outings from my previous visit. I could have spent hours just wandering through it. But though my friends had exclaimed over it and taken dozens of photos, it hadn't been as interesting to them as the flashy energy of Times Square or Rockefeller Center, so we hadn't gone back. There were no clubs, no stores, no theatres, just miles of twisting trails, statues, bridges and trees interspersed with fountains and lakes. I wouldn't presume to try to describe it as a non-New-

Yorker, but if you're into parks, and history, and nature, it's fantastic.

Our hotel wasn't far from the southeastern corner of the park, so we walked, hand in hand, wearing the lightest clothing we'd packed. I'd bundled my hair into a bun and taken a minute to dust some powder over my face and swipe fresh mascara on my lashes, but didn't have the energy for any more elaborate primping.

I felt kind of floaty with a mixture of weariness and happiness, content to let everything go for the time being and just enjoy the present for what it was. The park was as green and inviting as I remembered it, with long shady paths leading from one part to another, wide bright vistas showing views of the surrounding city blocks.

We wandered at will, not taking any pictures, not even talking much except to point things out to each other. We sat on benches and watched people walking by or sitting around us. We bought hot dogs and Cokes and ate them by the Carousel. We looked at the plaque by Strawberry Fields, Bethesda Fountain, the Zoo, the Shakespeare Garden. We circled the Alice in Wonderland statue and crossed the Bow Bridge.

Peter was so restful. Maybe because he spent so much time either with a dog or in a bar full of people talking to each other— by now I was convinced that *womanizer* was off the table—he was often quiet, keeping his thoughts to himself, but was always present when I spoke. It wasn't that he didn't talk; he asked questions and made comments and suggestions, but in between were comfortable silences. His friend in Queens, who had since moved back to Colorado, had collected old maps of the city along with interesting historical facts, a few of which Peter remembered and shared with me. But there was no need to talk, if we didn't want to.

It was the loveliest afternoon I'd spent in longer than I could remember, even with the lack of sleep and ever-present awareness about our improbable quest. I could mentally step away from that and just drift, my arm around Peter, my eyes and ears on the beautiful scenery around us.

It was on our way back to the hotel that we noticed the man following us.

■ ■ ■

Sometime before that, we decided to go to the Loeb Boathouse for a drink and a snack. I wasn't sure I wanted anything more to eat after the hot dogs, but found I did once we were seated at the outside bar, our table close to the edge of the lake. The sun had finally broken through or burned off the cloud cover, and a fresh breeze softened the sultry heat of the day to a temperate warmth. Over crab cakes and white wine, watching dusk fall over the wide expanse of water, Peter asked me about my job in LA, was I sorry to leave it, what did I want to do next.

"It's been awhile since I even considered that," I admitted, after briefly describing just how *not* sorry I was to be done with the sterile tedium of my last position. "I liked working in Silicon Valley, but I'm not sure I'd want to go back to doing that again. The problem is that I'm not really trained for anything in particular, not since I graduated. I've got a lot of experience in database programming, but... I don't know if that's what I want to keep doing."

Our appetizer arrived at that point, interrupting the conversation as we quickly devoured it with little to say for ourselves but a few murmured "yums."

"Do you think you would've quit your job if Marianne hadn't shown up?" Peter asked, putting down his fork and picking up his glass.

We both leaned back in our chairs, sipping wine, relaxed and replete.

"I... don't know," I said slowly. "I wasn't happy, but I was so used to it that I didn't really notice. My life was kind of... I was kind of on autopilot, not paying much attention to what was going on with me."

"Did you make a lot of friends? It always seemed like a social kind of town."

"Social… yeah, it is—but it's also lonely, in a way. I met a few women at workout classes or through work, we'd go out together to clubs or lunch. It wasn't always easy to connect, though. And I dated a lot, but that was more like a habit than anything else. I think I'd given up expecting to find someone I liked who actually liked me. They were into it, or I was, but not both of us."

"Mm. Define 'a lot?'" he requested, raising an eyebrow.

I laughed and ignored my slight blush.

"Not *a lot* a lot. I was on a couple of dating sites, and would meet guys for a drink or coffee a few times a month. It rarely got to a second date—and third dates almost never. Normally one of us would just fade out after it was clear that we weren't getting together again. It was usually obvious after the first couple of minutes, though sometimes I'd find somebody interesting and think he might be interested too, and then wouldn't hear from him."

"It sounds exhausting," he said frankly. "I hate dating."

"It could be kind of draining, but you get used to it. It becomes part of your routine, you know? Like exercising, or having your teeth cleaned."

"As fun as that?"

"Sometimes much less fun than that. The thing is, it doesn't work if you take it too seriously. I just went with it, kept my expectations low, had a good time when I could. So you don't date much, then?—I mean, *didn't* date much?"

He shrugged and made a face.

"Not really. I'd sometimes talk to women at the bar, and we'd meet up for coffee or something like that. I didn't… I mean, I wasn't exactly celibate, but opening and running the business has taken up so much of my time the past couple of years, I didn't really go out. And then lately—with the Hal situation—it's been easier to just lay low, which isn't great for your social life."

"What about in Tucson, before you moved out here?"

"That's... It was a different scene, I guess you could say. When Kathe and I first split up, I went out a lot—and I do mean a lot. Every night, or close to it. I wasn't dealing well, so there were some... it's embarrassing to admit. I had a few one-night stands and... partied pretty hard. That went on for almost a year, and did some real damage to my life. I got one DUI and then only a couple of months later I got another one—driving without my license with a small amount of drugs on me. It was... I wasn't in a good place, but that's no excuse. I'm just lucky nothing worse happened."

I didn't say anything, but met his eyes sympathetically. I knew he was ashamed. There was no point in dwelling on how wrong he'd been.

"Anyway, after I was arrested for the second DUI, Kathe helped me out. She arranged for me to start therapy and smoothed the way for a misdemeanor charge and sentence of community service. I quit my job—I'd been a bartender at a really wild place—and got hired as a manager at a hotel lounge, which was a crappy job but actually paid pretty well. I didn't like the therapist, much, but I think he helped me straighten myself out.

"I hung in there for a few years, got my license back—and had zero desire to go back to the party scene. I tried one of those dating apps and hated it. I cancelled my account after a month. And then Delia and Hal made their offer, and I figured, why not? It seemed like a good chance to start fresh, and I'd always liked the idea of living in California."

As I listened, I could see it, just like I had before. I could see his loneliness and desperation after his divorce, see the desire to lose himself in whatever seemed to offer the most distraction. The darkness of that time, the stricken, sobering recognition of how close he'd come to endangering himself and—even more disturbing—others, the slow determined struggle to get to a healthier place. His ex-wife had remarried, but he'd been alone.

Alone. Like me.

"I can relate," I finally said. "I understand wanting a fresh start—and feeling lost and overwhelmed and… doing reckless things to get away from it. Things that don't work, but you do them anyway."

"That's nice of you to say."

"It's also true."

"I know."

We ordered second glasses of wine. Dusk crept quietly through the park, muting the noise and movement of the city around us.

"It does explain one thing that I've been wondering about," I said in a lighter tone.

"What's that?"

"How you managed to stay a bachelor with hordes of single women around ready to snatch you up."

"Hordes?" he repeated skeptically.

"I saw hordes," I stated firmly.

"I'm not sure I'm such a great prospect," he said ruefully, with a laugh.

"Why not? You've got a lot going for you, the Hal mess aside. I think you're a *fantastic* prospect."

"Don't you think you're a little biased? Besides, you're one to talk—you were in town, what, a week? And already caught the eye of our fine young deputy."

"That was unexpected," I reflected, not bothering to deny it. "Nobody like him would pay any attention to me in LA. Poor Tom. Though come to think of it, he never made a pass at me, so it's just speculation that he was interested."

"It's more than speculation. And it's just as well he didn't."

His voice was neutral, but I caught the edge of something that surprised me.

"You aren't… *jealous*, are you? Because—"

"No, not at all," he assured me. "But I was. That first night in the bar, when he gave off that 'stay off my lawn' vibe—about you. It was incredibly hard to walk away and not drag you with me."

"Pleasant as that sounds, you wouldn't have had to drag me."

"Tom would've loved that," he grinned appreciatively. "You know," he continued, absently reaching for my hand and playing lightly with my fingers, "as much as I hate—and I really mean hate—that you've had to go through hell the past couple of weeks, and am going to do everything I can to help you get out of it, if it hadn't happened…"

We looked at each other. No meeting on the beach. No nights together in the camper and breakfast with Osiris. No New York.

No us.

"Yeah," I said, and we smiled.

chapter 10

We first noticed the man near the Bethesda Fountain. I doubt we'd have spotted him at all among the crowds of people out enjoying the mild evening, except that one of Peter's shoes became untied as we crossed Bethesda Terrace. He knelt to retie it, while I stood and looked idly around. The man was about twenty paces back, and staring fixedly at me.

When he caught my eye, he looked away and continued to walk in our direction, veering slightly as he passed us and continuing toward a sweeping set of stairs to the left, over the top of the Terrace Arcade. Other than noticing his stare when I met it, I barely registered him—just an average-looking man in a dark suit on his way somewhere for the evening. We moved more slowly, walking arm in arm straight down the center of the Arcade, under the decorative arches and through the tiled tunnel. It wasn't close to full dark yet, but the lights were on inside.

On the other side of the Arcade, we continued straight on until we joined the tree-shadowed Mall, following that down toward Center Drive and the southeast corner of the park where we'd entered. Not far along the Mall, Peter stopped again, needing, as so often happens, to retie the other shoe, and again I paused and glanced behind us.

And again the man was there.

Forty paces back now, but more noticeable since the lane happened to be fairly empty. He wasn't looking at me this time, but was staring straight ahead. I still probably wouldn't have thought anything of it—except that, out of my peripheral vision, I could tell that as he approached, he slowed his pace. Just a slight slowing. Just enough to show that he didn't want to catch up with us.

And that did catch my attention.

There are plenty of reasons you might adjust your pace while walking somewhere. Slowing down, speeding up, passing someone or allowing them to pass you. People don't always walk at the same consistent speed. The man might not have wanted to intrude—though it was completely obvious that Peter was kneeling to adjust a shoe, there wasn't any mystery to that. He might have had a completely unrelated reason for slowing down, which had nothing to do with us at all.

But a crinkly feeling went up the back of my neck, all the same. Maybe because for the first time in my life, I'd been warned to watch out for people behind me. Or because I knew there could be some danger of being followed—but not *here*, not in New York. I hadn't been consciously thinking about it for days, had taken no precautions.

And Marianne did say not to use my credit cards. Not to use my name at any hotels. I'd done both in the last twenty-four hours, along with a plane ticket stamped Lola Bright.

All of this took less than a minute to pass, and then Peter straightened again and we were on our way, the man behind us. It was my turn to change our pace, moving faster and pulling Peter by the hand along with me. I didn't want to run, so I kept it to a fast walk. Not hurrying-to-catch-a-train fast, but fast enough.

At Center Drive, I turned to the right, Peter following without comment. Using his shoulder and neck to shield me, I managed to sneak a quick look down the way we'd come. The man had dropped back some—*but not far back enough.*

He'd *had* to have increased his own pace to be as close as he was.

As the drive curved past the Carousel, now closed for the evening, I turned us quickly down one of the tree-lined paths beside it, circling around the Carousel buildings and heading northwest. A little way down, I stopped, pulling Peter off the path so that we were out of sight behind a bush, but could still see the gap of the drive where we'd turned in.

"What's up?" he asked quietly, holding onto my hand.

I didn't say anything, watching the gap with wide, anxious eyes. At first I didn't think it would happen. I started to feel relieved— and extremely silly—at my overreaction. He was just some guy walking through the park, some businessman on his way to drinks or dinner… and then he was there, in the gap.

He stopped, hesitating, looking down the way we'd gone, looking the other way, not seeing us in the deepening shadows. I realized I was holding my breath, as if it would help, and gave a quiet gasp. Peter was still beside me, not speaking or questioning my actions. After only a few seconds, the man continued down the path toward us.

I drew back in alarm, into the shadows—then stiffened in shock when Peter didn't join me. Instead he moved out to meet the man on the path, asking calmly, "Were you looking for us?"

I jumped—as did the man, though his surprise was more moderate, and more quickly controlled. He paused, staring angrily at Peter.

"I beg your pardon?" he asked stiffly, in a fair imitation of someone who'd been wrongfully accused. I saw his eyes flicker to me, probably just visible as a lighter shape in the gloom, before resting again on Peter. He was Caucasian with dark hair and regular features and no distinguishing marks or facial hair, but I thought I'd recognize him if I saw him again.

"Just wondering if you wanted something," Peter said in a deceptively helpful voice. "You seemed to be following us."

The man eyed him, and for a split second I wondered if he was going to break character and explain. But then the impression was gone.

"You're crazy," he said flatly. "Get the fuck away from me."

"No problem at all," Peter said with steely politeness, standing his ground.

Looking genuinely annoyed, the man turned and continued down the path by the ball fields, not looking behind him. He disappeared up ahead, turning left where the path met another of the streets that crisscrossed the park. Peter watched him go, and then fluidly pulled me with him back toward Center Drive, not running but moving at a rapid pace down through an underpass beneath the street, which even in my anxiety I recognized from movies and TV, down a series of darkening paths, past trees and small buildings. With steady speed, we passed the Zoo at the edge of the park, making a sharp right onto 5th Avenue.

We didn't talk until we were on the wide street, comfortingly bright with the last glow of daylight augmenting the streetlights, busy with late commuter traffic.

"You saw him too?" I asked breathlessly, holding tightly to Peter's hand.

"When we left the restaurant, he was standing by the bar."

I shivered, though I wasn't cold.

"Why do you think he was following us?"

"Maybe to see where we were going," Peter suggested, very kindly not pointing out what a stupid question it was.

We kept moving, crossing 5th Avenue, passing Barney's, turning again down Madison Avenue. We kept up the same very fast pace, panting openly now but not slowing except to step around someone or wait to cross a street. Rather than head directly south to our hotel, Peter lead us in a circle around it, diving at the last minute into a nearby Starbucks, waiting in line and ordering decaf mochas. I couldn't think what to order, and he didn't ask what I wanted. It was a good place to watch for anyone following, only having a few windows on one side. We stood in the lee of one of these while we waited for our coffees, our eyes darting from corner to corner.

The man didn't appear. We'd lost him—or someone else had taken his place. Someone we wouldn't recognize even if they were standing in line behind us. In addition to looking outside, I nervously watched the other customers as they came in, waited and went out. I couldn't help it. But nobody paid the slightest notice to us, and once our order was called and we walked outside, no one made a move to follow.

■ ■ ■

Back in our hotel room, Peter walked to the window and shut the curtains, keeping out of sight as he did so. Office buildings stood across the street with blinds hiding most of the rooms, no doubt empty now that the workday was over. I sat down on the end of the bed, and he paced in front of me. Our coffees sat untouched on the desk.

"They found us here," I said, rather blankly. "I don't even know who 'they' are, and they found us in New York."

He glanced at me, stopped pacing and came to sit beside me.

"It looks that way," he said. "How—and why, and *who*—is what I'd give a lot to know."

"Marianne said not to use my credit cards. And I did—I booked the hotel on my Visa."

"Then they'll already know we're staying here," he replied evenly. "Though it may have been something else that caught their notice. We've been asking questions about her past. Maybe this just means we're on the right track."

"That'd be good," I said without much feeling.

My exhaustion had returned at a new and furious pitch—it pinched between my shoulder blades, weighed down my neck, ached in my lower back and throbbed in my feet. My eyes stung on the inside, the nerves themselves seeming to twitch in pain.

With a sudden sense of vertigo, I found myself putting my head between my knees and moaning.

"Hey, are you OK?" Peter asked apprehensively, his voice sounding oddly tinny and far away. His hand rubbed my back.

"I got dizzy," I gasped, taking deep, shaky breaths from the edge of the bed. "And... I may need to throw up."

As soon as I said it, I knew it was true—and not only did I need to throw up, I needed to throw up *immediately*. I stood and moved quickly if unsteadily to the bathroom, barely making it to the toilet in time. There wasn't much to empty; what there was came up fast and left me feeling faint and clammy but as if it didn't need to happen again. Peter had followed me into the bathroom, hovering anxiously behind me at first, then kneeling to pull back my tangled hair, which had fallen down around my face.

"Ughh," I said, flushing and putting my head down on my arm, resting across the seat.

Peter stood and stepped away. I heard the tap running, and then felt my hair lifted and a cold, damp washcloth placed gently on the back of my neck.

"Mmh... feels nice," I murmured.

"Do you still feel dizzy?"

"Um..."

I waited another minute, then slowly raised my head, allowing the cloth to fall into my hand. The room wasn't spinning any longer. I just felt very weak and tired.

"No," was all I said.

"Can you drink some water?" He held out a plastic bottle with the top off.

I took it and sipped tentatively, drinking about a third of the bottle before I handed it back. It seemed like it was going to stay down, but you never know.

"Let's get you to bed."

If it had been up to me, I almost certainly would have curled up right there on the bathroom floor, maybe pulling a couple of towels down as bedding. Thanks to Peter's urging, I pushed myself into a sitting position, and with his help managed to stand up and walk to the bed. He pulled the covers back, sat me down, pulled off my shoes, then my jeans, then my shirt and bra. His hands moved with a gentle confidence that was very soothing. As soon as I was undressed down to my underwear, I curled up in a ball with my head on the pillow, and he covered me with blankets and turned off all lights but the lamp on his nightstand.

The last thing I remembered before sleep rushed over me was a soft kiss on the top of my head.

■ ■ ■

The next afternoon, we sat on the edge of a concrete planter, looking up at the United Nations headquarters. Today's sky was azure blue instead of gray, artistically brushed with windswept white clouds. The view across the East River offered low humps of islands basking below the Queensboro Bridge, skyscrapers on the opposite shore. Troops of schoolchildren marched past hand-in-hand, impelled along by teachers and parent chaperones, alternating with large tour groups of various nationalities.

When we'd arrived just before nine, the plaza had been mostly empty, the ticket lines moving quickly. Now, just after noon, the press of people seemed to be growing by the minute. It was chaotic and reassuring at the same time. If there was someone watching us from the crowd, we had plenty of insulation and cover.

On top of that, I had a vague sense of satisfaction in the idea that anyone following us was probably having a very boring day.

I'd slept deeply until about four in the morning, waking suddenly and alertly. My body still very firmly believed it was one, in spite of the undeniable numbers on the digital clock. I went to the bathroom, brushed my teeth, washed my face and drank two bottles of water. Feeling much refreshed, I slid back into bed and stared up at the ceiling for a while.

Once it became clear that I was unassailably wide awake, I found a granola bar in my purse and ate it, then played with the settings on my phone while my mind wandered. I wondered how late Peter had stayed up the previous night. I wondered if the hotel was being watched right now. If so, I wondered who was watching us.

The same man from the park yesterday? Would he only be assigned to the night shift now that we'd "made" him? I considered how that worked. Were criminals like law enforcement agencies, with set schedules and rotations? Guido on stalking duty, six to ten, relieved by Spike, ten to two?

Assuming it was a criminal or criminals, of course. Maybe it was just the one guy we already saw—Marianne's employer, say. Or boyfriend. That was somewhat less terrifying than the idea of a criminal network complete with real-time digital flags on my credit cards and flight reservations. It was still impossible to imagine how my cousin could be mixed up with crime, much less a sinister and resourceful group of criminals.

She'd never been arrested for anything, as far as I knew. She wasn't the type of teenager to get into shoplifting for kicks. She was a good student, driven to succeed in school, never making trouble for my parents or leading me into drinking or drugs. Honestly, part of the shock of this whole thing was that she was one of the last people I'd ever have imagined getting into serious trouble.

But how much did I really know about her life? Once she left California for New York, we'd remained close in terms of affection, but not in close contact. Even our emails and phone calls got a lot more infrequent once she quit the journalism program. Not long after that she moved into the loft with Mike and the rest of them, which had always been a bitter pill for me to swallow. I'd been so horrified at what I saw, I didn't say anything about the situation to my parents, knowing they'd feel even worse than I did.

Her involvement with the loft crowd, even before I knew the extremes that Mike Sorenson had gone to, had really shaken my perception of her, to the point that I hadn't wanted to admit to myself how shocked, offended, disturbed I felt. How betrayed.

I'd held it in, told no one about it—and experienced intense relief when she told me she was living in New York. My high opinion of her was once again vindicated. I didn't have to feel uneasy and sickened and disappointed by her choices.

But the truth was, I didn't really know anything about her choices. I still had no idea why she'd lived at the loft, or chosen to stay there more than a year. She'd never explained or excused that, other than her flippant adventure comment, which I discounted. Nobody purposefully put themselves through months of squalor and abuse just for a thrill. Which meant that whether or not I liked the idea, I had to accept the fact that the Marianne I wanted her to be and the real Marianne might be very different people.

There was always the possibility that whoever was behind all of this was actually not a criminal—was some kind of law enforcement. I didn't think it was likely, though. Admittedly my experience with and knowledge of the CIA and FBI were entirely limited to fiction, but I couldn't see them assigning someone to tail us through Central Park. Why would they need to? If those agencies wanted to track either Peter or me, they most certainly had all the resources they needed and then some to do so without sending some guy in a suit out to watch our movements in Central Park. At least, I imagined they did. I also imagined they might be better at covert surveillance.

At some point I drifted off again, waking up to Peter closing the bathroom door. It was six thirty, a much more reasonable hour to start the day. I'd come to learn that no matter what the time zone or day of the week, Peter woke up at six thirty. He couldn't explain why, he just had an internal alarm set for that time which never once failed to go off.

I was also coming to learn that he was extremely passive about suggesting fun activities for us. Unless work, food, dog care, exercise or some other impetus was involved—such as investigating my cousin's past—he tended to stick to his routines, and on trips would be fine with aimlessly wandering until we stumbled across something we wanted to do.

This would have been irritating beyond belief, except that he was always absolutely on board with the suggestions I made, and would, if presented with multiple options, give his opinion about which one was the better choice. It wasn't that he didn't want to do interesting things. He just wasn't interested in thinking them up or deciding on them in advance.

It was a new experience for me to be the activity director of a relationship—any relationship. I resented it at first, but soon began to value how easygoing he was. I could see how, if it had spread to other parts of his life like work or day-to-day tasks, being his partner would be like parenting a sluggish pre-teen—but it never went beyond activity planning. My awareness of this did, however, make me understand a little more how his ex-wife must have felt, managing a younger and less grounded version of this man.

All that to say that I suggested we walk to the UN on Tuesday morning, grabbing a quick breakfast of bagels and coffee on the way, and Peter unreservedly agreed.

"How are you feeling?" he'd asked, when he saw that I was awake.

"Much, much better," I said, reaching out for a hug. He smelled wonderful—clean and familiar. "I'm sorry to have been such a pain."

"You were exhausted," he said simply. "Combine that with the surreal experience of being followed in the park, it's understandable that you'd be upset. I didn't feel too great, either."

"Did you sleep well?"

"Not at first—it took me a while to relax. I took a shower and watched a movie on my iPad. I must've fallen asleep before it ended."

"Any new conclusions about the… situation?"

"Nothing very brilliant. I'm still not convinced they traced us here using your credit card. Something about that just doesn't feel right."

"Why do you think Marianne said not to use them, if it didn't matter?"

"I don't know—maybe someone involved could trace you that way, for the same reason she took your phone. I vote that we don't charge anything on them again or use any of your accounts, just to be safe. Truth be told, though, at this point *how* they found us doesn't really matter as much as *why*. Someone does know we're here, and seems to be highly interested in what we're doing," he kept his eyes on our interlinked hands—"...or better yet, who we're meeting."

He raised his eyes to mine.

"Marianne," I said slowly. "They're hoping we'll lead them to Marianne."

Peter nodded.

"That's the conclusion I came to. Of course we don't know, but..."

"But it's the likeliest reason for keeping us under tabs," I finished.

It made sense. Too much sense. If not for my safety—or not just for my safety, why else would Marianne send me into hiding, directing me to avoid police and stay off the grid?

To make sure that she couldn't be found through me.

Or... the thought made my stomach ripple anxiously... so they couldn't use me to get to her.

One way or another, they'd found me. Someone had. They knew we were in New York, and almost certainly knew we were at this hotel. The milk was soaking into the floorboards, and I found I had no desire to cry over it. It was too late to stay buried in Half Moon Bay, my head under the covers. Right or wrong, we'd stepped out and into their line of sight.

We couldn't change that now. All we could do was move forward. Going home wouldn't help. Maybe we could lose them on the way, maybe they wouldn't keep watching if they saw where we'd gone, maybe they'd keep me under observation until I died of old age or until Marianne made contact, whichever came first. We couldn't know.

And maybe they'd take matters into their own hands—rather than waiting for me to contact Marianne, decide to use me as bait, or something equally disturbing. Even as I considered the idea, part of my mind rejected it as far-fetched.

It was the same rational part that thought being tailed by a guy in a suit was far-fetched. Or meeting a stranger who felt like your soul mate from the first sound of their voice.

That part was losing ground fast.

I'd chosen door number three: to try to find out what Marianne had done, to discover anything I could about the bomb that she'd set off in my life. I'd known—or had a vague, uneasy sense that I didn't remotely know and didn't *want* to know—the risks involved. Whether or not we'd been prepared for it, and I definitely hadn't been, this was the consequence of that choice. Peter had made the same choice—to do this with me.

So there it was.

The anxiety in my stomach gave another frantic twinge, and then subsided to a low-level throb. A throb I'd been living with for nearly two weeks. Would be host to for the foreseeable future.

There was no going back.

■ ■ ■

I'd enjoyed seeing the UN, walking slowly through the exhibits in the Visitor Centre, seeing the chambers where the delegates did their work. It was soothing and inspiring. Coming together as a global community of people, rising above imaginary borders and national identities. The ideals it represented were so much nobler than ordinary human aspirations, the problems it struggled to solve so much bigger than mine.

For a while, in that bright high-security building, I could almost forget that shadowy figures lurked in our periphery, plotting who knew what for motives unknown.

For a while.

We sat outside people watching until hunger drove us to find lunch. Peter had a knack for leading us to good restaurants, without resorting to Yelp—though inevitably, if I checked later, the place he chose had high ratings. He'd worked in food service for most of his life, one way or another; whether it was an innate skill or learned from years of experience, anyone eating out with Peter benefitted, as long as you were willing to trust him. This was another reason why I didn't mind his dislike of planning things. He might not take the lead on the activity choice, but he'd make sure we ate regularly and well.

Today's chosen spot didn't look especially prepossessing from the outside, but offered the best Chinese food I'd ever had. It was crowded when we arrived, no doubt with eager Yelpers, so we were good and hungry by the time we were seated. While we worked our way through a platter of the house special shrimp dish and rice, we—or rather, I—planned our afternoon. After considering and rejecting museums, since it was too nice a day to be indoors, and tourist sites, since they'd be overrun and we'd both seen the major ones anyway, I pulled out my phone and started scrolling through a list of top things to do in New York.

"What sounds good to *you*?" I insisted, not yet having realized the futility of this question.

Peter took a large bite, chewed and swallowed.

"Being with you. Not being at work."

Frustrating and gratifying at the same time. I caught sight of a name I recognized.

"What about the High Line? I've never been there."

"The park? I haven't either."

"Does it sound good?" I asked, slightly desperate now.

"Sure. Is that what you want to do?"

"*Yes*," I said.

A train ride across town and a few blocks on foot later, we spent the rest of the day walking the High Line, a narrow, winding greenbelt converted from an old elevated railway line, from 34th Street all the way down to the other end at Gansevoort Street.

From there we joined the Hudson River Greenway and continued south along the Hudson River, through the Park and down through Rockefeller Park. Now and then we stopped and looked at the view. We bought expensive organic ice cream bars from a hairy hipster and ate them on a bench. We shared stories about the last time we were each in New York, and about other trips we'd taken and places we'd seen. Neither of us had been to Canada, but we'd both been to Mexico. Finally we turned, making our way to the 9/11 Memorial, where we stood at the edge of the fountain marking the original North Tower.

"A nice walk," Peter said, his eyes on the names of the fallen engraved in front of us.

"Very nice," I agreed, thinking it was good that we both liked walking. We'd come more than five miles, not counting the walk this morning.

"I didn't notice anyone behind us," he informed me in the same tranquil voice.

"Me, either," I said, though I hadn't been looking very hard. I hadn't *wanted* to see if someone was there.

If anybody was, I hoped they absolutely hated walking. I hoped they'd have blisters for days.

We took the subway uptown, stopping to pick up sandwiches and a bottle of wine at a deli next to the hotel, and didn't leave the room again that night.

chapter 11

"We made it," I said, as the shuttle pulled out. We were all crammed in together, those of us on our way to Rikers Island. There were a few other pairs like us—mothers and children, adult couples—but most of the riders had come alone.

It had been an easy trip to get here: we caught the subway near our hotel and rode straight through until we reached our stop. It was long past the morning commuter rush, so we'd found seats without any problem. Once in Harlem, we'd circled the block several times rather than wait on the corner for the shuttle, just on the chance that a) someone was on our trail and b) we might be able to lose them if they were. Not that my heart was really in it. I'd sort of gotten used to the idea that we were being watched.

Last night we'd gone over what we would ask Michael Sorenson. Peter would take the lead, unless it seemed like I needed to, but either way we'd try to stick to the plan, such as it was. Of course it was all moot if he refused to see us, wasn't allowed visitors, or someone else registered to visit him first.

We were silent on the fifty-minute drive. It was too crowded for easy conversation, so I leaned into Peter's shoulder and looked out the window. I kept remembering the last time I saw Mike, as I thought of him. The only time. Naked and scraggly and mean. Pushing Marianne up against the wall with a hard, sinewy arm. Screaming epithets into her face.

The memory didn't exactly make me eager to see him again.

Having grown up in the Bay Area, the concept of an island prison wasn't a strange one. Except that Rikers Island was still in use, while Alcatraz had all the charm of a slightly gritty, highly scenic tourist destination. The shuttle finally made the turn onto the long bridge that led to the island, past the oddly bright orange and blue sign, and after a few minutes we'd reached our destination.

It was different from what I expected. Less imposing, more like a military base. There were city-like streets curving around wide areas of grass, multistory buildings that could have been apartments or dorms, administrative offices. The shuttle pulled up in front of an unassuming structure that looked a lot more like a DMV than a jail, except for the large sign across the top proclaiming "New York City Department of Corrections" and all the uniformed officers around. The double doors were open and barricades had been set out as guards began the process of checking people in. A small line had already formed, swelling quickly as the shuttle passengers joined it.

Once inside, it was even more like a DMV. First we waited our turn to lock up our belongings. We'd read up on the procedures and had brought a dollar's worth of quarters with us for the lockers, changed by the hotel front desk. I'd left my purse behind, so we only had our phones and wallets to lock up.

We went through the initial security and search, then made our way to the waiting room of the jail where Michael Sorenson was incarcerated. Here we checked in with our IDs, received our Visitor Express Passes and were told that a shuttle bus to the jail proper would leave in about twenty minutes, then sat down in plastic chairs until they called us for the bus. Apparently there would be no problem seeing Michael Sorenson. We could only hope, now, that he was the right person.

"They're planning to close this place down, you know," Peter told me quietly. "Turn the whole island into mixed-use development."

"Really?" Sitting here, it was hard to imagine the prison not existing.

"Who knows if they will, but the idea keeps getting tossed around."

After a short ride, the shuttle dropped us off at the door to the jail. We went through a second set of metal detectors and were told that we'd need to lock up any other loose possessions, including jackets and jewelry. We had none to remove, and again sat down to wait. There were fewer people here, though every thirty minutes or so another shuttle arrived, until the waiting area had filled. Now and then names would be called by a guard and people would disappear into a secure area. An hour passed.

When my name was finally called, I jumped and scrambled to my feet, holding out my pass to show the guard. He checked it and nodded, then led me to a small room with a bench in one corner before shutting the door.

"Please remove your shoes and socks… Open your mouth… Lift up your hair… Show me your sleeves…" With the utter dispassion borne of frequent routine, the man snapped through the instructions, then told me to put my shoes and socks on and wait, shutting the door behind him. I sat down in the little room and complied. Everything about this was utterly surreal.

After a few minutes, the door opened and a different guard and Peter stood outside. He led us through two more high security doors into a long, light room surrounded by windows to a table about halfway down, then told us where to sit. There were four or five other visits going on, prisoners in orange jumpsuits on one side of the tables—all men—and visitors on the other. I could barely take any of it in.

Peter said nothing. I could tell he wasn't as calm as he seemed, noticing the tightness of his mouth and determination in his eyes. I didn't know where to look, so I looked at him.

"I shouldn't have made you come," he whispered.

"You didn't make me," I whispered back. "I wanted to."

"It was my idea."

"It's our only lead."

A door at the far end of the hall opened and a guard came in, leading a prisoner. They walked over to our table and the prisoner sat down.

"Hey," he said, eyeing us with understandable curiosity.

I stared at him. I couldn't help it.

The past five years hadn't been good to Mike Sorenson, but even so I recognized him. His hair, which had been long and dirty, was buzzed short and receding off his forehead. He sported a neat goatee and some kind of scrolling tattoo on his neck. He looked tough and worn at the same time. His eyes, which I only remembered as being enraged and bloodshot, were a startling light blue. He must have been very handsome when he was younger, I realized. I hadn't noticed at the time, distracted by too much other nastiness.

"I'm Peter, and this is Lola," Peter said.

"Uh huh. Should I know you?"

"We think you used to know our friend, Marianne DiGregorio."

Mike leaned back in his chair, considering us.

"I knew Marianne, yeah. A long time ago." His eyes focused on my face and narrowed. "You showed up once. At the loft."

It wasn't a question. He recognized me, too. I'd had a forlorn hope that he might have been too drugged out to register the encounter.

"Yeah," I said.

"Your face rang a bell when you said Marianne's name."

"I was only there a couple of minutes."

"Really? What happened?" He genuinely seemed to want to know.

"Nothing—you yelled at her and wouldn't let her leave with me. And then I left."

He shrugged slightly.

"Don't remember," he said. "So what do you want?"

"We want to know anything you can tell us about her," Peter told him, using the only part of our original strategy that still held.

"Why?"

"We're looking for her. If you can think of anything it might help us find her."

"Mm. What's it worth to you?"

I know I must have looked stunned at the question, though Peter took it in stride.

"Some," he said imperturbably.

Mike laughed once, a hard, harsh sound.

"Don't worry. I don't know much so it's not worth much. You probably figured that out. But I'll tell you what I do know if you spot me fifty bucks at the comm. Call it a 'thank you' for my time."

Peter looked at me before replying.

"Deal," he said briefly.

"I'll trust you. What've I got to lose, right? Send a money order for my account."

"Fine. What can you tell us?"

"Marianne… She wasn't like the others. Drove me up the wall. Nothing seemed to get to her, you know? I never got why she hung with us."

"Where did you meet her?"

"She worked for the agency where I was under contract. I was a model for a while, but the whole thing was so corporate and shallow and—*fucked up*—I just couldn't handle it. Blew my wad and quit. Marianne and me'd gone out a few times and stayed in touch. Then I rented the dump in Newark and got some people to move in, thinking it'd be kind of a 'fuck you' to the establishment." He cracked his knuckles, making me wince. "Did some seriously fucked-up shit. It became like this mission—screw the man by screwing each other. We got into some petty shit, theft and dealing, enough to scrounge food and stay stoned. Stopped paying the rent after a while, but the old guy who owned the place said we reminded him of the sixties." He laughed. "Peace and love and all that shit. Except I wanted to *blow—shit—up.*"

His large blue eyes had deep lines around them. He shook his head.

"I was an angry little shit," he said. "Went about it the wrong way. The establishment's going to have to go down from the *inside.* I get that now. Just watching it implode a little more every day. Before you know it, that one percent at the top is just going to go 'pop' and all their money and power will be gone."

He sounded more resigned than impassioned. Whatever fervor had driven Mike to reject the system so sordidly and completely— inspiring him to make bombs and take hostages and whatever other appalling choices he'd made—apparently hadn't survived his incarceration. He didn't scare me anymore. Six years ago, this man had shaken me—his malevolence, his vicious and brutal treatment of Marianne, his filthy savagery. And now he was just a washed-up model in prison, a protest leader who'd never accomplished anything worthwhile. I almost felt sorry for him, but stopped short of that. He wasn't a pitiful figure. Just a failed one.

"Mmhm," Peter replied neutrally. "When did Marianne end up leaving your group?"

"Not sure. Before I got arrested. She hung with us a year or so."

"Did she just take off one day, or…?"

Mike thought back.

"I guess so… something like that. She—no, wait. Some guy came and talked to her—this older guy. I must not have been too fucked up that day, 'cause I remember now."

"An older guy," repeated Peter. "Did he say who he was?"

"Nah. Never caught a name. Or forgot it. He looked like one of those dicks from Wall Street—suit, slicked back hair, shiny shoes. Didn't like getting them dirty on our floor. He pushed his way in and said some shit to Marianne... something about... her time was up. She looked kind of freaked—and *nothing* freaked this girl. I got up on him and he didn't even flinch, just stared at her and said some more shit about making her choice and then left. Cold fucker. Ice cold. Marianne didn't say anything—yeah, no, she just left. Didn't take her stuff or anything, she just stood there while I yelled at her and then walked out. Never saw her again."

Peter and I glanced at each other.

"She didn't come back for her stuff later?"

"Nah. There wasn't much. Some clothes and couple notebooks and shit. What we couldn't sell we tossed."

My stomach sank. I hadn't really expected Mike Sorenson to give us any leads, but it was just such a final dead end. The appearance of the older man raised a lot of questions—who was he, what did he mean by "her time was up?" Assuming Mike even remembered right—but gave us nothing more to go on.

"Well, thanks," Peter was saying.

"Told you it wasn't much." Mike grinned, showing nicotine-stained teeth.

"We'll get that fifty to you."

"Cool."

Mike nodded to the nearest guard and stood up, while we continued to sit, as instructed. He was a few steps from the table when he turned around and came back.

"Just thought of something—doubt it means anything..."

"What's that?" Peter asked, his tone betraying the same sense of pessimism that had settled over me.

"She sent us a postcard after she left—from some foreign place. South America, maybe. It was weird, though. It just said 'Pegasus,' and her name."

"Pegasus?" I repeated.

"Crazy, right? It became like this running joke. Unicorn, Pegasus, Loch Ness Monster. She went off to find them, like those fucking stupid shows on the Discovery Channel. Anyway, that's it."

"Thanks," I said this time, since Peter already had once. "We appreciate you seeing us."

"No prob. It's not like my social calendar's real full, you know?" He got up and strolled back the way he'd entered without another glance at us. A guard met him at the door and opened it, and Mike had disappeared.

■ ■ ■

At a little after four, we were on the shuttle heading back to Harlem. We'd gotten back to the main exit to find that it was already almost three thirty, and had spent the remaining half hour or so stretching our legs around an unrestricted grassy area and talking about what we'd learned.

"Pegasus doesn't mean anything to you?" Peter had asked me.

"Nothing. Marianne wasn't into things like that," I said. "Fantasy or mythology. At least not when we were growing up. She liked true crime and mysteries."

"So whatever it referred to, it probably wasn't a winged horse— unless there's some other inside reference with the loft people that we don't know about."

"Wouldn't Mike have known about it?"

"Maybe not. She could have meant it for someone else there. He didn't remember the postcard being addressed to any one person, but I'm not sure that means a whole lot."

"I'm kind of surprised he remembered as much as he did."

Peter looked blank and said nothing.

"You think he was lying?" I asked, wondering why I should be surprised.

"Maybe not deliberately, but yeah, I think it's possible he added a few details. Still, what he said about the Wall Street guy did line up with Napoletti's story about the guy who asked about the loft for his daughter. He might have been looking for Marianne, or looking for information about her."

"Who do you think he was?"

"I was kind of hoping you might have an idea about that. What about her father?"

That did surprise me.

"Uncle Leonard? But…" I trailed off, considering this for the first time. For some unknown reason, I'd only met my aunt and uncle twice, once when I was very young and once as a pre-teen, brief visits while they collected Marianne to spend a few weeks traveling with them. "I never saw him dressed like that," I said slowly, trying to remember. "His hair was short, I think, kind of pepper and salt, and he had a beard. I don't know her parents at all."

"Who was related to who?"

"Our moms were half-sisters. They didn't grow up together— her mom was a lot older than mine. They've always spent most of their time overseas."

"Nobody said anything about a beard, but he could have shaved it off."

"I guess her father makes as much sense as anybody, though I'd never have said he cared much about her welfare. They started leaving Marianne with my parents not long after I was born."

"Is she close to them now?"

"I highly doubt it. Though she might still be in touch with them, I don't know. They didn't reach out when either of my parents died."

"Her time was up…" Peter mused to himself. "Seems like that implies an ultimatum of some kind."

"She reacted like it did. I thought she left the group because she finally got fed up with—well, with all of it, but it sounds like it was this man coming that made her leave."

"Definitely puts a different spin on the situation," Peter agreed. "Not long after that, she tells you that she's working for a travel agency and living in Manhattan, right?"

"Yeah. She never gave me the address and I never visited her again, but that's what she said."

"What agency, do you know?"

I shook my head.

"I wonder if there's one called Pegasus."

There were three in the greater New York area, though only one listed an address in Manhattan: Pegasus Destinations. It came up on the search as a business listing, but other than the address, had no website or other information. Another Pegasus was in Long Island, with an impressive, up-to-date website, and a third was in Brooklyn, which, according to Yelp, had closed a few years ago.

"Narrows it down," Peter said, putting his phone back in his pocket. "Though it might be a stretch to put the two things together."

"It's something," I said. "And it's our only lead. Where else would we start looking? I mean, it could mean anything."

"We've come this far, we might as well check out the Manhattan address," Peter agreed, though I could tell he didn't believe we'd find anything.

I didn't believe it either. It just seemed so *wasteful* to have come this far and still have no clue what, or who, Marianne was protecting me from. All we knew for sure was that someone had been following us on Monday afternoon. Everything else was a tangle of speculation and unanswered questions, bringing us no closer to a resolution. We had one more day here, less than a day, and still had no clue as to what was going on. Only *Pegasus*, that was the single piece of information Marianne had left behind in New York, lodged in the decidedly sketchy memory of a convicted felon.

After we found nothing at the address, because of course there would be nothing to find, we'd go back to California on Thursday, empty handed and possibly tailed by person or persons unknown. It was a discouraging thought for a lot of reasons.

Never mind that, deep down, I knew it was the best possible scenario.

Because as long as we knew nothing, we were safe. At least, that's what I wanted to believe. "Safe" had become kind of an ambiguous concept lately. A man had definitely followed us in the park—and it was really only by chance that we'd noticed. Someone might be watching us at all times. If so, our visits to Napoletti and Rikers might not have advertised our interest in Michael Sorenson and, through him, Marianne. But they also might. If whoever was keeping an eye on us had extensive enough resources to track us down in New York City, they probably had enough background information to figure out what we were doing.

In which case, it wouldn't matter much either way if we followed the next lead.

That's what I told myself, anyway.

■ ■ ■

The shuttle dropped us off in Harlem where it had picked us up, not quite as full on the way back but full enough to make private conversation impossible. We spent part of the time figuring out our route to the address listed for Pegasus Destinations, the rest thinking our own thoughts. After we got off the bus, Peter was hungry and stopped to get a bagel to eat on the way. I didn't think I wanted food, but as soon as I walked into the shop and smelled fresh toasted bread, I got one as well. We waited until we got off the subway at East 14th Street and 1st Avenue before we pulled them out of the bag, still slightly warm and oozing with cream cheese.

The address was near the East Village, in the neighborhood called Alphabet City, about a fifteen-minute walk from the subway stop. We cut south through Tomkins Square Park and found the street easily, just off Avenue B, a few blocks north of Houston. It seemed to be mostly residential, with monotonously severe brick apartments marching down one side of the street and a mixture of apartments and a few businesses on the other.

Not quite halfway down was a tall, narrow building of four stories, older than those around it. The ground floor space looked like it had been commercial at one time, with an unlit "Open" sign in one of the windows, rather the worse for wear, but no other signs or indications that a business operated here. Colorful graffiti covered the base of the walls, the closed metal door and one of the ground-floor windows.

We stood at the bottom of the short stoop and looked at it.

"It's definitely the address listed," Peter said, without me having to ask.

"They don't seem to be open," I said lightly. Just as with our visits to the Newark warehouse and to Mike, I'd known there was little chance we'd find anything of value.

And I was disappointed, all the same.

Chances were, Marianne hadn't meant anything with her postcard. Maybe it was just a way to mess with the people at the loft. Or a private joke she shared with her roommates that Mike never knew or forgot about. We couldn't depend on his memory to hold onto something like that. And she might have been working for any one of hundreds of travel agencies around here. The fact that Mike had thought the postcard was from South America could be a clue, but it also could have been something she picked up at work, or part of the joke we didn't know.

We were amateurs at this investigation thing. Even with Peter's instincts, which struck me as being unusually strong, and my knowledge of Marianne, we'd only managed to get ourselves here.

An empty and dilapidated building.

A true dead end.

"Should we knock or something?" Peter asked me.

"I don't see the point," I said depressingly. "I doubt anybody's in there."

As soon as the word "there" left my mouth, we heard a muffled grating sound from the building. The door—the very door we'd just been discussing—swung open, revealing a dark space beyond. A woman stepped into the doorway, a large purse hanging off one shoulder, obviously on her way out. She came two steps before she saw us, then stood frozen on the stoop, one hand on the open door.

We stared at each other.

"Marianne," I said.

"Oh, *shit*," she said, and turned quickly around.

chapter 12

I only had time to feel a kind of sickened shock—both at seeing her and at her reaction—before I felt Peter tug at my elbow.

"She wants us to follow her," he said in my ear, and I noticed that Marianne, rather than disappearing back into the building, was standing in the doorway beckoning urgently. We hurried inside after her, and she closed and locked the door with a rush, shutting the three of us into musty darkness. Dim light filtered down from an upper story, showing us the stairwell leading up.

"What the hell are you doing here?" she hissed, starting up the stairs. We followed.

"Looking for you," I said, my mind still unable to fully take in what was happening.

"Of all the idiotic…" I heard her mutter as she led us up.

We continued all the way to the third floor, where she unlocked and opened a door at the back of the hallway. It was a dingy little room, bare of furniture except a camping-style cot made up with sheets and a blanket and pillow, a desk, a chair and, incongruously, a mini-fridge. One corner held a rack of clothes, dark lumps of shoes below. The only source of light was the single dusty window, the daylight diffused through a yellow shade. Marianne closed and locked the door behind us, then crossed over and switched on a low desk lamp, throwing her heavy bag down on the floor.

"How'd you find me?" she demanded, turning to glare at us.

"Michael Sorenson," Peter said, after it was clear I wasn't capable of answering. "He remembered the postcard you sent. And the fact that Lola knew you worked at a travel agency. This address is listed for Pegasus Destinations."

"Great. Just fantastic. And who the fuck are you?"

I woke up.

"This is Peter—Owen. He's my—he's been helping me."

She eyed us, then abruptly sat down in the chair and lit a cigarette. No wonder the room smelled so stale and sticky.

Marianne didn't smoke. But this woman was Marianne—a tired, pale, thin Marianne with the same drawn, worried look she'd worn in my apartment a few weeks ago. Her long sweep of dark brown hair, her sparkling brown eyes, her features too sharply defined to be beautiful, but so vivacious you didn't really notice, all as familiar to me as my own. And she was undoubtedly smoking.

"Sit," she said, waving at the cot. We sat. "You're telling me that toxic joke actually remembered the postcard I sent when I left? What rock did you find him under, anyway?"

"Rikers," Peter said briefly.

"Hmph. I should've guessed." She smoked furiously for a moment while we waited. I took in her clothes: tailored jeans, white shirt, high boots, light khaki jacket. She looked elegant and fashionable. An elegant, fashionable stranger who smoked. "What else did he say?"

"He remembered about the man who came to see you—an older man in a suit—right before you left. Not his name, just what he said about your time being up, something like that."

"Mm. How'd you track down Mike?"

"Richard Napoletti—his landlord in Newark."

"Damn. If I wasn't so irritated, I'd be impressed," she said, and then laughed suddenly—and there she was, the Marianne I'd known all my life. "Did you even go to Uncle Joe's?" she asked me, sounding less angry.

"I did—just like you told me. That's where I met Peter."

"Ah. And the two of you decided to come hustling across the continent to—what, look for me?"

"Find answers," Peter told her. "It was that or wait indefinitely until you made contact. Lola chose not to wait."

"Your idea?" she asked.

"My suggestion," he admitted. "It didn't seem likely that you'd be showing up to relieve her mind anytime soon."

"No," she agreed. "But at least she'd be safe. Well, *safer...*" she stubbed out the cigarette on a plate overflowing with butts, her movements jerky. "How long have you been in New York?"

"Since Monday," Peter said.

"Someone followed us in the park on Monday night," I added, finding my voice.

"Oh? Fantastic. So you're back on the grid, then." She glared at me, and I tried not to feel guilty. "They must know you're in town. Let's just hope that's all they know."

"'They' being...?" Peter asked, before I could. My brain was still moving on the slow side, trying to take it all in.

"Look, we can't talk here. I've got to go—but I'll meet you later tonight. Bar Sixty-Five at nine, OK? At Thirty Rock. Ask for Jojo's table."

"Wait," I said, my panic building as she stood up and started for the door. "You haven't explained *anything.*"

"I will—tonight. As much as I can. Hurry *up*, Lo. I'm already late."

Without any further conversation, she herded us back down the stairs and out the front door, shutting and locking it firmly behind us—Marianne still inside. Peter kept walking calmly along the way we'd come, his hand keeping a firm clasp on mine.

"She must have used a back door," he said, as we turned the corner and Marianne didn't appear.

"I've never seen her smoke before," I said irrelevantly.

"She seemed... on edge," he said.

"You think?" I asked wryly, the shock finally wearing off. "I can't believe we found her."

"Sheer luck, I think."

"No—you have really good instincts about stuff like this."

He laughed, shaking his head.

"My ex used to say the same thing. I always figured out the mystery before she did. It drove her crazy."

"See? And she's a trained detective."

"What I want to know is, why did Marianne send the postcard with a clue on it if she didn't want to be found?"

"Maybe she didn't expect anyone to figure it out. Who knows? It was a while ago. Maybe things have changed since then."

"I get the feeling you're right, and a lot has changed. Well, we'll either know more tonight or we won't. After all this, I could really use a drink and something more substantial to eat. How does an early dinner in Soho sound?"

"Perfect," I said. "Lead the way."

■ ■ ■

Bar SixtyFive wasn't the kind of place you expected to go for a clandestine meeting, which is probably what made it ideal for anyone planning one. It was far too swanky, an expensive fusion of power suits and enthusiastic tourists. We'd looked on its website and saw that it had a recommended dress code of "cocktail chic," which sounded a lot like something you'd hear in LA. I didn't have any fancy outfits with me, but settled for a semi-casual black shirt that could almost be dressy, my darkest jeans and black boots versus sneakers. Peter pulled a polo shirt out of his bag, slightly wrinkled, but when it was tucked into his khakis he looked quite nice.

Neither of us looked particularly cocktail or chic, whatever that meant, but at least we had made an effort and weren't wearing sneakers.

A pretty girl with lots of makeup greeted us with supercilious politeness, hearing our request for "Jojo's table" almost as if she didn't believe we'd said it, and then directing one of the lower beings to guide us through the elegant, crowded room. Outside on the balcony, tables were lined up along a glass barrier overlooking the city. At the end of the row was an empty table for four with a "Reserved" sign on it, set slightly apart from those around it in the corner of the balcony. Our host led us to this premium spot, waited while we sat, handed us heavy menus and disappeared.

We settled ourselves and looked around. I couldn't help feeling self-conscious, but nobody was paying much attention to us. Everyone was too busy looking at the view, eating, drinking or talking to the people they sat with.

Before we had a chance to more than glance at our menus, Marianne appeared and sat down, dumping her bag on the chair beside her and asking an attentive waiter to get us three gin and tonics. She wore the same outfit as earlier, and looked even more tired.

"Hi," I said.

She studied me, then her face warmed into a smile.

"It's good to see you, Lo," she said. "It shouldn't be, but it is."

"You come here a lot?" Peter asked, gesturing toward the table.

"Frequently," she said. "It's the perfect place to bring potential—clients. They eat it up. I thought it'd be better to meet somewhere I go often, though at this point I don't know that it makes much difference. The damage has been done, now we have to figure out how to get you back out of sight."

The drinks came with a speed that proved Marianne's value as a customer.

"Hope you like gin. Well, cheers."

We clinked glasses and drank. Then we waited. Marianne met our stares then looked away, out over the city.

"How'd you meet, anyway?" she asked after a moment.

"*You* get to ask questions?" I protested, feeling the old childish heat of perceived unfairness rise up under my skin—but it quickly evaporated under Marianne's calm, discontented gaze. I gave in. "We met on the beach near Uncle Joe's. Peter and his sister own a bar not far away, and we met again the same night. That was kind of…" I made a vague circling gesture with my hand "…kind of it." How to explain the mysterious, intense connection we'd felt from the beginning, without sounding corny or crazy? It wasn't possible.

"Interesting. All those years of fruitless dating, and you just run into each other one day, poof." I didn't especially relish the "all those years" comment, making it sound like decades, but let it go. "So, Peter, you own a bar? What's it called?"

"The Hideout. Our drinks are cheaper, but we can't offer this quality of booze. Or the view."

"Mm. Well, you seem OK. Trustworthy—I've learned to read people fast and you give off a trustworthy vibe. Not that I really have a choice." We didn't say anything, and after another long sip of her drink—emptying her glass—she nodded. "All right. I'll explain. I won't tell you everything, but you deserve the truth. I just don't… The problem is where we go from here."

"Just start—we'll get to that later," I urged, failing to hide my impatience. Marianne acknowledged it with a wry look, signaled the watchful waiter for another round, and then began to speak.

"I was young when I first realized that my parents weren't—quite kosher. Those times I stayed with them I saw all these little signs that added up to something that I didn't like. I couldn't put my finger on what it was, but it was there. Stuff like… Always paying in cash—big fat bundles of it. Changing plans mid-trip, going to Guatemala when our flights were booked for Greece. Never having a settled place to live, even though it seemed like they could afford it. All that money without any obvious source for it. I assumed it was investments, or family money. I didn't ask. The truth is I didn't really *want* to know.

"They claimed to be dedicated activists—working to expand human rights and eradicate human suffering across the globe. That's their favorite line. Not bad, is it? The great humanitarians, striving to end poverty and homelessness and educate the children. The thing is, there weren't ever construction plans to approve, or a house to build, or a remote village to visit. You'd think they'd use their kid mingling with villagers for PR or something, but there was no PR, no press. They mostly stayed at high-end hotels or resorts, disappearing for hours at a time for 'meetings.' They didn't talk about work in front of me, and barely talked *to* me either. I spent most days alone reading or watching TV in hotel rooms, or wandering around by myself. Sometimes they'd pay a housekeeper to watch me."

"As I got older I stayed with them less and less—and noticed more when I did. Your parents were so natural and... *kind*, Lo. So normal. Mine were cold. Cold—and exacting. Nothing was good enough. Either that or they ignored me, which was worse, in a way. I never talked about it to anyone. I figured I'd just lost the genetic lottery and looked forward to making my own living one day so I wouldn't have to accept their help. After I started college, they mostly left me alone, though they'd show up once a year or so and take me out to dinner, like they were testing me or something. That's what it felt like—they didn't ask direct questions, but it always felt like a job interview with some real asshole employers. It only happened a few times, so I'd just—pretend that nothing was wrong and keep focusing on the future. I wanted to be a journalist more than anything. I pushed and worked and eventually got accepted to the graduate program. I was over the moon— remember, Lo? This was going to be It."

The waiter appeared with three more gin and tonics. I hadn't even realized I'd finished mine. They were extremely well made, going down far too easily. After he exchanged the new drinks for empty glasses and moved away, Marianne went on with her story.

"Halfway through my first year in New York they showed up. *Mom and Dad.* They took me out to drinks—not here, but the same kind of vibe—and told me it was time for me to join the family business. They'd invested in my education, and now I owed them… everything."

A short silence fell. Marianne drank.

"This business…?" Peter prompted gently.

"Yeah. Hell." She took a deep breath. "OK. So they're con artists. Grifters. World-class grifters, but grifters all the same. They usually operate in countries that have fewer restrictions and more bribable officials—South America, Central America, Asia, Africa. They pretend to set up causes—they sell these ambitious but viable schemes for bringing potable water to a village, or establishing schools—shelters—health centers. Aid to Syrian refugees, malaria vaccines for children, new homes for earthquake victims in Haiti. They target business investors as well as rich donors, selling them on the 'profit of public opinion' if they're seen to be backing the little people. It's all fake, of course. They disappear and the money goes into financing the next scheme and into their pockets—except for the cut they give to the people who help them do it. Like me."

I stared at my cousin. Her eyes were on her glass, her hands cupped around it. Neither of us spoke, but Peter touched my knee under the table. His fingers felt warm and comforting—something real in a world suddenly gone rather mad.

I hadn't liked my aunt and uncle, had barely known them. But it still wasn't an easy thing to hear about people you're related to—who all of your life have been described as "humanitarian activists," serving the greater good.

When really what they should have been called was "world-class grifters."

"So that was it," Marianne continued flatly. "They expected me to pack up and join in. They said they were done paying my way, and they wanted a young, educated woman to—facilitate certain aspects of their scams. Just my luck, they'd decided I'd do for the job. They were willing to cut me in on their deals and sign me up for life. I told them *hell no*, and they said too bad, and I said I'll quit school. So I went home and grabbed a few things and left. I moved into a hostel. After a few weeks, I found a temp job as an admin at a talent agency and just… just prayed that I'd heard the last of them. But of course I hadn't. They weren't in New York often, but my… he kept in touch. He kept saying it was just a matter of time. I thought about going to the police, but they'd said I'd regret it if I did and… I don't know, I believed them. Besides, what proof did I have? Who'd believe me, even if I knew who to tell?

"Not long after that I met Mike at work and we went out a few times. He was really hot back then and had a great sense of humor—before he lost it and went all Charlie Manson. I didn't see what a lunatic he really was. He came in furious one day because he didn't get some modeling contract he wanted, and said he was leaving to rent a loft in Newark and bring down the system, or something. I saw an opportunity and I took it. Maybe I could lie low long enough for my parents to lose interest. They'd find some other woman to do whatever it was they wanted me for. I joined the ridiculous group at the loft and—gritted my teeth… and dealt with it, knowing it would be worth it if my parents left me alone. They found me after a while, of course—I knew they would—but my delay tactic seemed to be working. I put up with eleven months of it, slowly watching all of my ambitions and connections trickle away—but *it was worth it.*"

She finally looked at me.

"I knew how you felt about it, Lo. I didn't blame you. I don't know why I told you to come there. I guess I was just feeling so… isolated from everyone and everything that mattered to me. I missed you—I wanted you to be a part of my life again. I'd gotten so used to the—the squalor and the drugs, I forgot just how… repulsive it would be for an outsider."

"It doesn't matter," I said, and reached out to squeeze her hand. She let me, but then pulled it back and put it in her lap.

"Well, no. But your visit did have a consequence that I didn't— I *should* have expected. It made my parents remember how much you meant to me. I don't know why it took them so long. They knew we grew up together. But neither of them has siblings—our moms are steps, you know, not half-sisters like we always thought. They only met when Rosemary was a teenager and your mom a baby. I guess it hadn't occurred to them that they might use you as leverage. They knew there was nothing I wanted—they couldn't bribe or threaten me with anything else. I'd proven that by the way I'd lived for almost a year. And then, not long after you visited, they sent a message—an email to an account I thought was secure, with no words but a picture of you and your parents. That was it. I didn't know what they were threatening to do. I didn't want to know."

No. I wouldn't have wanted to know, either.

"Before long they showed up again, and I knew I'd lost." Her face was expressionless, unreadable. Whatever pain she'd experienced, she'd had to put it away. Bury it under layers of resignation and endurance.

"The man who came to the loft, that was your father?" Peter asked, after a short, heavy silence.

"Yeah. Our Leonard, champion of the little people. He told me my time was up and I had to make my choice. I knew I couldn't risk Lola and her parents being hurt. They knew it too. Whether or not they really would've done anything, I didn't know. Not then." She finished her second drink. "Now I do."

There was a long pause before she continued. My skin crawled at the quiet hatred in her voice.

"So I joined them. I learned fast, and I did well. Well enough that they didn't object when I kept in touch with you, though I didn't have much time for socializing." She gave a bleak laugh. "I don't know why I sent that stupid postcard. I guess it was just… a last-ditch effort to stay connected to my previous life. I can't believe that creep remembered it, after all this time."

"That building where we found you—that's where you work?" I asked.

"Some of the time—it's kind of a base of operations. They own the building and set up the dummy company years ago. Comes in handy for certain cons that pretend to have headquarters here—all under fake names and layers of bureaucratic camouflage, of course. They have an office in San Francisco, too—a west-coast base—and a few others. I'm here most of the time, sometimes I go wherever they happen to be. Finding marks—people with more money than sense, corporations that want a PR boost. There's an endless supply of them, and most jump at the chance to come to New York. I make initial contact, welcome them to town, wine and dine them, convince them it's all legitimate—whatever cause they're being asked to invest in. I lie to them, dazzle them with glossy brochures and falsified budgets. Then I them over to Rosemary and Leonard, the true professionals, waiting to close the deal in whatever part of the world. It's impressive to watch, if you can see past their cold-blooded greed."

"How do they manage not to get caught?" Peter asked with interest.

"They move fast and talk a good game—most of our targets don't realize their money didn't go where it should, and those who do figure it out too late and don't have enough to go on. I mean, they're wanted criminals in at least ten countries, but they're too slippery to get caught. By the time the authorities have gotten around to opening an investigation, they're long gone. They don't even trust the people who work for them enough to know their location, not exactly—and that includes me."

"What about you? Could *you* get caught?" I demanded.

She moved restlessly in her chair and spoke with a kind of weary frankness.

"Yeah, well, I'm slippery, too. I... I got really good at it over the years. Selling their bullshit—staying out of sight. But I never wanted it. I've never *liked* it, Lo. I've hated everything they made me do. Most of all how they took me from my real family. When Aunt Gina was diagnosed... Her death really threw me. I knew how alone you were—even with your dad still around, it wasn't the same. You'd lost me, and now your mom. I had a feeling it wouldn't be long before your dad went, too—he looked so gray and… kind of defeated at the funeral. I was glad *she* didn't even consider going. I think she really hated Aunt Gina."

I nodded. I wasn't sure what else to do.

"Anyway. It got me thinking that maybe there was a way out that I hadn't seen. If it came down to just you, I might be able to protect you. If I could get collateral—find something to *bargain* with, maybe we could call it even. I could get out for good, and guarantee our safety until the two of them are caught or killed or die of old age in the Bahamas somewhere. I don't care what happens to them. I'll have to watch my back for the rest of my life—both our backs. But it could be done. As insanely paranoid and careful as they are, sometimes they've slipped. Left something undone, missed a trick. And the next time, I'd be waiting to catch whatever fell out of their dark little cracks.

"With your dad gone…" her face tightened. "Well, in one way it made things easier. One less person they could use against me. So that's what happened. I waited—put the word out in a few places that there'd be value in something like that. Then earlier this year I got my first bite. A deal in Rio went south a couple of years ago, and nearly came crashing down on them. They barely got out with their tailfeathers intact, and though they didn't know it, they left a paper trail that tied two of their aliases to everything. About a month ago, I bought the only copy of a file one of their associates had kept on the deal. It had been taken from a dead man's office, mine for the price of substantial bribes to find the low-life who had it and a whole lot of patience.

"I made contact with the guy, and eventually we reached a deal—I paid, he scanned everything and sent me instructions for how to get it. He said he burned the original. I had to trust him, but—somehow they… they caught on. Maybe they were watching my contact—or bribing the same people, or something. They couldn't know for sure—I was *careful,* they couldn't trace anything back to me—but if they heard there was a buyer looking for dirt on them and had the slightest whiff of it from Rio, it'd be enough to set them off. That's how they've stayed in business as long as they have. They don't wait for proof. The guy ended up in an alley in São Paulo with a bullet in his head—a week too late to stop him, but still not good news. As soon as I got word I moved to get you out of sight fast, the only way I thought they wouldn't notice. I flew into Mexico City so it would look like a routine banking trip and drove hell for leather up to LA. Then it was back here for business as usual."

I couldn't take this in. Bribes to informants thousands of miles away. A dead man in an alley, shot in the head. A frantic race to Mexico, and from there to LA, where I joined the story. My mind circled dazedly around her words, listening even as it struggled to arrange and comprehend.

"They're watching me even more closely now," she went on. "They've always known they can't trust me not to give myself up and destroy everything they've built. I'm the best contender to be plotting against them, even if they can't prove it. They know I'm not cut out for this—'don't have the stomach for it,' as Leonard would say. You're the only leverage they have on me, and they'll use it. But as soon as I get my hands on the collateral, we'll be free."

The words were positive, even triumphant, but were flattened by the bitter resignation in her voice. She didn't really believe freedom was possible. She believed they would win, just like they always had. I could see it in the tightness of her eyes, the angry gestures of her hands. Marianne thought we'd probably lose this fight.

Maybe they'd get to me and do whatever she was afraid they'd do—I couldn't let my mind go there, beyond that blank white wall of unknown terror—or maybe they'd wait and get us both the next time she tried to act against them. It would happen sooner or later. Her acceptance of the futility of her plan settled across my tight chest.

"Where did the São Paulo guy put the evidence?" Peter was asking.

Marianne blinked and came out of her abstraction to wordlessly order yet another round.

"On the darknet. He told me how to get it, it just isn't safe to try right now. They're monitoring everything I do—it's not some Word doc I can download on the free computers at the library. There's no one I can trust to help—not anyone on their payroll. It's too big a risk. I don't even know for sure that it's there."

"Assuming it is, you'd be able to access it?"

"If I had the time and equipment, yes."

"And what'll you do with it once you have it?"

She met his steady gaze. Hers didn't falter, and I saw a gleam of the old defiance in it.

"Set up a hundred fail-safes. A thousand, if I have time. And then show them enough to prove I have it—and walk away."

"Is it enough to convict them?"

"If it's what the guy said it is, it's enough. It proves that they were mixed up in a nasty case that Interpol would give their left nuts to solve—and would probably lead to more convictions."

"And even so, you wouldn't turn them in," Peter said evenly.

Her dark eyes flashed.

"You think I'm afraid to be arrested? I couldn't care less. But— they can do a lot from prison. If they even get there. I know how officials can be bribed, even the law isn't immune to corruption for the sake of hard cash. Not to mention, they'd see the cops coming from a mile away—assuming I could even *say* exactly where they are. No. This is the only way to keep us safe."

I knew by "us" she meant the two of us. Her and me. My big sister Marianne. Protecting me this whole time. Turning herself into something she despised so my parents and I wouldn't suffer whatever punishment two sociopaths dreamed up for us. She hadn't sent me into hiding to protect herself, or to stop me from leading someone to her. It was only for me.

I hadn't ever really known her. I couldn't have imagined the depth of her ingenuity or bravery or strength.

She deserved so much better than this. So much more than what she'd been dealt. Immured in that sad dingy room, in beautiful clothes, completely alone.

I'd have taken up smoking, too. At the very least.

"And then... what?" I asked gently.

Marianne let out a little gasp of laughter, a tiny burst of hysteria that held no amusement.

"I have no idea," she said. "But... I'd start with never seeing them again."

I reached across the table and took her thin, cold hand in mine. This time she didn't pull away.

■ ■ ■

Peter asked if we could order some food. I was starting to feel a slight buzz from my third gin and tonic, though Marianne appeared to be as stone cold sober as when she arrived. Peter hadn't touched his third. After considering his suggestion, Marianne waved the waiter over and asked for "the usual eats," which he approved with a respectful nod.

"I can't stay much longer," she said. "I'll settle the bill before I go. Don't let them charge you for anything."

I didn't want her to leave. Upsetting and strange as it was to see her like this, to see the real Marianne at last, something in me reared up in anxious protest at the thought of losing sight of her again.

"I've been thinking," Peter said slowly, as if Marianne hadn't spoken. "I might know someone who could help us." At our equally blank looks, he explained, "A hacker. He's legit now, but he got into a lot of trouble when he was younger breaking into high-security systems. Now he teaches cyber security at U of A."

Marianne's eyes rested on me, somewhat speculatively, but she spoke to Peter.

"You trust him?" she asked.

"Absolutely," Peter said.

"And you think he'd be up for it?"

"It's possible. It'd be an interesting experiment, I think. He's bored with his job, but no tech firm will trust him because of his record. The university took a chance—and they keep a tight leash. I think the government has tried to recruit him a few times, but that doesn't interest him."

Marianne thought furiously for a moment.

Across the silence, the waiter gave us each a small white plate, then set a long board filled with delicacies in the center of the table. Olives of all shapes and sizes, two thick slices of pâté, small wedges of toast, thin curls of cured meats, stuffed mushrooms, devilled eggs, tiny tarts bubbling over with melted cheese... Suddenly ravenous, I reached out for the first thing that came to hand and stuffed it indelicately into my mouth. Marianne nibbled unenthusiastically on a piece of toast with pâté while Peter and I finished everything else.

As I ate, I wondered, with a kind of distant curiosity, if Peter's friend really could help us. I knew of the darknet, but not much about how it worked. The whole situation seemed too impossible to be true, but then my aunt and uncle were vicious criminals and my cousin had been blackmailed into working for them for years, so what did I know?

Only once the board had been taken away and the small plates cleared did Marianne respond.

"I don't know what else to do," she said. "I don't want to wait until they've dropped their guard—it could be months. Longer. It's too risky to wait. They're spooked by São Paulo, and when they're spooked, there are consequences. They're out of the country now, as usual, but... What do you propose?"

"We change our flights tomorrow to Tucson, and I talk to my friend and see if he can help us. Knowing him, it'll be best if I ask him in person. If he's willing, we give him your instructions and spend a little time in the area while we wait. Should it take long?"

"No, not for someone who knows what they're doing."

"After that, we go home and... wait and see."

She glanced between us, considering.

"You'd go together," she stated, and at Peter's nod and my murmured "of course," she gave a worn version of her old grin. "What will the two of you do in Arizona?"

"I lived in Tucson before I moved to California. I can show Lola around, visit some friends in the area." Peter took an unhurried sip of his drink. "My ex-wife, for one. She's a detective with the Tucson PD."

I wasn't sure exactly why he told her that, but when Marianne had taken the information in, she seemed to understand what he was saying.

"Right," she said composedly. "Every fail-safe possible."

"Will they send someone to follow us?" Peter asked.

"Mm... I don't think so. I don't see why they'd bother. They probably only had one of their people keeping an eye on you because they saw Lo was out here and it was unusual enough to make them curious. Once they know you've left town—and see that I'm still where I'm supposed to be—I don't think they'll pay much attention. Not until they notice that you're off the grid, which might be a while."

"Won't they be afraid that you gave them away to us?" I asked. I couldn't seem to think of the people behind this as anything other than "they," even though I knew their names perfectly well.

"I doubt it. It wouldn't occur to them. They don't trust anyone but each other—just like they don't give a crap about anyone else. It protects them, but it also means that nobody knows what anybody else is doing. I'm sure whoever was following you has no idea who you really are. No one knows I'm their kid, thank God."

"So, Tucson?" Peter asked.

"So Tucson," Marianne agreed. "Well, if this is happening I'll need to hand over the information to give to your friend—and you need to leave town *immediately*. The longer you stay the more suspicious they'll be. Go tomorrow, as early as possible."

"Understood," Peter said. "And once he's gotten what you need—assuming he does?"

"A copy uploaded to where I tell you. I'll know when it's there. Then delete *any other copies,* burn any paper trails and get the hell back to California. And... there won't be any way to stop you, but I recommend that you don't read it."

Peter didn't say anything.

I was too tired and keyed up to absorb these instructions. I couldn't make sense of all the implications of her plans. Too much had happened in the past two hours—two days—two *weeks*—for me to process any more just now, especially with a mind hazy with gin.

"Was it you who called the burner phone?" I demanded suddenly. Marianne looked surprised, then slightly guilty.

"I wanted to make sure you weren't using it," she said.

"That doesn't... whose number did you program in? Is that even yours?"

"The local police department. Another fail-safe."

I hadn't even registered that the number had a 650 area code until now. Half Moon Bay police. What would Deputy Tom have thought about a panicked and confused call from the area's latest cause for gossip? I couldn't begin to imagine.

"We got rid of the item you left in Lola's luggage," Peter said mildly, seeming out of nowhere—until I made the connection.

I'd forgotten all about the gun, but of course if I had called the police and they somehow found it, chances were high they'd have arrested me. Marianne didn't seem fazed by this news.

"Did you? Maybe for the best. I'm not a big fan of any deadly weapon, though they do come in handy in certain parts of the world. When I have to use one, I prefer a knife, though *they* like guns. Typical. Leonard even had a machine gun once, thought he was Rambo or something."

My face must have shown my reaction to her casual observations about weaponry.

"What?" she asked. "I've never used it on anyone—well, except for this one time, but the guy *asked* for it. And he didn't *die* or anything."

"As long as he didn't die," I said in a hollow voice.

"Just as well you got rid of the gun I gave you, anyway."

"We assumed it was untraceable, but still a bad idea," Peter explained.

"Wait—so can they track our phones?" I asked, trying not to get sidetracked by the alarming new subject of bodily violence. "And credit cards? Is that why you told me not to use them and took my phone?"

She swished the ice around in her empty cocktail. I wondered if she was going to order another, but she didn't.

"No—and yes," she replied, sounding tired. "They can't track phone numbers through the usual systems. But there are lots of ways to find people. If you've got the time and equipment it's not hard to get into someone's accounts and see exactly where they are—credit cards, email, social media apps. They're monitoring most of yours—because of me. They use a couple different freelance hackers for that kind of thing, one of them told me how it works. These day's a phone's basically a hand-held bloody *tracking* device, even if you don't check in every five minutes. If this was going to work, I didn't want to make it easy for them to find you."

"Oh. So my phone is gone, then."

"It's gone." She made a tossing gesture with her hands. "I made sure everything was backed up, if that helps. You must've used one of your accounts to get here, that's how they traced you. Sloppy, Lo. Don't log into anything again. Not even to change your passwords. It's not safe."

"I won't," I agreed weakly, more overwhelmed than I could ever remember being.

"I've got to go."

I saw Marianne pick up her bulky bag and stand, saw her looking down at us. Something in the fierceness of her gaze told me not to get up.

"Good luck," she said briefly. "Don't do anything stupid, OK?" She turned, then stopped. "Oh, and Lo... happy birthday," she said. And walked quickly away.

chapter 13

We stayed on a little while after Marianne had left, taking time to finish our drinks and look out over the city. The waiter came by once, but when we said we were fine, didn't check in with us again. Presumably the tab had been paid. It had to have been at least a few hundred dollars—twenty a cocktail times six, along with a generous helping of appetizers… It seemed that crime did pay for good restaurants, if nothing else.

The night had grown cool, but not uncomfortably so. I slipped on my jacket and leaned into Peter's arm, cradling my nearly-empty gin and tonic in one hand. Spread out in a tapestry around us were lights of all hues and brightness—headlights, lit windows, streetlights, signs. I knew I'd need to drink water before I went to bed, but having such high quality alcohol and a solid snack were helping keep my buzz to a low hum.

"I… can't really believe it," I finally said—the first sentence I'd been able to form since Marianne had gone.

"I know," Peter said. "Honestly, if it wasn't for what I've seen with Hal, I might *not* believe it. But having a brother-in-law who's mixed up with violent cartels kind of opens your eyes to the fact that this kind of crime—stuff right out of a movie—is real. There really are people out there getting away with theft and fraud and murder. It's unimaginable, but it's there. And the humanitarian angle is clever—people are less suspicious when they think their money's going to a good cause."

"Yeah," I said inadequately, relieved to hear that he understood. "So you believed her?"

"I did… as much as I didn't want to."

"Do you think it's—dangerous for her to have told us the truth?"

He considered the question before answering.

"It sounds like you were already in danger from these people. Even if Marianne kept toeing the line, she could never be totally sure that they wouldn't decide to force her hand with something more dramatic."

"Something more dramatic," I repeated.

"Well… Framing you for a crime and making sure you got sent away for it, comes to mind. With the right contacts, they could easily make your life inside bearable or hellish. That'd keep your cousin on a tight leash."

"Oh. Yeah, I guess it would."

"I mean, there's no way to know," Peter backtracked, seeing how fixed my expression had become. "Chances are they'd have left you alone."

"No, you're right. It's better to face it. They probably wouldn't bother to kill me—not unless they found something else to use against Marianne. But that doesn't mean they wouldn't have— have found new ways to keep her quiet."

"She took a big risk in getting that evidence, but I can see she didn't have any other choice. Not being the person she is."

"Yeah. It does all make sense now. I mean, most of it."

"I almost don't want to know more." We were silent for another long minute. "Do you realize the two of you aren't actually related?"

"I guess not. Not by blood."

I didn't need to say that it didn't matter. She would always be my cousin, just like she had always been my sister at heart, even though we had different parents. That didn't change because I'd learned that our moms were stepsisters, only related by marriage. We were family, the rest didn't matter.

Though deep down, in the dark private recesses of my heart, I felt intensely glad to not share a single genetic tie to her parents.

"What this about a birthday?" Peter asked, pulling me out of my thoughts.

"Oh—it's Friday. I'll be thirty-two," I said.

"Were you going to share this interesting little detail at some point?"

I laughed feebly.

"I sort of forgot about it. I haven't been paying attention to dates for… almost two weeks, I guess. It feels like longer than that. Honestly, it just hasn't seemed important enough to talk about."

"Delia's a big believer in astrology. You're what, Cancer?"

"Gemini. What about you?"

"Virgo. September fourteenth. I have no idea what that means."

"Me, either. I'm going to say it's an awesome match. Truly exceptional and… er, long-lasting."

"Here's to that. How do you feel about spending your birthday in the beautiful and cosmopolitan town of Tucson?"

"I thought you'd never ask."

"We should probably get back and see about changing our tickets."

We were about to rise when the waiter appeared next to us, slipping something onto the table with a murmured, "This was left for you," before moving away again.

It was a sealed envelope with the logo of the restaurant on one corner, unaddressed. I ripped it open; inside was a business card for the manager of Bar Sixty-Five, nothing else. I looked perplexedly at this, before Peter reached to gently turn it over in my hand. A series of numbers and letters had been scribbled on the back, filling the small white space—the instructions, presumably. There was also a phone number, short one digit: (601) 167-943. I recognized Marianne's handwriting, but not the number.

"So that's that," I said, and tucked the card into the back of my wallet, behind all the credit cards it wasn't safe to use.

With a final glance at the view, we left Jojo's table (was Jojo an alias of Marianne's? Or someone else?) and walked back to the hotel. For the first time since Monday night, I didn't worry whether or not someone was behind us.

■ ■ ■

The following morning we rushed to put on our shoes and collect our belongings after clearing security. Our flight was leaving in thirty minutes.

"We're cutting it close," I murmured as we hurried toward our gate.

The flight to Tucson was already boarding when we arrived, breathless, at the gate, humbly joining the end of a long line. We'd waited at TSA for nearly an hour, until the powers that be finally relented and opened up more lanes.

I watched with rapidly growing unease and impatience as other passengers slowly, *slowly* filed into the jet bridge, far too many of them trying to haul oversized baggage onto the full plane, being stopped, having to check the bag. Now that the key to the evidence was actually in hand, and we were about to leave town with it, my anxiety spiked. That tiny piece of paper—and the pictures Peter had taken of it with his phone as backup—could mean our lives.

We were so vulnerable. Anyone could attack us here—not with a gun, maybe, but a jagged piece of broken glass would do the trick nicely. I couldn't help thinking that the last person who had access to the evidence, besides Marianne, had ended up dead.

Dead, because Marianne had been connected to him. Just like she was connected to us.

I shifted restlessly from leg to leg, dropping my bag, picking it up. Would this endless line *never move*? Nobody arrived to wait behind us; we were going to be the last people to board. Peter was his usual calm, quiet self, but I saw the tension around his eyes. The departure time was in ten minutes… eight minutes… seven. We were going to miss this goddamn plane because these idiots didn't know how to follow simple directions. We shuffled slowly forward. I gritted my teeth, trying not to look as irritated and panicked as I felt.

Finally, four minutes before our departure time, we made it to the gate. The airline representative glanced over our bags with a practiced eye as she scanned our boarding passes and nodded us through. I would have run down the jet bridge in sheer relief, except for the twenty other people in front of us still waiting to board.

Our seats were near the back, but luckily were on the far aisle, which was empty as we rushed down it. Peter stuffed our luggage into two of the nearest overhead compartments and we threw ourselves into a middle row, tucking my purse down at our feet and snapping on our seat belts. The kid next to me had headphones on and was doing something on his phone, not taking any notice of us. After only a minute, the flight crew came through doing a final check of overhead bins and seatbelts, and we were cleared for departure. Peter had pulled his iPad out of his bag and now opened it.

I was too restless to concentrate on a book or magazine, staring out one of the side windows. The day had been a blur so far. Peter had managed to change our flight the previous night, racking up another nearly thousand dollars on his credit card, which I hated but he was philosophical about. We still had about two thousand dollars in cash, enough to cover the fees then and there, but he continued to feel we should save it for immediate expenses and settle up later. The flight to Tucson left at ten, which meant we had to be out of the hotel before seven to give ourselves enough time to get to Newark and through TSA. This also meant that we were fighting commuter traffic the whole way there. I'd barely managed to choke down a granola bar on the train from Penn

Station, feeling too apprehensive about the trip ahead of us to think about food.

I had coffee as my complimentary beverage, sweet and milky, and felt somewhat better. We shared the rest of the candy I bought before we left. Eventually I picked up my book, but still couldn't focus my mind on the story.

"Worried about Marianne?" Peter asked, when I put the book down for the third time.

"I don't know. Yes. No. Worried in general, I guess."

"Tell me," he invited, closing the flap on his case.

"It's just… We don't know if your friend can help, if he'll even want to help," I began in a low voice, "and whatever Marianne said, she can't be positive this will work even if she does get what she needs. We're spending all of this money flying all over the country—and I feel terrible about that. I feel terrible about what my cousin's been through. I don't know what to do with everything she told us. And I'm—I'm *completely* nervous about meeting your ex."

Peter choked on the bite of Snickers he was chewing, swallowing before he responded.

"You're—really? You don't have to be."

"It's not logical, I know. I just… she's important to you, and I hope she—you know, approves of me."

He carefully set down the rest of the candy bar on his tray and took both of my hands in his.

"That's the sweetest, most misguided thing I've ever heard anyone worry about. Kathe's going to *approve* of you so much, I'm worried that she's going to propose on my behalf while we're there. You think I'm kidding."

I laughed—though for all I knew he really wasn't kidding, or only half-joking. His reassurance should have helped, but… I didn't know what it was that made me nervous to meet her, exactly. It didn't bother me that she was his ex. Maybe it should have, but it didn't. Not only did I not for a second doubt the strength of what was between us, but I knew she'd moved on and was happily married to someone else. I wasn't jealous or anything like it (not then, anyway). She just seemed both intimidating and impressive. She was a *police detective*. She solved crimes and arrested people. I was an unemployed programmer who lived in a camper.

I knew that Peter didn't need, and wouldn't give a damn about, anyone else's approval of me. But how awful would it be if Kathe—and Delia—and all the people who cared about him—didn't end up liking me? Osiris was an easy victory; he liked anyone who threw a stick for him. Other than Marianne, I didn't really have anyone on my side to give an opinion, and she wasn't in much of a position to judge. Anyway she'd already made it clear she trusted Peter, which I took as a whole-hearted endorsement.

Maybe it was misguided, but I couldn't help but feel the pressure of meeting Kathe hanging over my head—adding to all the other pressures that had piled on over the past few weeks. It made all the difference in the world to have somebody to share this with, a warm hand to hold and warm body to hug. I'd felt so alone and isolated before meeting Peter. I didn't take it for granted how lucky I was to have met him—at all, but especially right now. I didn't even know how to feel all the gratitude that rose up in me every time I looked at him, or thought of him, or did anything else.

But I'd also pulled him into a messy and dangerous situation. This trip was only possible because we were spending his money. True, I could cover a lot of the costs, but how much more would we need to spend? We still had to get back to California. He was taking time off work—time away from his own business, which I knew wasn't an easy thing to do—to take these risks with me.

It was his choice, of course, but given the kind of person he was, and the connection between us, did he really have another option? If he was arrested tomorrow in connection with Hal's crimes, would I be able to tiptoe away? Pretend like it didn't matter, go on with my life and let him face his troubles alone?

There wasn't a chance of that. Just like there wasn't a chance that he'd have chosen not to help. We still hadn't exchanged a single declaration or promise—but they were *there*, all the same. We were in this together.

■ ■ ■

I must have fallen into an uneasy doze at some point, because I was startled to hear the announcement that we'd be landing shortly in Tucson. I'd missed the last three hours of the six-plus-hour flight. I just had time to dash to the bathroom—meeting a disapproving but resigned flight attendant on the way—before we were circling around for the final descent. I couldn't see much of the landscape from the center of the plane, but got a sense of blinding white light, palest blue sky, flat, sprawling city.

Once were off the plane, we quickly made our way outside, not having to wait for checked luggage. The heat was the first thing I noticed—heat and light. It had to be at least ninety, dry with broiling sunshine. I followed Peter as he turned to the right and made his way to the rental car area, noticing the clean, modern landscaping with more greenery than you might expect from the desert.

I'd never been to the southwest before, not counting Vegas a few times, which I didn't. I was surprised at all the green: trees of all varieties, even orchards at the edges of town, cacti and succulents and other plants as well. It wasn't the lush, dense green of the forests south of my home, or the rolling brown-green brushland and foothills near Uncle Joe's, nor were the trees half the size of valley oaks or redwoods, but they were still trees. Tucson is high desert, more than two thousand feet above sea level, on a plain centered between five small mountain ranges. I noticed the mountains almost as soon as I noticed the green—starkly purple against the sky, they ring the city in almost all directions, some nearer and some farther.

I would definitely need to buy some cooler clothing. My jeans and short-sleeved shirts had been bearable in New York, but already made me feel like I was zipped into ski gear. I could feel sweat pooling and trickling under my clothes on the short walk to the nearest rental car office—followed by the instant and glorious bliss of cold air when we walked inside. We didn't have a reservation, but Peter seemed sure that there would be cars available, and he was right. Twenty minutes and two hundred dollars later, we accepted the keys to a small red Nissan, put our bags in the trunk and climbed inside.

"Ugh," I said, sweltering even as Peter switched on the ignition and turned the A/C on high. The air helped, even if it was unpleasantly warm at first. "I need to pick up some shorts or something." My feet felt like small ovens in my sneakers and socks. I resisted the temptation to tear them off and set my fiery toes free.

"That can be our first stop," he said. "After that, I know of a couple of good hotels we can try close to the center of town."

"Perfect," I agreed, relaxing into my seat.

As a recent former resident, Peter easily navigated to a nearby big box store. Bringing only my purse—and in it, the precious card—inside with us, we split up in the clothing departments and spent about fifteen minutes grabbing whatever we could find. I didn't want to bother trying anything on, so picked a pair of classic white denim shorts in my size, a couple of light, loose tank tops in the same style but different colors, and—at the last minute—a long, soft, belted sundress in a summery floral pattern. It would be cool in the heat and, I told myself, would be a nice change from the shorts. Not to mention I could wear it when I met Kathe for an extra boost of confidence.

Peter, a bundle of clothing under one arm, found me in a women's shoe aisle, awkwardly pulling off a sandal I'd just tried on. He went to see about flip-flops, and I ended up getting a pair as well. In less than half an hour we were checking out—using some of the remaining cash, as we had for all our meals—and climbing back into the already baking car.

Do people actually get used to this? I wondered. LA was warmer than the Bay Area, but only rarely did we get temperatures much above ninety. The car thermometer told us it was one hundred and one degrees outside, at barely three in the afternoon.

"You're a fast shopper," he commented, pulling out of the parking lot.

"I'm not always that fast."

"Still," he said, and left it at that. I supposed some people would have been pickier about what they bought, given that we weren't in a particular rush. It just didn't seem like the moment to worry about building the best wardrobe possible.

"Nothing from Brendan?"

Last night, Peter had texted his hacker friend—whose name was, improbably, Brendan—and told him he'd be in town the following afternoon and would like to get together. So far there hadn't been any response, which Peter didn't seem too surprised about, but which made me antsy. We didn't have time to waste—at least, I supposed I did, but Peter didn't. I was increasingly conscious of every day that he spent away from the bar, Delia, Osiris, his responsibilities back home. It was already Thursday; how much longer could he justifiably stay away?

"Not yet. Don't worry. I'll call him once we get checked in. If he doesn't pick up, we'll track him down tonight—there's only a few places he could be."

This was encouraging, but until Brendan had agreed to help, until he had the instructions in hand, until our plan was in motion, it didn't feel like we were making any progress at all.

■ ■ ■

We found Brendan at a pub in El Presidio, the oldest neighborhood in Tucson, according to my guide. Peter had chosen a well-kept economy hotel less than a mile north of the downtown area, with rooms for about sixty dollars a night. It was a lot cheaper than New York, but would add up fast the longer we stayed. In spite of the cash in my luggage and purse, I felt a twinge every time he handed his card over. It wasn't that I had a lot of extra money in my accounts—I didn't—but it bothered me not to be able to throw down my Visa or debit card, even just to reserve the room.

After we'd checked in, Peter had called his friend's cell, then left a message on his office line, and finally sent another text that he wanted to meet up—tonight, if possible. While he waited for a response, we showered and changed into our desert-appropriate clothes. The hotel had a small but sparkling clean swimming pool, which looked so tempting that I wished I'd thought of buying a swimsuit as well.

We rested awhile in the cool of the room, not talking much. There were so many things I wanted to hear about in Peter's life, to share about mine, but in spite of how pressured I felt about the situation we were in, I didn't feel any particular rush to communicate everything about ourselves. I liked how organic and relaxing our conversations were. It wasn't anything like the awkward process of getting to know a stranger on a series of gradually more intense dates.

It felt like hanging out with someone deeply valued and long missed—like seeing Marianne again. Or rather, like seeing her every time but this most recent one. This had the same qualities of familiarity and security mixed with pleasure to be with her and anticipation to catch up on how she was without any objectives. We never needed to dive right into all our news, but could talk about the past, or about nothing in particular, and then somehow it would remind me of something and I'd start telling her about my life.

Only now did I recognize just how little she'd had to say about herself the past five years. How dark and hidden and disturbing her unshared stories had been. Knowing that changed the flavor of the memories, but didn't change the satisfaction and comfort seeing her had given me.

That was how it felt to be with Peter. Soon enough, I'd meet his ex-wife—we'd arranged to have breakfast with her the following day. I was here, in a town he'd lived in for most of his adult life, near his college, surrounded by familiar places and people he knew. Eventually, I'd hear his stories about living here.

Almost as if he'd read my thoughts, he spoke out of a long silence. He was lounging in the room's sole armchair, his feet stretched out onto the bed, while I lay on my back across it diagonally with my paperback lying open next to me.

"We don't have to see Kathe tomorrow," he said.

"Why wouldn't we?" I asked, turning my head to look at him with some surprise. He'd checked with me before he made the suggestion to her, saying of her response only, "She can't wait."

"It's your birthday. I'd totally understand if you wanted to do something other than meet up with my ex."

I rolled over and put my chin on my hands. My birthday.

There were several reasons why I'd avoided thinking about it, only some of them having to do with my flight from LA. I wasn't sure I was ready to put them into words—hadn't actually allowed myself to examine them, or how they made me feel.

"It's not a big deal," I said. "Honestly, please don't think you have to make a thing out of it."

"OK, I won't," he agreed evenly, "not if you don't want me to."

I shook my head. He was silent, but I could feel the waves of empathy coming from him. That, more than anything he could have said, was my undoing.

My throat closed up. Tears built up behind my eyes and spilled out over my cheeks in un-dramatic little drips. Peter, without getting up, put his feet on the floor and leaned over to rest a soothing hand on my head.

"It's just—it's nothing," I snuffled, wiping my nose on the back of one hand. "It's just my first birthday since my dad… The first one I won't talk to him on. I'm… it's hard to think about it." Peter hugged me for a little while, saying he understood completely. He didn't ask me to explain any more than that, which is probably why I volunteered it. Reverse psychology, or something. "Even after my mom died, he always called on my birthday, you know? He wasn't… I didn't come up to visit much, he didn't have room for me to stay and he always seemed distracted and… I don't know—distant—when I did come up. But he always remembered—he always called at three twelve, the time I was born."

"What would you have done if you were still in LA?" he asked, after a moment.

"In… Oh. Nothing, probably. Maybe gone out with one or two friends to a bar or something. Probably stayed home by myself and cried."

"You're welcome to cry all day, if you want."

"Oh, sure. 'Kathe, meet Lola, my sobbing drag of a girlfriend.' I'm sure she'd be really impressed."

"We can cancel, seriously."

I sniffed a few times and wiped my cheeks with my hands, sitting up and facing him, one leg bent up on the bed.

"I know. I appreciate that. But I think it would be easier to just… just go on, you know? Pretend that it's just one more day of this trip—a weird trip, but still. I don't need it to be a special occasion—or an excuse to be depressed."

"It's good to feel your grief," he said. I knew he wasn't just saying that, he'd gone through deep loss himself. "Let it out when you need to."

"It is good to let it out," I agreed. "But it's also good to move forward with things that make you happy."

He looked searchingly at me for a few seconds, then nodded.

"OK. Getting hungry?"

I thought about it and realized that I was. The combination of candy and anxiety had kept me full for most of the afternoon, but it was after six, and we were definitely due for a solid meal.

"What did you have in mind?"

"Some of the best tacos in town, followed by drinks at Brendan's favorite hangout. If he's not there, we can start looking at his second and third favorites."

We were in luck, or Peter just knew his friend well. We hadn't been in the bar, a low adobe building like all of those around it, for more than three minutes when Peter said, "There he is."

We'd parked the rental car around the corner; even though the place was walking distance from our hotel, it was still over ninety degrees at seven, the sunlight streaming hot and orange from the far west. The tacos had been as good as advertised, a small dingy stand at the edge of downtown, not far from campus. We'd eaten them standing up at an unsteady table outside, juices and sauces dripping down our hands onto the paper trays. Peter had six, I had four, along with a pile of barely-salted, thick tortilla chips dunked in dusky chipotle salsa. There was no shortage of fantastic and authentic Mexican food in California, along with the trendy Cal-Mex variety, but there was nothing quite like a corner taco stand in the southwest.

Pleasantly full, hair and skin damp from the heat of the day and the spicy food, it felt good to step into the cool, dim bar and contemplate a long, very cold drink. The warren of rooms was fairly crowded with people; more than half of them looked like tourists, while the rest had the relaxed proprietary air of regulars. You could just tell they felt they belonged there, suffering the tourists as a necessary and unavoidable evil.

The music was loud and old-school country, TVs showed the usual mix of sports. The walls were the most interesting part of the place, almost entirely covered with historical ephemera from the area—framed deeds, documents and photographs, wanted posters, beer logos, ranch signs, horse shoes, and, the unmistakable star attraction of the place, a large buffalo head wearing a cowboy hat on the wall opposite us. I knew without asking that the head was a "he" and had a name like "Butch."

"That's Brendan, sitting in the end seat," Peter said.

At the far end of the bar in the second room we entered, separated from the first by a dangerously low, dark-beamed opening, sat a man with long light hair tied into a ponytail. Peter led the way over to him and tapped on his shoulder.

The man turned with a jerk, staring suspiciously at Peter over the rims of the John-Lennon-style sunglasses he wore, and then grinned.

"Figured you'd turn up," he said.

chapter 14

For whatever reason—maybe the fact that he didn't seem to believe in using deodorant—the stool next to Brendan was open. After introductions, Peter insisted I sit down, leaning between us. The bartender, a platinum-haired, deeply tanned woman in her fifties, greeted him like an old friend.

"Where you been, Pete?" she asked, coming out to give him a motherly hug. "We missed you around here."

"Peter's gone California on us," Brendan said dryly.

"That's right—how's the business going?"

"Not bad. The first couple of years were rough, but it's going all right these days," Peter said. "Val, I'd like you to meet Lola." Val shook my hand warmly.

"Nice to meet you," I said.

"You too, honey. What's your poison?" She looked between the two of us.

"I'll take a Stella," Peter said.

"A gin and tonic, please," I said. I knew they wouldn't be anything like the ones we had in New York, but it still sounded good. Val returned to the bar and poured our drinks, ignoring the crowd of customers who'd been waiting before we arrived.

"I worked here for a couple of years in college," Peter told me. It explained not only Val's reaction, but the trickle of people who came up to greet him throughout the evening. Even as he shook hands and exchanged hugs and answered questions, Peter remained focused on the task at hand, always returning as quickly as possible to our low conversation with Brendan.

He was older than he looked at first, more light gray in his hair than the original pale blond. His face was lined and sallow, as if he didn't spend much time outside of a computer lab, his body lean and slightly hunched. His drink appeared to be straight whisky with beer chasers, and though he consumed a number of these, didn't seem to be affected by the alcohol.

"Why the sudden urge to get in touch?" Brendan asked, barely getting through a polite exchange of greetings.

Peter glanced at Val, busy at the end of the bar, which Brendan didn't miss. His eyes moved restlessly at all times, darting to Peter, to me, to the people nearby, taking everything in.

"We have a situation that requires your skill set," Peter told him in a low, casual voice.

"You do, do you," Brendan said, eyes flickering between us over the sunglasses. "What kind of 'situation?'"

"Information stored on the darknet that we need retrieved, copied and sent to someone."

Brendan stared at his friend for a long moment.

"Interesting," he said neutrally. "Is this information of value?"

"It is to us," Peter said.

"Anyone else?"

"There's a good chance that Interpol wouldn't mind a look," Peter admitted. "Among others."

Brendan laughed and finished the last of his beer. Another round already stood ready for him.

"Damn. What did you get yourselves into?" He took a sip of fresh whisky. "Don't answer that. It's rhetorical. And you need someone to grab this—information—and put it in a safe place for you."

"That's right."

"Urgently, I'm assuming. From the number of messages you left."

"As quickly as possible. And thanks for not responding to any of them," Peter told him.

"No problem. Well, it's an interesting request. What do you think?" His eyes swiveled suddenly to me, silently listening and slurping down my drink.

"What—um. Well, I hope you'll help us," I said awkwardly.

"Do you think it's wise? Safe? No risk involved?" he persisted.

I looked at Peter, who looked back at me, raising one eyebrow in inquiry.

"No," I said honestly. "It's probably a huge mistake to get involved."

"Excellent. When do I start?"

I choked on my drink, but Peter must have expected this response.

"As soon as possible. Everything you need should be on this card…" Peter pulled the business card from his pocket.

Brendan accepted it and looked at both sides, squinting at little at the scrawled information on the back.

"The phone number is short a digit. It's a Mississippi area code," Peter informed him. "There's supposed to be a place to upload the information once we have it."

"Not a phone number, an IP address," Brendan said without hesitation. "Not a bad way to hide it. You can just make out the dots. That'd be the server address for uploading, yeah?"

Peter and I looked more closely, and saw what he meant. Very, very lightly, so that there almost wasn't any ink at all, were marks between some of the numbers, which translated to: 60.116.79.43.

"I think that's got to be it," Peter agreed, handing the card back to Brendan. We were interrupted again by a couple of regulars greeting Peter, two old-school cowboy-types who had to be at least seventy. They weren't satisfied with a passing exchange, reminding each other of old times and leaving Brendan and me to ourselves for a few minutes.

"Thanks for doing this," I said.

Brendan's gaze swung past me as he shrugged.

"Gambling keeps life interesting. I'm too cheap to play for money and too bored not to play at all. Have another drink. Val, another round," he called, then turned back to me. "You don't seem like the kind of person who'd be into anything nefarious."

"I don't feel like it, much, either," I conceded.

"But this is you—the situation is about you," he said. He wasn't asking.

"Yeah. Someone I—it's about someone I care about," I explained inadequately. "She's in trouble—*we're* in trouble. Peter offered to help."

"I can tell. Otherwise it'd be out of character for him to ask for something like this. I've known Peter since he came to town for school—gotta be fifteen years, now. More."

"Were you on the faculty then?" I asked.

"Not yet. Getting my doctorate. We met when he started working here." He took a swig of beer. "One of the few people who didn't dump my ass when I—ahem—crossed a few lines. Ethically."

"He mentioned something about that."

"Mm-hmm."

Not wanting to pry, I shifted the subject.

"So you must know Kathe, then."

"Oh, sure. I was at their wedding."

"We're having breakfast with her tomorrow."

Brendan's sharp, bark-like laugh rang out.

"Are you. Impressive lady. Scares the bejesus out of me, but she never trusted me." He considered. "Not that I trusted her, either."

"Because she's a cop?" I wondered.

He shook his head.

"Because she's *her*. You'll see."

Tomorrow morning suddenly felt even more intimidating than it had already. And that was saying a lot.

■ ■ ■

I stared around the edge of the table at my toenails. The scuffed and peeling red polish was painfully apparent in my new sandals. It was too late to do anything about it now, but as we waited at the diner for Kathe to arrive I was agonizingly conscious of the scruffy state of my feet.

I remembered that I'd planned to get a pedicure after work the very day Marianne showed up—the day I went into hiding. Attractive toes hadn't really been on my mind since then. It somehow made the gap between my life now and in LA even wider and more impossible, like that was just a trip I'd taken a long time ago, a passing interlude, and this had been my reality for years.

At least I'd been able to put a little more effort into the rest of my appearance. My hair was clean and tied up into a loose French braid. I'd put on eye makeup and lip gloss, and wore my new sundress. My time on the beach at Half Moon Bay and walking in New York had given my skin a healthy kind of glow, even if it did bring out a few freckles.

If only she didn't look *down*, I was more than presentable.

It had been a later night than I'd expected, with more and more people arriving who knew Peter and wanted to catch up, buy us a drink, tell stories about the past. Brendan had left not long after we chatted, a backpack slung over one shoulder, muttering to Peter that he'd be in touch. I wished, not for the first or last time, that we could know exactly how long it would take him. Hours— days? Would Marianne be OK in the meantime? Would we all be safe from suspicion?

It seemed like she'd been right; nobody appeared to be following us here—or they were keeping their distance to such a degree that we couldn't tell. It made sense that her employers (also known as her parents) wouldn't be especially interested in our movements now that we'd left New York, not if they believed they could easily keep tabs on me with access to my accounts. I just hoped our visit with her hadn't raised any red flags. They knew we had stayed in touch, it wouldn't be so surprising for me to want to see her if I was nearby. In hindsight it was a good thing that we'd gotten some sightseeing in.

It was nearly midnight when we went back to our room, tired from our travels and socializing, relieved to have made contact with Brendan. We'd set an alarm for six to meet Kathe at seven, and so far Peter had kept the birthday stuff to a murmured "happy birthday" and kiss when he saw that I was awake. Followed by quick and satisfying birthday sex, though he didn't say anything about it being birthday sex, specifically. That was just how I thought of it.

We got to the diner a few minutes early, finding a booth and ordering coffees. It was a typical breakfast menu, heavy on the southwest influence. Peter thought he'd probably have the chilaquiles, his favorite here, while I was torn between two kinds of omelet. Kathe was a few minutes late. I wished I didn't feel so nervous and tucked my feet further under the table.

"You know it's our anniversary?" Peter asked suddenly. "Or... weekiversary?"

"So it is," I said, not at all convinced that it had only been seven days since we met, in spite of the fact that it had only been seven days since we met.

"We'll have to celebrate later."

Before I could respond—was he just determined to celebrate *something* today?—the door of the diner swung open and a woman walked in. She looked around, spotted Peter and walked quickly over.

"I'm so sorry I'm late," she said, stopping by our booth and smiling down at us. We slid out and were hugged, lightly and fragrantly, in turn, before we all sat down. I tried to think of something to say in response to her greeting and managed a choked, "Nice to meet you."

This was not what I'd expected.

It was much, much worse.

It wasn't just that Kathe was beautiful. She was, but many women are beautiful, it wouldn't have bothered me in the least to learn that she was more attractive than most. It was something else about her—a mixture of vitality, elegance and authority. She was one of the most confident people I've ever met. She just *exuded* self-assurance.

Her hair was in a stylish pixie cut—how many women can really pull off a pixie cut? The dark, almost black cap was untouched by gray, except for a striking patch of white just left of center above her forehead. It was undoubtedly natural, and completely unforgettable. Her eyes were a smoky hazel, her features aquiline, her skin a rich, smooth bronze, her body lean and graceful. She wore a clinging white silk tank top and gray pencil skirt, and I felt positive that a matching suit jacket was hanging in the back seat of her car, ready to slip on. Even in the most drenching heat, her clothes would be perfect, she would look cool and composed. Nothing I could wear, even had it cost twice as much, would look half as good on me. Her jewelry was tasteful and expensive, diamond drop earrings and heavy gold bracelet. She wore open-toed low heels and when I caught a glimpse of her feet, saw that her pedicure was perfect.

To hate Kathe for her looks and poise would be like hating a concert pianist for her talent. Sure, it made the rest of us feel like grubby, underdressed, gawky teenagers picking out "Heart and Soul," badly, on a tinny upright. It wasn't her fault. It just crumpled the last of my nerve.

All of this took very little time to notice and feel, while I looked (I hoped) intelligently between Peter, on the bench beside me, and Kathe, across from us.

"How are you?" Peter was saying.

"Appallingly busy—as always—but great. Isaac sends his regards. He's out of town at a conference or he'd have come with me." Her voice was somewhat deep, with an appealing rasp in it.

"Say hello for me."

"I will." She flagged the waitress with a subtle gesture and ordered a coffee. "Thanks for meeting me for breakfast—I'm working insane hours the rest of the weekend and wanted to be sure to catch you before you left town. Did you meet in California?"

This to me. I met her clever, curious gaze and resisted the impulse to fuss with my hair or smooth my dress.

"In Half Moon Bay," I confirmed.

"You live there too?"

"No—well, I didn't, though I'm in the process of moving back to the Bay Area," I said, hoping I sounded more collected to everyone else than I did to myself.

"Lola inherited some property not far from the bar," Peter broke in. It sounded very sophisticated, inheriting property. "She came up to spend a few days there and we... bumped into each other." He half-smiled as his glance crossed mine.

"Thanks to Osiris and a gull," I added inconsequently.

Leaning back and looking across at us with tolerant amusement, Kathe repeated, "Osiris?"

"My dog," Peter said.

"You got a dog? You're kidding," she laughed lightly. "I remember you being adamant about *never* getting one."

I sensed a slight tension in the air and took a sip of coffee, keeping my eyes down.

"I had no objection to dogs in general," Peter said equably, and Kathe laughed again.

"Just my kind of dog. Well, fair enough."

The waitress brought Kathe's coffee and asked if we were ready to order. I chose my omelet, Peter his chilaquiles, and Kathe cottage cheese and fruit, without comment. I realized that she had to watch her figure, and, in spite of the curves she had which I so visibly didn't, in spite of the fact that we weren't in any sense *rivals*, felt slightly better about myself. Even if I didn't have a stunning face, natural style and regal posture, at least I got to eat what I wanted.

"So, Lola—that's such a pretty name—where were you living before?"

Kathe really wasn't hard to like, once you got past the daunting parts. She seemed genuinely interested in getting to know me, and genuinely happy that Peter had met someone. Her questions were personal but not nosy, and she kept the flow of conversation light and rapid. I told her some of my background, about Uncle Joe and his camper, about my dislike of LA and desire to start fresh. What she inferred from this, she didn't say, but she was obviously too shrewd not to see the implications.

We didn't just talk about me, though. Kathe shared a few updates about herself, some prompted by Peter: a recent trip she and Isaac had taken to Iceland, updates on her family. She asked Peter about the bar, how long we planned to stay in town (he said only a day or two), about Delia and Hal. She seemed to know the details of the situation, and gave it as her opinion that if the DEA knew where Hal was and had the option, they might even be working on extradition. She thought he must be hiding out of the country, most likely with associates in Mexico.

"We deal with a lot of traffickers down here," she told me, "though it's not my area."

"What kind of cases do you work on?" I asked—the first question I'd voiced to her.

"Homicide," she replied, holding out her cup for more coffee and, once filled, drinking it black.

I had nothing to say.

■ ■ ■

"We'll have to plan a trip out to see you," Kathe said, giving us a repeat of her fragrant hugs as we stood in the shade of the diner's awning. The second we stepped outside, I started to sweat, the heat was already that overpowering. Kathe's silky blouse didn't even look like it was sticking to her.

"You should," Peter said, and I seconded this with a warmth that surprised me.

"We'd love that," I told her. Peter took my hand.

She smiled, showing very even, very white teeth, then laughed.

"Isaac will be *so pissed* he didn't get to meet you," she gloated, eyes alight with glee, then said goodbye, stepping into a sleek gray BMW convertible, the top closed against the blinding sun.

We turned and walked to where the rental car was parked, hands still linked. As Kathe passed us, she honked twice, then sped away with a final wave.

"Why will Isaac be pissed?" I asked idly.

"No idea. Must be some private joke between the two of them." The utter detachment of these words was far more reassuring than a thousand declarations of being over his ex could have been. "So, what did you think?"

I waited until we were in the car with the A/C blowing before I answered.

"She's great," I said. "I really like her."

"I'm glad. She liked you too. She told me she approved when you went to the bathroom."

"At least she didn't propose."

He laughed. "Wait for it," he warned.

"Now that I've met her, I just can't see you two as a couple," I said slowly, trying to picture it. "I mean... I can see why you would go out with her—and her you, of course. But..."

"But not married?"

"Yeah. Not married."

"It's even hard for me to see it now," he confessed. "It was falling apart way before the actual ceremony. I wasn't mature enough to see what she wanted—somebody who would go along with her but give her a hard time about it, which is what Isaac does. He's his own guy, but she gets to run the show. Even if I'd known what I was doing—been ready for that kind of commitment—I don't think we would have worked."

"No," I agreed. "She definitely needs a specific type of person. You're too... too independent, but also too easygoing, I think."

Peter looked impressed.

"Yeah, that's very astute. I didn't know what I wanted, I just knew I didn't want what Kath wanted *for me*—so she pushed, and I gave way and resented her for it, and she resented me for not pushing back. It wasn't pretty."

"I can imagine…" I murmured. He didn't say anything more, so I asked, "What kind of dog did she want to get?"

"Hm? Oh," he rolled his eyes, grinning. "Pure-bred *chihuahuas*. She loves them. Last I heard they had four."

"Oh no," I laughed. "You've got to be kidding."

"I wish I was. She had one as a kid, and always w—"

Peter's phone, sitting on the console between us, rang, and he broke off to ask, "Do you mind seeing who it is?"

"It's Brendan," I said, my stomach twisting in sudden anxiety. "Do you think there's a problem?"

"Only one way to find out…" Checking the mirrors, he quickly and adeptly pulled over, picked up the phone and answered. "Hey, man," he said into it. I could hear a voice on the other end, buzzing in speech, but not what Brendan was saying. "Seriously? Already?" He glanced at me and did a thumbs-up. "That was fast… Of course, I stand in awe… Sure, we can be right there… Right, I know where it is. See you in a few minutes… OK." He hung up and looked at me. "It's done—Brendan finished downloading it and wants to us to stop by."

"Really? It was that quick?"

"He pointed out that only someone with his brains and expertise could have done it in such record time."

"Kind of him."

"He wants us to meet him at his place up in the foothills. It's not far, just a few miles north of town."

When traffic was clear, Peter made a U-turn and began to weave his way through the city. I looked out of the window at the passing scenery and wondered why my stomach had suddenly dropped and started to knot up. This was what we wanted, wasn't it? To give Marianne the evidence she needed to use as leverage against her parents? Within minutes, if not already done, it would be uploaded to the IP address she gave us and she could start the next phase of her plan. That was a good thing… right?

My anxiety didn't seem to think so. It ratcheted up even higher the more I thought about it, a sense of dread creeping over me, up my arms, around my neck in a vise-like grip. Something about this felt so wrong. I tried to pinpoint what it might be… Was it Brendan, did I not trust him?… No, that wasn't it. Peter trusted him. Was I afraid for us—that someone was after us, behind us, closing in?

No. I hadn't been afraid of that for a few days now. It made a nice change, but didn't explain the heavy sense of fear, of a threatening storm about to break.

Marianne…?

My body shuddered with an unpleasant electric spasm at the thought of her.

Marianne. She was in danger.

This wasn't going to work. They were going to kill her and risk the evidence getting out, believing that she wouldn't have trusted anyone else enough to have a backup. They didn't know about her fail-safes, about our role in this, but by then it wouldn't matter. She'd be dead.

I shook with the certainty of it, even as I sternly told myself not to overreact. They needed her, didn't they? She was their *daughter.* In spite of everything they'd put her through, killing her would be an extreme way to go.

They're capable of anything, a frighteningly calm voice spoke out of my dread.

Not that, I argued desperately. *They can't know for sure that she hasn't protected herself. They'd wait to see if—*

They won't care. They killed that man in Brazil without proof. They'll kill her too.

No. They can't. She's their kid.

They know she isn't loyal to them, she said so. They're watching her. They know she'll do anything to protect you.

Then we'll turn them in. We'll expose them. We'll—

You won't know. Don't you get it? She isn't going to be in touch with you again—she knows it isn't safe. They'll take her out the minute she shows them her hand, and you won't know anything about it.

Defeated and dumb, the voice of hope fell silent.

Fear was right. This was what Marianne herself expected, after all. Even as she set this plan in motion, she'd known that it would most likely end this way.

Her parents were more than just liars and thieves. They were murderers, too. Dangerous and ruthless and cunning. She knew she'd fail.

But she was doing it anyway.

And there was nothing we could do to stop it.

chapter 15

It didn't occur to me, then, to worry about what might happen to me once Marianne was disposed of. Whether her parents would bother to remove me from the equation or ignore me, knowing my only connection to them was through Marianne. Later on, when I did examine the possibilities, I thought they'd probably leave me alone. I knew my life didn't mean anything to them, but it would be an unnecessary risk to take me out, a waste of their resources. They couldn't know that I knew what they really were. Or that Peter and I had access to evidence that could convict them of at least one of their crimes—maybe even to lead Interpol to them in the future.

That might change their calculations.

I hunched over, tense and silent, for the rest of the drive. Peter put his right hand on my knee, and I clutched at it with all ten of my fingers. He didn't ask me what I was thinking about. I wouldn't have been surprised if he guessed—and had come to the same conclusion. He'd probably figured it out before he even suggested we come to Tucson. I just didn't have the perspective to understand until now.

I hated that we were wasting everyone's time. Hated that we were driving ourselves closer to Marianne's death, every mile bringing us nearer to the moment that the information would get uploaded and she'd show it to her parents. But it wasn't like we had a better choice. Stopping now wouldn't help. Marianne had to try. I understood that, even while I understood just how dangerous and futile the whole stupid plan was.

I wondered how she would show it to them. Email them a screenshot? Text a photo? I couldn't imagine. How did criminal conspirators communicate with their networks? Encrypted text apps? Marianne had said they weren't in New York, now or often, which at least put some distance between them. Probably scamming some unfortunate victim on the other side of the world.

It should have been a reassuring thought. It wasn't.

From everything Marianne had said, they were just as dangerous far away as they were nearby.

I barely noticed that the city was gradually thinning out to a more sparsely-populated neighborhood, until we crossed what looked like a dry riverbed, covered with low trees, and began to weave through brown foothills. Straight ahead was one of the five mountain ranges, etched against a cloud-swept blue sky. Peter made a right turn onto a road that was paved, but had no sidewalks or streetlights or other signs of urban development. Only power lines crossing above and the driveways we passed showed that we were still in a city, otherwise we could have been dropped into the middle of nowhere.

I paid attention now, interested by the scenery. The high desert has a beauty all its own. Scrubby trees and shrubs grew thickly along the road and around the properties, interspersed with tall cacti and low, crumbling ridges of rock. Unlike in so many parts of California, no grasses covered the hills, not even the scorched brown grass of summer. The soil was sand and rocks, out of which sprung, somewhat miraculously, every shade of green from dark forest to pale chartreuse. I caught glimpses of the houses we passed, each standing on its own property at least a few hundred feet, usually more, from its nearest neighbors. They were built in various styles, from Mediterranean to ranch, some much bigger and grander than others.

Finally, after winding our way for several miles, we turned left onto a road that wasn't paved, slowly churning up the brown dust, passing a gated property with flagstone driveway on the right. The road ended in a dirt driveway, which wound steeply up to a small house shaded and partially hidden by several stout, rounded pine trees. As we pulled up in front of a closed garage door, I could see that the house was made of concrete blocks with a flat roof and few windows. Peter parked the car and we got out. It was pleasantly cool here in the shade of the pines.

He knocked on the front door, was about to knock again when it suddenly opened and Brendan waved us inside.

"Good, you made it," he said briefly, barely allowing Peter to pass before shutting and locking the door behind us.

We found ourselves in a dim, empty hall, facing another doorway that provided the only source of light. Walking through into the room behind, I was vaguely surprised to find it spotlessly clean and comfortably furnished as a living room-study combined. An inviting leather couch stood to one side, facing a fireplace, flanked by armchairs and side tables. The other half was filled by a large U-shaped desk holding various pieces of computer equipment and monitors, the cords neatly tied and organized. Colorful artwork hung on the white walls, landscape paintings and posters. A large set of doors along the back wall opened to a private, walled patio. The view beyond this, ringed with dark trees, showed a glimpse of the mountains above.

I don't know what I'd expected; Brendan's appearance, combined with the word hacker, had made me think of a dark, cramped underground bunker filled with shelves of canned food and unwashed dishes. I felt slightly ashamed of myself for making assumptions about how he'd live. Especially given my background, raised by software developers and trained in the same field, I should have known better.

"Sit down anywhere," Brendan said, waving a vague hand and moving purposefully over to the computer chair.

"You had no problems, then," Peter said, moving over to sit on the cushioned hearth and pulling me with him.

Brendan snorted and continued to type.

"As if," he said. "You handed me basic account credentials, all I had to do was go where it pointed me and use them to decrypt the data, which got me to the exit node. It finished downloading last night."

"Did you look at it?" Peter asked casually.

"Yep," Brendan said. He spun slowly around toward us. I noticed he was wearing the same clothes as the day before. "You know what it is?"

"Not... exactly," Peter said.

I shook my head.

"Well, you two have gotten yourselves into some interesting shit, that's all I can say. What are you planning to do with it, if I may be so bold?"

Peter looked at me.

"I'm... we're not sure," I said. "My—my friend is the person you're sending it to. She has plans for it."

"We'll be taking a copy, as well," Peter said in his level way.

"Oh, you will? That's neat. And your friend has plans for it. I can only imagine how much I don't want to hear what those plans are."

"Have you already uploaded it to her server?"

"Not yet. If you still want me to, it won't take long."

"You want to do this?" Peter asked me quietly. I met his eyes, and saw regretful understanding in his face.

"We want you to," I said out loud, trying not to sound like the voice of doom I felt myself to be. "What other choice do we have?" I added to Peter.

"Well..." he pondered, considering me before looking at Brendan. "I have an idea—but I'd like to see the files first."

"Be my guest, man," Brendan said, pushing back from the desk and standing up. He stretched his long body and made way for Peter, who had walked over to join him, to sit down. "It's all there…" he pointed to something on one of the monitors, and Peter leaned forward to study it. Brendan disappeared through another doorway and I heard the sound of clinking glass.

I stayed where I was. I didn't want to see. This felt a lot like sticking my head in the sand, however, and after a shamed minute I went to stand behind Peter and look over his shoulder. It wasn't fair to put this burden on him. The least I could do was to share it.

"Do you want to sit?"

"No," I said, resting my arms on his shoulders and scanning the document on the screen.

It didn't make much sense to me, this document or many of the others we saw. Out of more than thirty files in the open folder, there were at least twenty scanned PDFs in a language I didn't recognize—not Spanish, so I guessed Portuguese, which made sense given that whatever it was had happened in Brazil. They looked legal, like contracts or laws—long outlines of articles and sub-articles, many of the pages with initials scrawled here and there.

Eventually we came across something that wasn't unintelligibly legal: a scanned page out of a notebook, which had words and numbers printed on it in a list, three words with three sets of numbers beside them. It looked to me like names and phone numbers. Two of the names were foreign—*Espinheira, R* and *Perez, T*, but the third was Anglo: *Debrett, H + J.*

Now that we'd seen that name, Debrett, Peter pointed out that it was on nearly all of the legal documents, something I'd missed completely in the paragraphs of foreign text. Two people named Heidi and John Debrett, their names repeatedly listed along with the English words "Human Habitat Coalition," had been involved in whatever this was. I had a strong suspicion who this "Heidi and John" might be.

"You don't happen to read Portuguese, do you?" Brendan asked from the doorway, holding three bottles of beer. He walked over and offered two of them to us. I straightened, stretching out the kink in my back, and accepted a bottle, as did Peter. It was barely ten in the morning, but then this was a vacation of sorts. The cold beer, some kind of local IPA, tasted good, settling into my stomach with a pleasant fizz.

"No, do you?" Peter asked, after taking a sip.

"No. I translated some of it. Looks like an investment scheme of some kind, to do with that habitat thing. Those three names were putting together a deal, but doesn't look like it ended well. You didn't get to the newspaper article, did you?"

"Article?" Peter turned and quickly clicked through the file names, previewing as he went, finally stopping on one and opening it. This was a scanned article from a newspaper website, O Globo, printed from the online version rather than on newsprint. The headline had the word "homicídio" in it.

"Roughly translated, it says a man was found dead in an apparent homicide. The police were investigating several leads. It's dated two years ago."

Peter scanned down the text.

"Raul Espinheira," he read.

"The dead dude. His partners were wanted for questioning—Tomas Perez and a couple of foreigners, names unknown."

"The Debretts," I said, my throat suddenly dry.

"Looks to me like you got yourselves a fat little conspiracy there," Brendan commented, not seeming too disturbed by the idea. "Most of the rest of it's more of the same—legal docs, and a couple of brochures for some kind of housing project in a depressed area—there, see? 'Casas para os sem-teto,' roughly 'homes for the homeless,' according to Google Translate. Looks like these guys were investors, or something."

This fit all too well with the kind of fraudulent schemes Marianne had described. The brochures, both colorful tri-folds with images of happy, nice-looking children with dark hair and large dark eyes and families standing joyfully in front of little bungalows, had been flattened and scanned, like everything else, but still came across as slick and glossy and quite convincing. They were both in Portuguese as well, but it was obvious that they advertised affordable housing projects.

Brendon gave us a moment to absorb these before adding, "The only other scorcher is the passports."

At almost the exact moment he said this, Peter clicked the file and opened it. It was a color PDF of two scanned passports for Heidi Debrett and John Debrett, both ostensibly issued by Canada. The photos were of a late-middle-aged man and woman—the man clean-shaven with longish pepper-and-salt hair and glasses, the woman dark-haired with a stylish up-do. Neither had any distinguishing marks or features; they looking like average, well-to-do people in their sixties.

The first two pages of the PDF were the passports. The second was a handwritten list of names—each appeared to be the name of a couple, a man and a woman. Wendy and Phillip DeVere. Jonathan and Sara Devlin. Paul and Lina Desano. Nan and Harry Dunn.

"Aliases," Brendan suggested.

"Looks like it. Is this...?" Peter asked, scrolling back up to the passports and looking up at me.

"Yeah. It's them," I confirmed. "They didn't look like that the last time I saw them, but it was a while ago."

"You know these people?" Brendan asked, lounging against the desk behind me.

"Not well," I said shortly. "But yes, I've met them."

"Guessing those aren't their real names."

"I doubt it—I knew them as Rosemary and Leonard DiGregorio."

My eyes briefly encountered Peter's as Brendan said, "Ah."

I didn't feel the need to mention that the woman was my step-aunt.

■ ■ ■

"So what's your idea?" I asked Peter, walking over to one of the armchairs and plopping into it, beer in hand. It was going down very fast and very smooth. Peter came to join me, sitting on the couch, while Brendan wandered around the room.

"It's probably a really bad idea," Peter warned me.

"Bad how?"

"Dangerous… stupid… destined to fail." He smiled ruefully, and I couldn't help but smile back.

"Let's hear it," Brendan said, taking the other armchair. "I love a good dangerous stupid idea."

"Can I tell him a little background?" Peter asked me, and I nodded. "Lola's friend, Marianne, works for these people. They're her biological parents, as a matter of fact, but we won't hold that against her. From what she told us, they're behind a lot of crime abroad—fraud, mostly, using the humanitarian angle as their cover, and some more violent crimes like murder. Marianne wants to get out, and managed to get her hands on these documents—some source or stash her parents missed when the scheme went south—which she plans to use as leverage. She's going to show them she's got this evidence and try to make a deal."

Peter drank a long sip from his beer before he continued. Brendan waited, fingers busy peeling bits of the label off his bottle, eyes skimming the room.

"I've become convinced—I think Lola is, too—that it's not going to work. Marianne's going to tell her—employers—that she has this evidence, and they're going to kill her the first chance they get."

I had to swallow hard to manage to get out a murmured "Yeah." It was what I'd believed for almost an hour, but was still hard to hear it said out loud in such a matter-of-fact way.

"We can't stop Marianne from going forward with this, and we can't help her once she does. So I was thinking… what if we take matters into our own hands? Send the evidence to Interpol—the FBI—the police—the whole goddamn lot of them—and give Marianne a chance to run, if that's what she wants."

I looked at him in surprise.

"Really?" I asked.

"It *would* be the responsible thing to do, turning it over to the cops," Brendan acknowledged.

"I can't help thinking there's no other way to stop them—our best bet is to get them into custody. Marianne has a fighting chance that way—so does everyone involved," Peter explained, with slight emphasis on the "everyone." Meaning me. If they wanted to retaliate against their daughter, there'd be no better way than to track me down and take me out.

"Yeah, but these are slick customers, man," Brendan protested mildly. "I'm sure they've ditched these names and buried themselves behind new ones. Interpol's probably been looking for them for years."

"Well... That's the other part of my idea," Peter confessed. "We set up a trap for them, with Marianne—and the evidence—as bait."

We stared at him.

"Definitely stupid, and probably destined to fail," was Brendan's opinion, after a moment of consideration.

"How?" I wondered. My brain didn't seem to be processing things clearly. Maybe it was the beer, which I'd finished. I did feel slightly fuzzy, which wasn't unpleasant. I just couldn't seem to connect all the conversational dots without extra help drawing the lines. "How would we set a trap? Why would they fall for it?"

Peter finished his beer before answering, and as I watched him set down the bottle on the nearest table, I realized that this must be really hard for him. He wasn't even involved in this mess, and here he was trying his damnedest to think of a way out of it. He didn't want to scare me more than I already was, he didn't want to involve Brendan any more than he already had, but at this point he had to push forward anyway. I reached out and took his fingers, squeezing reassuringly, and he squeezed back.

"We use what we already know—what Marianne told us about them. She said that they're monitoring your accounts—credit card, email, social media, whatever they've been able to hack into. We know they can trace your credit card because they found us in New York. So, we use that to our advantage. We book plane tickets and hotels, fire off emails and log into anything and everything, sending them to a certain place and time that we'll supposedly be meeting up with Marianne to get the evidence from her—or a contact of hers."

"Waving a red flag in front of the bull," Brendan said, getting up and walking into the kitchen.

"Would they buy it?" I wondered.

"They might," Peter said. "They don't know you know anything concrete—and even if it occurred to them to be wary it might be too tempting not to come check it out. I don't know that they could afford to ignore it, even if they didn't buy it."

"But... where would we go? Back to New York?"

"Maybe... It's possible you could have left town and come back again in a few days. But I think it makes more sense to do it somewhere else. Somewhere that might seem safer to you, since it's not far from where you grew up. Remember she said that her parents had a West Coast base in San Francisco? I don't know anything about them, but I bet they'd be more inclined to show if they felt they were on familiar turf. Otherwise I'd suggest we do it here."

He'd really thought this through. I still couldn't grasp the whole plan, so waited for him to explain further.

"You think they'd come themselves?" Brendan called from the kitchen.

Peter rubbed his eyes and dropped his hands to his lap.

"I don't know," he said slowly. "I just don't think there's anyone else they'd trust to send. Marianne said they only really trust each other, right? Worst case, only one of them shows up— but that's better than nothing."

"How'd you plan on letting our friends in law enforcement know about this little sting?" Brendan asked, returning with another round.

"I was going to ask you about that…"

"Oh, swell."

"Would there be a way to get it to them through the darknet?"

Brendan, after handing us each a bottle, took a thoughtful swig.

"That's a thought," he said. "Especially if you don't want them to know who sent it, which is what I'd recommend."

"I'd like to keep our options open. I don't know much about how it works, though. Do you, Lola?"

"Very little, I'm embarrassed to admit," I said. "It always sounded so ominous… the *darknet.* Like a horror movie."

Brendan snorted kindly at my ignorance.

"Nothing so dramatic, sorry to say. It's basically web content that only exists on darknets—overlay networks that use the net but require specific software or authorization to access. It's all *there,* you just can't see it unless you've got the configuration or decryption. There are a couple of networks that access it—Tor is a big one."

"And it allows people to remain completely anonymous?" Peter asked.

"That's the idea. The darknet encryption tech routes data through a gang of different intermediate servers, and that protects a user's ID and location. It lets people communicate and transact without anyone knowing who they are, or being able to access their data. It's reasonably ingenious, and such a complicated system makes it damn near impossible to reproduce the node path and decrypt the data. Sites aren't able to track the IP of their users, and users can't get the IP or location of the host, so you get complete confidentiality."

"It seems like a perfect breeding ground for crime," Peter said.

"Oh, it is. Crazy shit goes on—everything from the worst kinds of pornography to fraudulent Bitcoin transactions and illegal drug sales—even terrorist groups use it. But most of what's on there is just people not wanting big brother to see everything they're doing. Whistle-blowers, political groups, stuff like that. Lately it's getting a lot more popular with people who just want to avoid ads and data mining."

"Would there be a way to send this to the FBI or Interpol, like Peter said?" I asked.

"Oh, sure. They're always monitoring what they can. Interpol has indexed thousands of darknet sites. If we push it to a place they're looking with the authorization they need, it should land in their laps—theoretically."

"So, theoretically, they'd have this file full of evidence, along with anything else we wanted to include, and would be able to decrypt it without seeing who sent it?" Peter asked.

"That's the idea, yeah."

"And then what?" I asked Peter.

"We bait the trap—and hope to God it works," he replied.

"And Marianne?"

"She doesn't need to know anything about it until we know it's failed—or succeeded," Peter said. "We can keep in touch through the IP address she left us and let her know if it worked—or if she needs to run."

"She won't run unless she knows I'm safe."

"I know. So we'll have a back-up plan—if they don't show up, or something goes wrong, you tell the cops or Feds everything you know and see if they can't help protect you."

"I'd be turning Marianne in, too, wouldn't I."

"I don't know what other choice we have. And honestly, at this point, I don't think she'd mind."

"She prob'ly even intended it," Brendan drawled, lounging down in his chair as if his spine had melted into the leather.

"Why do you say that?" Peter asked quickly.

"Seems to me there are a few holes in your plot—no offense, man."

"None taken. What holes, exactly?"

"How about, why did this Marianne tell you so much? Seems weird that she just spilled all her deepest, darkest secrets like that. You could put her in some serious trouble if you passed any of it along. Trust is nice, and all, but nobody's going to incriminate themselves without a reason. So, what was the point of filling you in? Did she say?"

"No," Peter answered thoughtfully. "No, she didn't say."

"Seems fishy. And why didn't she just pull this stuff off the darknet herself? Anyone with half a brain and some knowledge of servers could do it, and I'm betting she knows plenty. These parents of hers probably use it in their little operations. So why not just download it and—what did she say she was going to do with it?"

"Show her parents enough to prove to them she had it, and make a bargain," I said, since Peter seemed too abstracted to respond.

"Huh. Well, why couldn't she have done that? She didn't need you to do it, did she? Something else was stopping her."

"She knew it wouldn't work," I said.

"Yeah, exactly. So you two come along and offer to do it for her when she says it's not safe—am I getting warm?—fitting nicely into her new plan. You'll pull the evidence—and use it to turn in her folks. My bet is the lady's already long gone."

"She set this up," Peter agreed thoughtfully.

"Right," Brendan said.

"She set this *up*?" I echoed, apparently the only one who found the idea surprising.

"It makes sense. Why else tell us everything she did?"

"She couldn't know we'd offer to get the evidence off the darknet," I protested. "Would you have suggested that if you didn't know Brendan?"

"No, but she could have gotten it to us some other way. She knew we'd want to use it somehow—to help her or to turn it over to the police. It turned out that we did know someone who could get it for her. This way was just an extra fail-safe."

One more fail-safe.

It made sense, now that the idea had been shoved into my lap. Marianne had played us. She'd used our appearance in New York to her advantage, weaving us into her plan. Now that Brendan had pointed it out, it seemed so obvious. Without us, she had no chance of making a deal with her parents. The collateral she'd collected at such a high price, and I believed her story about that, would only be useful for one thing—to put her parents away. She could have sent it to Interpol herself, tried to set up a sting, but there was no guarantee it would work. Her parents already didn't trust her, they were watching her every movement. What was her excuse for not turning them in herself—that they could do us harm from prison? Maybe that was true, but now that I thought it about it, it was ambiguously thin. More likely she'd already decided that we could do it for her.

She had her exit plan in place. That's why, at long last, she was willing to share the dark side of her life with me. Show me the criminal schemes spun by the DiGregorios, or whoever they really were. Because after this, it wouldn't matter anymore. One way or another, she'd be gone. She'd do everything she could to protect me, set up every safeguard possible, and then go. The final fail-safe would be handing myself and everything I knew over to law enforcement, so they could protect me if it came to that.

I could only hope, with all my heart, that it wouldn't come to that.

chapter 16

"So she knew we'd want to use the evidence," I said, some minutes later. Peter and Brendan had already moved back over to the monitors and were animatedly discussing the best ways to bait the trap and send the files. I'd listened with half an ear, the rest of my mind still processing our theory about Marianne. It was only a theory at this point—and it directly contradicted what she'd told us she planned to do. But all the same, it was too plausible to ignore. My partners had already decided that this version was the correct one, and deep down I felt they were right.

"What was that?" Peter inquired, after a short pause. I got up and joined them, leaning up against one of the desks.

"She knew we couldn't just send it off and sit on our hands," I said. "When do you think she decided to bring us into it?"

"Before she agreed to meet us for drinks," Peter said. "And after we showed up at her bolt-hole. We'd shown some tenacity in finding and interviewing Mike Sorenson, not to mention tracking down her address. I think she saw we could be allies."

"*Unwitting* allies," I amended, with mild bitterness. I couldn't help but feel used.

"Somewhat unwitting, maybe. Though there's no reason we couldn't have figured it out—as we did."

"Why couldn't she just have *asked* us to take it to the police? Why all the—the maneuvering? It seems so pointless."

"Well, what if we didn't want to? It was a lot to ask, and might not have done much good. At least we were warned, and maybe even protected to a degree. The worst thing that could happen was that we got the information to her and she was no worse off than before."

There was no debating this, so I left it alone and drank the last of my second beer.

"I think I've got the sending part figured out," Brendan volunteered, clicking rapidly through a number of windows. "I can send it through a posting server to a couple of agencies in D.C. Domestic and international. All we need to do is figure out what we're going to tell them."

"And how to bait the trap," Peter said. "And where to set it."

"Just a few small details, really," Brendan said.

"Do you remember anywhere your aunt and uncle went when they were in the city?" Peter asked me.

I thought back. My memories of them were brief, vague and impersonal. When they infrequently came to town, they stayed at a hotel—did I ever hear which hotel? Or was that even true?—and either sent for Marianne in a taxi or drove by to pick her up without coming inside. It was sort of odd at the time, but with the serene self-centeredness of childhood I never questioned it. Only once did they get out of the car at our house, and once we met them in San Francisco, when I was about thirteen. It wasn't far from Union Square, on Market…

"The Four Seasons," I said suddenly. "We met them in the lobby once, to take Marianne home after she'd been staying with them. We happened to be in the city for the day—it was right after Christmas. I don't know if they were actually guests there or not, but Marianne was waiting in the lobby and they were in the bar. My mom was kind of annoyed about it, I remember."

"Swanky scene," Brendan commented.

"Anywhere else?" Peter asked. I shook my head, feeling discouraged. "We don't have any idea how to find their dummy business, or else that would be ideal. What we really need is someplace they'd feel confident in coming to, but couldn't get away from easily."

"Alcatraz?" I suggested wryly.

"Too remote," Peter said, "but you're on the right track."

"I was kidding."

He looked up and smiled.

"Sorry. I've been wishing I knew the city better. I'm sure we'll think of something."

"All you need to do is to set the bait," Brendan said. "You don't actually need a place for it. In fact, it'd be better *not* to have one."

"Why is that?" Peter asked curiously.

"They'll catch onto it—anywhere you pick will be too obvious."

"So what do you suggest?"

Brendan unhurriedly spun his chair around in a circle.

"You mention this supposed meet—all nice and obscure, you don't even really need to say where it is, right? Then you set the real trap in your hotel, say—somewhere they think they'll be able to come at you unawares. Vulnerable. Before the fake meet is supposed to happen. If the Feds buy it, they'll be watching the entrances, ready to nab our friends if or when they show up."

"Use their suspicions against them," Peter said slowly.

"Well, yeah. Otherwise they'll smell a rat. I mean, they probably will anyway, but it might just get them where you need them to be. And, eventually, in custody."

"How do we avoid getting arrested ourselves? Or do we avoid it?"

"Well, that's the trick, isn't it? You'll have to chance getting caught in the crossfire, so to speak—tell the authorities where to look for these DiGregorio people, and show yourselves to the DiGregorios so they think they've got you cornered and feel confident about making a move. Then turn yourselves in or get the hell out, whatever doesn't get you killed."

"That's kind of brilliant," I declared, thinking it over.

"It's smarter than anything I had in mind," Peter said without resentment. "I don't like the idea of putting Lola in any danger—or myself, or anybody else—but I can see how these people are too devious to be caught easily. You're right—the trick is to convince them that we're trying to trap them somewhere else. They'll only show up if they think they've outsmarted us. If they have the upper hand." He sat in brooding silence, rubbed his eyes again. We waited, watching him. "Will it work, do you think?" he asked Brendan finally.

"I'll be honest with you, man," Brendan said, avoiding our eyes and turning back to the nearest screen. "I seriously doubt it."

■ ■ ■

Suddenly everything seemed to be moving faster, now that we'd come up with the beginnings of a plan. Brendan, who must have had nothing better to do with his Friday than drink beers and advise us on how to catch a pair of lethal criminals, began to build the package we'd send to certain servers flagged by the FBI, the Justice Department and Interpol in Washington. As far as Marianne had said, Interpol was the only agency actively investigating her parents as most of their crimes were committed outside of the U.S., but it couldn't hurt to throw a homegrown acronym or two in there.

Peter and I pulled chairs from the kitchen to sit closer to Brendan while he worked, discussing the best way to present our trap, along with all the incriminating files. In the end he suggested a text file, programmed to open automatically on download of the zipped package. I peered over his shoulder while he put this together, asking the occasional question and finding that none of it was more complicated than other programming I'd done. It was just a matter of using different tools and servers to do it.

To my surprise, Brendan was a good teacher; I'd forgotten that he taught for a living, that "hacker" wasn't his profession. He answered my questions patiently and went out of his way to show me how to use Tor to access the darknet, which was straightforward enough. I'd forgotten a lot of what I learned in college, only working in database development for the last few years, but much of the language and intuitive processes started to come back to me as I watched Brendan work.

Peter wasn't half as interested as I was, not even pretending to listen. He'd pulled over a blank piece of paper and was writing intently on one of the desks opposite. Once Brendan had finished setting up the text file programming, he turned to Peter and said, "So, what are we putting in this love note?"

Frowning in concentration, Peter read out what he'd been writing. I should have guessed that was what he was working on.

"'Enclosed evidence regarding suspects of international fraud, extortion, murder, wanted for questioning by Interpol. Alias Heidi Debrett, John Debrett (aka Wendy DeVere, Phillip DeVere. Sara Devlin, Jonathan Devlin. Lina Desano, Paul Desano. Nan Dunn, Harry Dunn. Rosemary DiGregorio, Leonard DiGregorio). Suspects may be at this location at this time'—we'll need to figure out where and what date—'possibly under new alias. Best wishes from a concerned citizen.'"

Brendan chortled, nearly choking in his mirth.

"Oh, man!" he guffawed. "'A concerned citizen…' Priceless!"

"Too much?" Peter asked, grinning.

"It's good," I assured him, wishing I could find any of this as funny as they seemed to. "I don't see what else we can say."

"What day are you going to do this?" Brendan asked, still shaking with laughter.

"I don't know. Soon. How quickly could they take action?"

"As fast as their analysts can get through it. I'd say no more than a day or two. They'll have to run it through their security software a few times, once it's deemed safe it'll get pushed through for processing. My guess is Interpol will be the first dogs in the water, if any of those names show up in their system. After that the Feds."

"So possibly as early as tomorrow or Sunday, if we send it today. If we send it tomorrow, maybe Monday at the latest."

"Sounds about right."

"The timing will be the tricky part. We can't risk moving too fast on either side—having the DiGregorios show up before the police are in place."

"We'll just have to push them to come soon—make it a tight window between the pretend-trap and the real one," I said, finally feeling like I had a grasp on what we were going to do. "We can reserve a hotel room there under my name, and keep walking through the lobby or hanging out in the bar—places where the agents or whoever can keep watch."

"Makes sense," Brendan approved. "Which hotel?"

"The Four Seasons," I said without thinking. "Go big or go home."

"Great choice. The management won't like it, but let the authorities deal with that. They're good at cleaning up awkward messes."

Peter looked more concerned than impressed by my plan.

"I know this was my idea, but I hate the idea of you being such... such *visible* bait," he said, his voice strained. "We'll be sitting ducks for some very dangerous people."

"In public—surrounded by cops," I reminded him.

"There's no guarantee of that. We can't force the authorities to set up a sting—anything might prevent them from taking action."

"In which case a couple of baddies know you're holding the goods on them," Brendan added helpfully. "But hey, that was always the risk, right? Dangerous and stupid plans have that disadvantage."

"Right," Peter agreed reluctantly.

The nerves in my stomach—previously steadied by the beer—gave an anxious lurch. There was no getting around it. If our plan to have them caught failed, we'd have walked ourselves directly into the DiGregorios' line of sight. We could always throw ourselves onto the mercy of the FBI or the police, but as Peter said, there were no guarantees.

"Then we just have to hope it works," I said, and hoped I didn't sound as terrified as I felt.

■ ■ ■

Brendan completed the "love note," as he kept calling it, including the name of the hotel and the date range of now through Monday. We had to push everyone to act. It was soon—too soon, ominously soon, but we had no reason to wait and every reason to get it over with quickly. Peter had already missed almost a week of work. If our plan succeeded, and we weren't in jail, he might even be able to return to the bar on Tuesday. Delia had kept in touch via text and told him everything was fine, but he didn't feel good about not being there, for her or the business. On top of that, time might be ticking away until Hal's indictment came through, setting more problems in motion.

If our plan failed, well… We'd just have to figure things out from there. I could only hope Peter was still an unknown factor, one that the DiGregorios would dismiss if I, or Marianne and I, were out of the equation. If that meant we were dead, or framed for crimes we didn't commit (or did commit, on Marianne's part, but only under duress), I couldn't worry about it. I just couldn't. It was unthinkable—and I'd had considerable practice, in the last weeks, of avoiding unthinkable fears. My dread was with me, heavy in my heart and stomach, but I forced it down and worked to focus on what was directly ahead of us.

The evidence would be sent this afternoon, immediately. Before it was done, I booked a room at the Four Seasons on my credit card, making a reservation for three nights—Saturday, Sunday and Monday. Three nights in even the cheapest room cost more than a month's rent in LA, but I had just enough credit to cover the cost. Peter suggested we drive home, since we had time, leaving early the following morning and arriving in San Francisco Saturday evening. It was about a thirteen-hour drive, if we went through LA and up Interstate 5, joining the same route I'd taken on my mad rush north, and would save us hundreds to rent a car versus booking a last-minute flight.

Though it seemed like an inopportune time for a road trip, I thought it was a good idea. Short of cooling our heels for an extra day in Tucson, the only other option was to head back to the Bay Area early. It was tempting to think of going home for a quick stop; the camper had become home, my tiny sanctuary. Even more so for Peter, who could check on Osiris and Delia. But it would be harder to get away again if we went back, we both saw that. While we didn't want to show up in the city too early, getting there late Saturday and staying in our room should be safe enough. After all, the DiGregorios, as I still thought of them, no matter how quickly they'd want to strike, would also need time to travel from wherever they were. Out of the country, Marianne had said, though giving no indication where. From what she said, she might not know.

Before we left his house, Brendan used his Tor account to upload, encrypt and push the information to sites the agencies would be monitoring, flagged and programmed to catch their notice in ways he didn't bother to describe in detail, and neither of us questioned. It had to do with whistleblowers and anonymous tips. Each agency had many of their own accounts on Tor and other darknet browsers, according to him, though like everyone else they were impossible to identify. He described what he was doing as similar to commenting on a public blog with links, except it was more layered than that, which would take them directly to the downloads he'd set up.

On Brendan's suggestion, he also uploaded an encrypted copy of the folder to Marianne's IP address, along with a key. Whether she'd feel safe enough to access it, or took steps to use it, we couldn't predict or control, but he pointed out that anything she did could only help our cause.

"The doomsday clock has officially started," he said, as soon as he'd finished. He went for a third beer, offering us the same, but

Peter refused for both of us, suggesting that we head back to town to figure out what we were going to do next.

"Welcome to stay," Brendan said, yawning and gulping down more beer.

"Thanks, but we've got a few other things we should take care of," Peter told him. "Sorting out the rental car, for one thing."

"Sure," Brendan said amiably, getting up to walk us out— though I suspected this was more to make sure that the door was secured behind us than out of politeness.

"I can't thank you enough—for all your help," I said earnestly, feeling slightly ridiculous as he herded us down the hall. Now that we were leaving, Brendan was more than ready to have us on our way.

"Wouldn't have missed it," he said, not bothering to suppress an even bigger yawn. "Hope to see you again sometime."

"We'll let you know what happens," Peter said.

"Yep. Do that. Bye-bye," Brendan said, ushering us out and closing the door with a definitive thud.

The air outside rushed over my skin like a soft, hot blanket, making me realize how chilly the house had been. I checked the time and was surprised to see that it was after one. The strange little interlude, both exhausting and exhilarating, had left me feeling somewhat blank.

"Sorry about that," Peter said, unlocking the car. "He doesn't mean to be rude."

"He wasn't rude—his mind's just moved on."

"Exactly. I'm glad you see it. It puts some people off."

He rolled the windows down and started the car; the seats were warm but bearable after being parked in the shade.

"He told me Kathe didn't trust him," I said.

"No, they didn't get along. She found him... shifty, was her word, I think. And socially inept." Peter started the car and turned the A/C up to full blast, carefully backing out of the driveway.

"He's not inept," I protested. "He's just... a little abrupt. Not everyone cares about being liked."

"Kathe does, of course. Being liked and respected matters so much to her that it's hard for her to relate to anyone who doesn't feel the same."

That made sense. Even more reason why she and Peter wouldn't have worked—she placed a much higher value on societal approval and recognition than he did, which was made clear by the professions they'd chosen. He ran a small bar in a small town, content to stay behind the scenes, while she made her mark as a homicide detective in a growing city, no doubt often in the public eye. Even if their relationship hadn't fallen apart when and how it did, it was easy to see how Peter wouldn't have fit with the image she cultivated. I wondered briefly what her current husband did for a living, but before I could ask, Peter changed the subject.

"As soon as we get back to San Francisco you can start logging into your accounts on your phone—whatever tracking stuff it does. Aren't there ways to sort of check into where you are?"

"Almost every social media site lets you check in, if you have location services turned on," I said. "It might look suspicious if I suddenly flooded my accounts, but one or two check-ins on the way and once we get there should do it. It probably won't surprise them to see I'm in the Bay Area, I could easily be visiting friends or taking care of business up there."

"Right. So we have to make them sit up and take notice. Any ideas?"

I thought for a moment, looking out the window as we turned back out of the twisting neighborhood streets onto a main road.

"I think I need to email Marianne," I said slowly. "She has the evidence now. Even if she guesses what we're doing, she still might try to force their hand by showing it to them. I can tell her that I'm worried… that I know she said not to write but that I don't think it's a good idea to meet her right now. That everyone else is convinced that this will work, but I'm not, and I don't want to go through with it."

"As if you're panicking, but it's out of your hands?"

"Yeah, exactly."

"That should get their attention. Do you think she'll see the message?"

"Maybe. If she still looks at that email account. But if you're right that she wanted this, she'll understand what we're doing—and anyway the point is for *them* to see it."

"True. It might not make a difference, you know."

"I know. But we have to do everything possible to get them to show up, don't we?"

"We do, yeah. If the plan has any chance of success." After a minute, he said, "I'm leaving a copy of everything with Brendan. He said he'll get it to Kathe if anything—goes wrong."

"When did you decide that?"

"You were there, but I think your mind was on something else when we were talking about it. If he doesn't hear from me, he'll take it to her and explain... Well, I have no idea what he'll say, but he'll convince her to look at it."

"Not that I'm questioning, but... Why didn't you want to go to her—from the start?" I asked. "She could've sent it to the right people."

"Of course—and she'd have done everything possible to help us. But we couldn't avoid being the center of a swarm of police, answering awkward questions they might not believe the answers to—and there's no way they'd agree to work with us to set a trap for the DiGregorios. Marianne would be in just as much danger, or more—her parents might decide it was time to do something drastic to keep her quiet, to her or both of you. Not to mention someone might arrest us for collusion or something. It wouldn't help that I'm closely associated to a suspected drug trafficker. It—doesn't exactly inspire confidence," he concluded with a curt laugh.

I pinched his arm very lightly.

"I'm glad we're doing it this way," I said, and it was mostly true.

■ ■ ■

After a quick visit to a nearby office of the rental car agency, where we extended the rental contract and arranged to return the car in Oakland, and a second stop to pick up sandwiches and large iced teas, we went back to the hotel. I wanted to clear my head and wash off the day with a shower, after which we could discuss our plans in the cool privacy of our room. Our intention was to leave early the following morning, not rushing, but aiming to get to Oakland by about eight, return the car and take BART into the city.

We could have gone to the airport and driven my car instead, since it was—I hoped—still parked there, but the cost of parking at the hotel was astronomical. On top of that, we'd be less encumbered without it if we wanted to get away quickly. It was about the same length of drive to SFO as it was to Oakland, but it just felt safer, somehow, to approach the city from a different route.

We'd agreed to all of this, and I was settling back onto pillows propped against the headboard, holding my phone in preparation for loading apps and logging into all the accounts Marianne had warned me to stay out of, when something occurred to me.

This was my life now.

From the minute Marianne called on that Friday so many weeks ago—two weeks, I realized... *two weeks ago*—everything had shifted to a kind of bizarre alternate reality, where I considered how fast I'd need to get away, who might follow, who would be watching. Where people I grew up knowing as distant and unlikeable humanitarians became menacing figures who forced my only remaining family to work for them under the threat of harming me. Where I'd recklessly risk my present and future safety because the alternative was that much worse.

Where I had a partner—the first partner I'd ever really had. Someone to plot the downfall of villains with me. To support me through danger and investigations and the dismantling of old beliefs. To fall asleep beside every night, our arms or legs touching, damply satisfied from making love or simply relaxed and tired from a long day of travel and adventure. To wake up to every morning, stale-breathed and tousled, doubting what the day might bring, but never doubting we'd be together for whatever it did.

In just fourteen days, everything I'd ever known or thought about my cousin, my past, my future, had been unwritten. I'd always just assumed that the disturbing things that happened to other people, other families, hadn't had a chance to touch us. Cancer and illness and death were terrible. Brutal beyond endurance. But they weren't malicious or sordid. No person was responsible for deliberately depriving me of my parents; no one had devised that aching tunnel of grief and forced me into it; no malevolent plot or actions led to their deaths. The wounds inflicted were painful but pure, just as the gray dim doldrums I'd lived through the past five years were soul stifling in their own shallow way, but still wholesome, the way plain, unsalted oatmeal is wholesome.

Without ever recognizing I had these assumptions, I believed that we were removed from and untainted by the evil that exists in the world. Separated from it by an invisible, impenetrable barrier that could never be violated. I was profoundly naïve, sincerely convinced of this truth.

I'd been so wrong.

Just beyond my sight was a vast darkness, a thick black web of greed and lies and violence. It touched me, had touched my parents, though we never knew it existed. And now that I'd seen it, I couldn't ever go back to unseeing. I was a part of it now. Connected by a dozen different strands, held fast by its sinister influence.

The DiGregorios, as I still thought of them, were the architects of that spreading ugliness. How they became what they were, I'd probably never know. And it didn't matter. They had done such harm to someone I loved, done such irreparable damage to the daughter they should have honored and cared for, that even if they'd been innocent of any other crimes, I would have despised them for that.

As it was, they were thieves and crooks and killers. They were without conscience or common decency. Catching the unwary in their snares, we were tightly bound and sucked dry for their swollen avarice, at their narrow pleasure.

Even if this didn't work, I knew it was what I wanted to do. I wanted to bring them down. End their reprehensible schemes for good, free my cousin from their control. Maybe I wasn't the person to do this, but that was just too bad. I was given this chance, and was willing to try. Even if we were arrested or—worse.

As far as Peter was concerned, it was far too chilling to imagine he might be hurt in any way, so I couldn't consider that. They didn't know him. They knew *me*. They'd want me. He had a chance of getting out of this even if our clumsy schemes fell apart. Believing that was the only thing keeping me from screaming aloud in panicked rage at the thought that those awful people might do him harm.

I didn't want to die. I had no desire to be recklessly daring. It wasn't that I was prepared to martyr myself for him or anything so dramatic. But if it came down to it, it was fair for me to be the one in the crossfire. He was only part of this because of me. It was his choice, but it was still because of me.

Maybe we'd just get arrested.

At this point, that really didn't sound so bad.

chapter 17

"OK, what do you think of this?" I asked Peter an hour or so later. In that time, while he mapped out our trip, I'd downloaded several social media apps and logged into my accounts, keeping location services off for the moment. I'd also added my email accounts to the phone and downloaded my contacts from the cloud. By tomorrow, I'd be traceable again. I planned to turn everything on in LA, as if I'd gotten a new phone in SoCal and was driving up from there.

"'Marianne, please don't do this,'" I read aloud. "'I know you said not to write but I can't sleep and I don't know what else to do. There's no other way to reach you. I'm on my way to LA and will be in the city by Sunday. I DON'T WANT YOU TO COME.' (That's in capitals.) 'Let them figure it out without you. You did enough by getting the files—the police have everything they need to find these criminals and put them away for good. Please please stay out of sight. *Please.* Do this for me. It isn't worth it. I love you, Lo.'"

"I like it," Peter said.

"That's the first one. I figured I'll send it tonight around two, and maybe another on Saturday night saying the same kind of thing along with the fact that we're at the hotel as planned. I don't know how to work a fake meeting location into that—but maybe it doesn't matter at this point?"

"I don't think it does," he replied. "Since we're counting on the idea that they'll move on us first."

"Do you think it's enough?"

He rubbed my back a few times and smiled.

"I really hope so. I'm somewhat out of my depth in all this, if you couldn't tell."

"I'm *totally* out of my depth—but you know," I said reflectively, "even though I'm doubting all the time what I'm supposed to do next—what the right thing is… I'm not doubting that this—that it's the right thing for us to do. Like it's… an opportunity that I know I don't want to miss. Not only to help Marianne, and not just to do something crazy or risky. But to—to…"

"Make a difference," Peter said, his dark eyes thoughtful.

"Yeah. I've never done anything remotely *heroic* before—never helped anyone or saved anyone. Even if this plan doesn't work because we don't know what we're doing, even if they get away and we're all in danger for it, I'm—I'm glad of the chance to try, you know?"

He didn't speak, but pulled me into a long, deep kiss, one of his hands tangling in my hair while the other slid around me. I'd gotten somewhat used to kissing Peter in the week we'd known each other. Even with the other distractions of the trip, we'd managed to put in some time making out as well as having a few sexier interludes. Of course our relationship was so new, everything we did was novel and exciting, but even so kisses and holding hands had become the norm, comfortable and natural.

This kiss, though, knocked me sideways.

Sweeter, more intense, more full of love and longing and intimacy than any other physical touch we'd shared. I felt an ache welling up in my chest—a good ache, as all the pain and loss of the past few years rose up and pushed forward. At long last, it could be shared, and understood.

As we moved tightly together, breaths and mouths mingling, I felt more reverence than passion, as if my very heart was expanding, my soul reaching for eternal, starry bliss. It would be impossible to describe in any other way than a spiritual experience, born of the body and carried out of it into the realm of poetry and song and wildly ecstatic drug-induced trips, unlike anything I'd ever felt.

After a long moment—or maybe several millennia—we pulled slowly apart and stared at each other.

"Damn, Lola," Peter laughed shakily, "I really hope you feel the same way I do."

I reached up to touch his cheek, which seemed to be slightly damp; only then did I realize that I was crying. My eyes had gently overflowed onto both our faces, since his—though bright with unsaid things—didn't appear to be wet.

"I feel..." I began, then stopped. "I... I do," I managed inadequately.

"I can't imagine what would have happened if Oss hadn't..." he said, as inarticulate as I was.

"We'd have met some other way," I stated, having no doubts in the matter. "At the bar—around town. It would've been the same no matter what."

"It does feel like that. Like so many things were pushing us toward each other without us even knowing it..."

"Like the tides," I offered, leaning my head against his shoulder.

"I used to think people were being stupid when they talked about meeting someone and just *knowing*—love at first sight, and all of it. I still think most of it's a combination of attraction and timing—and no small amount of wishful thinking. But this... it's... indescribable. I don't believe I've only known you a week."

"I know," I agreed, nestling comfortably into his neck.

"It's… It seems wrong, or like it should be wrong, to be taking any risks just when we've found… But I know it's right to go forward. I feel the same way you do—I want to do it. I've only ever watched from a distance—been a kind of side act to people like Kathe who are actually doing something to make things better. It's a fight you lose more than you win, and we might lose this round in a spectacular way. But I'm—thankful to have the chance to do it. I'm glad to be doing it with you."

We fell silent, and sat like that for a long time, safe in our own small, private bubble, the air sweet with rare and friendly understanding.

■ ■ ■

Peter asked if I wanted to go out for my birthday, and I said no. Instead we picked up more of his favorite tacos and ate them in the shade by the hotel pool, where several small tables had been set up with umbrellas. A family with four children ranging from a chubby toddler to a thin, leggy girl of about eleven splashed happily and noisily at the other end of the pool, overseen by relaxed and indolent parents on nearby lounge chairs. The evening light stretched and grew dimmer, we bought and drank a bottle of cheap prosecco from a nearby convenience store, sipping and talking idly about nothing in particular.

Now was the moment I asked him about Tucson, his time at school, the places he'd worked, friends he still kept in touch with. There were long periods of comfortable silence, while I watched the family dreamily with a magazine in my lap and Peter read on his iPad.

As seven thirty became eight, eight became eight thirty, the shadows grew darker, the last of the lights around the pool came on and the family collected various belongings and toys and moved in a disorganized group back to their room. We planned to leave before seven the following morning, so gathered our own things and made our way back upstairs. I unlocked the door and opened it, and felt Peter's arms come around me and his body move against mine.

I turned, dropping my bag, meeting his kiss with a rush of instantly enflamed lust, barely registering that the door swung shut behind us. We threw ourselves at each other, pulling impatiently at buttons and straps, clumsy with the force of our desire and pulsing with expectant heat. We didn't make it the twelve steps to the bed, using a nearby wall to prop us up until we slid fluidly to the floor, my back cooled by the tile of the entryway, in no way disturbed by the hard ceramic surface. I was too absorbed in Peter—Peter's mouth, Peter's skin, Peter inside me moving me in ways I'd never thought to imagine—to be bothered by anything outside of us.

We'd made love quickly before, and slowly. Though we hadn't talked much about sex outside of the act, we'd begun to learn each other's likings and had been relatively successful in coming to mutual release, one way or another. This time was different from all others before it. It was faster, wilder, more intense, deeper on every level—and it was with a kind of blissful, wide-eyed astonishment that we came at the same moment, moving together to kiss and breaking away to gasp as our bodies shuddered with pleasure.

As our breathing and heartbeats slowed, we lay on the floor for a time, limbs casually tangled. I marveled at this thing that life had brought me—this person. Nobody had ever made me feel like that... so wanted, *craved* even. So safe and so fiercely aroused at the same time. What was between us felt so utterly right, it was tempting to be afraid of it—to call it "perfect" and stumble quickly from there to "nothing is perfect, so it must not be real," to "it can't last." The fear of loss hangs so easily over those things we grasp the tightest.

But I couldn't think of it as perfect, so the rest didn't follow. I couldn't think of Peter as perfect.

Not only because of the strained, criminal-ridden situation we found ourselves in, which wasn't ideal. It was more than that. The sex was, admittedly, *really* good. And we got along with an ease and effortlessness that might have been boring or false, except it wasn't. It wasn't that we were so alike, just that we were alike in not feeding off of or enjoying drama. At the same time, just because we hadn't had our first fight yet didn't mean a first fight wasn't coming—I wasn't so besotted as to believe it would always be as easy and exciting as this past week.

No, it wasn't perfect. It was an insane lucky beautiful unlikely blessing, one that neither of us had ever thought to hope for in our years of solitude and unhappy relationships. It was something real and precious and worth whatever it asked of us, because it wouldn't ask us to give up ourselves. It had flaws, just like we had flaws—but it worked. I wasn't scared of losing it because it was so good. I was just endlessly, utterly grateful for it, down to my core, no matter what the future held.

If we found in a week or a year that it wasn't working, it would be devastating. But we'd survive it, and walk away knowing that we took the chance with the best intentions. I knew that like I knew my own name.

"You know," Peter said sleepily from my hair, "this floor is really cold."

As soon as he mentioned it, the tile was freezing and hard and extremely uncomfortable. Together we pulled ourselves up and crawled, drained and drowsy, into bed.

■ ■ ■

At two o'clock I woke up—was startled awake, from a nightmare I didn't want to remember. I was sweating under the light blankets and pushed them off, then got up to go to the bathroom and drink glass after glass of water from the tap. When I finally lay down again, cooled and hydrated, I found that my eyes wouldn't close.

Tomorrow we'd be on our way. If all went well, tomorrow night we would be in San Francisco, checking into our extravagantly expensive room. And from there… whatever happened would happen.

I was lying on my back, staring at the ceiling, when my phone alarm began to trill. I couldn't remember, as I frantically groped to silence the sound, why I'd set it for such an odd time, two twenty-four, and then memory returned. I needed to send the email. Maybe my brain woke me in anticipation of that task, unconsciously aware of it hanging over my head. I quickly found the draft I'd written and hit send without looking at it again, then set down my phone and tried to go back to sleep.

After another twenty minutes, I knew it wasn't going to happen. My mind was too busy spinning endlessly through what might be true and what could happen, too anxiously occupied to let me relax again. I resolutely pulled out one of the novels I'd brought on the trip but hadn't yet read, a cozy mystery, turned on the low light by my bed, angled so that it didn't reach Peter, and forced myself to focus on the words. To this day I don't remember what happened in that story, even though I read every line and made myself pay attention. When Peter finally stirred at six thirty, dawn had brightened the edges of the curtains and I was on the last chapter.

"Morning," he said, rubbing his eyes and yawning.

"Morning."

"How long have you been up?" He rolled over and sat up, stretching.

"A while. I couldn't sleep," I said, not bothering to add that I'd privately resolved to wake him if his internal clock hadn't done the job first. "But I can always doze in the car."

Peter nodded and wandered into the bathroom. After a minute or two, I heard the shower going, making me realize that I really should have gotten up earlier and started getting ready to go. I began to pack my things, pulling out clean clothes (nearly my last) for the long drive ahead and shoving everything back into my duffel. If this adventure went many days longer, I'd need to do laundry.

As soon as Peter got out of the shower, I was ready to jump in, rushing through washing and conditioning my hair, soaping and shaving dangerously fast with Peter's razor since I'd forgotten to grab mine out of my cosmetic bag. He hadn't bothered to shave his stubble since we left on the trip, but I think we both felt the unspoken need to smarten ourselves up for our arrival at the Four Seasons. We didn't want to be Those Guests, standing out in any way because of our scruffiness.

We were doing a last check of the room and on our way shortly after seven, stopping to grab coffee and breakfast burritos before we got on the freeway. Our route on Interstate 10 would take us through Phoenix, Palm Springs and LA, where we'd join Interstate 5 north through the Central Valley.

About an hour outside Tucson, I noticed that I had a new email from an address I didn't recognize. It consisted of a lot of numbers and letters, so I would have trashed it as spam except for the subject. One word: "Lo."

I made a strangled noise and urgently waved the phone at Peter, who continued to drive with commendable steadiness.

"What happened?" he asked patiently.

"A message—from Marianne!" I nearly shouted, quickly tapping to read it.

stop it lo. it's going to be fine. you're freaking out over nothing. we have this handled, ok? just relax and stay far away. I know the people running this thing told you to be there but you have to ignore their bullshit. it's too dangerous and I've been through too much to have you screw it up. it was good to see you in ny but that's it. stop contacting me and CHILL OUT. love m

"She totally *got* it," I said excitedly, after reading this aloud to Peter. "She understood what my message was for and is helping us set the trap!"

"Looks like Brendan was right," Peter said, smiling sideways at me. "She hoped we'd take this chance."

"*Planned* for it, you mean," I corrected. As excited as I was to see this sign of her support, it still rankled the tiniest bit.

"True, but... Look at it this way. She's going on faith—trusting that we're taking some kind of action with the dirt she managed to pull together on her parents. We were the ones who tracked her down in New York. Up to that point, she did everything she could to keep you out of it. You chose to walk back in, and she's taking that at face value and making the most of the opportunity."

"You're right," I admitted. "But why didn't she just—arrange everything with us? The night we saw her?"

"We can't know that, but I still think it was a snap decision. She thought of it once she saw us—and it's possible she wasn't even sure she was going through with it until after she had a chance to talk to us. She didn't know how you were going to react to the truth, Lola. It might have been different—you might not have *wanted* to help."

"She knows me better than that," I said, but even as I spoke understood that the statement wasn't fair. Marianne knew everything about me... except how I might respond to her story. She'd had to take a huge leap of faith in sharing it with us—not only with me, who might very well have turned on her, but with Peter, a total stranger I brought along.

Peter said nothing; he knew he didn't need to point this out.

He had some music loaded on his phone, a mix of genres, so we turned that on and drove in a companionable silence. Somewhere during the Eagles Live I dozed off, eased into sleep by the motion of the car and the changeless landscape. I must have been more tired than I realized—from my sleepless night, from everything that had happened—because I slept for nearly five hours. I woke up with a guilty start to find that we were already well into California, entering the eastern edges of the LA area.

"I'm so sorry—I completely conked out on you!" I said repentantly.

"You didn't miss anything," Peter assured me, smiling. "You were tired. But I'm about ready to take a break and stretch my legs. I thought we'd stop for gas in Pasadena, if you can wait another twenty minutes or so."

My full bladder, probably the reason I woke up at all, was now clamoring for my attention, but it could stick it out for twenty minutes.

"I can wait. You've made really good time."

"Not too much traffic on the roads. It was a little slow in Phoenix, but since then I've been able to go around eighty."

"Let me know if you want me to take over after we stop."

"I think I'll be OK, but thanks."

First car trip, I thought. *He'd rather drive than be driven.*

I began to collect empty wrappers and water bottles and other trash, ready to clear out when we stopped. It was just as well the wait wasn't longer, because now that I was conscious I was increasingly uncomfortable, just about at bursting point when Peter smoothly took us off the freeway and pulled into a Chevron.

"I'll be right back," I gasped, dashing for the door of the station shop.

Fortunately one of the two bathrooms was unoccupied and I was able to find quick relief. After washing my hands and checking myself in the small, scratched mirror, I came out to see Peter through the window filling the rental car's gas tank, and took the time to stock up on more snacks and drinks. With a ten-cent plastic bag in hand full of bottled water, sodas, chips and candy, I came back outside just as Peter returned the nozzle to its dock. He took his turn at the bathroom while I washed the bug-spattered windshield, then we were back in the car.

Nearby was every kind of fast food imaginable, and he opted to stop at Wendy's before we got back on the freeway, ordering a burger and fries while I chose a chicken sandwich. It was long past noon, and though we'd bought a bagful of snacks in Tucson, there's nothing like hot greasy fast food to satisfy hunger on a road trip.

We ate in the shrub-lined, shady parking lot. While Peter took our wrappings to the nearest trash can, I went into my phone settings and granted Facebook and Instagram permission to access my location services. I then logged into the Facebook app and allowed it to tag me at this business, Wendy's in Pasadena, double-checking that my privacy settings were set to "public." I did the same with Yelp, giving it five stars. I thought that was enough to start with. Before we left LA, I'd log into my bank account and use location services on the app to find a nearby ATM. As soon as we got to San Francisco, I'd do it all over again—at the Four Seasons and nearby.

Either they'd know it was a trap and stay away, or they'd think I was an idiot and come to find me. Or a third option I couldn't think of—and didn't want to try.

■ ■ ■

I found I didn't have any desire to sleep any longer, feeling wide awake, distracted and uneasy. The closer we got to the Bay Area, the more my anxiety grew. Peter seemed lost in his own thoughts, his eyes on the road. We had no more plans to make. Whatever was coming, we'd already set it in motion.

I knew Peter felt responsible for suggesting that we go to New York in the first place, that we download the evidence, and that we not only send the evidence to the police but set up the trap, using Marianne and me as the only available bait. Of course they were his ideas, but I was just as responsible for agreeing to them. If it hadn't been for me, meeting me and hearing my problems, he'd still be living a quiet life in Half Moon Bay, helping his sister prepare for the coming storm.

I was the catalyst that set him on this path, just like Marianne had been my catalyst. *Like vampires siring each other*, I thought vaguely, not that the metaphor really fit. Maybe it was the sense of doom that hung over me that made me think of horror stories. I wasn't even a fan of the genre.

It was just after six when we merged onto I-580 West, continuing to make good time in spite of sporadic mires of traffic on I-5. Bay Area freeways were crowded, as usual, and as I navigated us to the rental car office in Oakland, traffic continued to crawl. I wasn't sure whether to be glad or sorry that these last miles were taking so long. On one hand, I desperately wanted to be out of the car. My body was cramped and I had to go to the bathroom again.

On the other hand, the sooner we arrived, the closer we'd be to the center of the web.

There was no going back now.

We finally got off the freeway at MacArthur Boulevard and were soon turning into the returns area of the rental car office parking lot. After a hectic minute spent clearing out the clutter of trash and belongings, Peter checked the car in, we loaded up our bags and headed in the direction the employee had pointed out to us, toward the nearest BART station. It was a short walk, maybe half a mile, and tired as I was it felt good to move my legs.

We only waited about two minutes for the next Richmond-Daly-City-bound train, finding two seats in the middle of a semi-crowded car, shoving our bags at our feet. Just like in New York, plenty of people used BART to get to the airport, so it wasn't unusual to see fellow passengers towing suitcases or strapped to large backpacks.

I felt sick as we swayed our way through the tunnel under the bay, staring out the blank black windows. The train was stuffy and my stomach full of too-salty and too-sweet food without any nutritious value. It didn't help that every mile drew us closer to an unknown end.

"Hanging in there?" Peter asked me quietly. I nodded and held on. He slipped his arm around my back, and I leaned into his shoulder, breathing in his now-familiar smell. It helped.

Once we reached the city, our stop was the second after Embarcadero. We stood as Montgomery Street neared, hauling up our bags and pushing out with the crowds. I was anxious to get to our hotel room, the privacy and the quiet. The air in the city was fresh and cool, the sky just fading in the last of the western light. It felt so different from the desert, here on the edge of the cold, unfathomable Pacific Ocean. Half a block down were the subdued glass doors of the Four Seasons.

Entering, we were instantly transported into a world of gleaming floors, polished wood walls and ambient lighting. The lobby was dotted with people, milling around, standing at the front desk, sitting in tasteful groupings of chairs. Of those I noticed, most looked like tourists, the expensively-dressed kind who could afford to stay here, with a smattering of businesspeople who were probably taking advantage of their per diem.

We waited a few minutes for the next available clerk, a politely effusive young man. He checked us in efficiently and with considerable aplomb, making sure we knew all of the many amenities that the hotel offered its exalted guests. It was such a far cry from our bargain motel in Tucson, I had to smother a laugh on our way to the elevators. We'd refused the help of a bellboy; no need to waste five dollars on a tip when we only had light bags.

We made our way up to the sixteenth floor and followed the signs to our room. The door opened to a low-lit, beautifully-decorated space with a clean, modern design. A large part of the open space was taken up with a king-size bed, but there was also a café table with two chairs, an armchair with matching footstool, the usual dresser-console below the flat screen TV and a long, padded window seat. The curtains were open, the views spectacular. Our room looked over the city, versus the bay, alight with activity as the dark of evening settled.

I went to the bathroom then made way for Peter, conscientiously pulling out my phone to check in my location at the hotel. I also did a quick ATM search, and made sure that the map apps were registering where I was. I sat down on the pristine white expanse of bed, the phone in my hand, unsure what to do next.

A soft knock on the door had me up on my feet, meeting Peter as he came out of the bathroom.

"Someone's at the door," I whispered urgently.

Without answering, he walked calmly over to it and looked through the peephole.

"It's an employee," he said in a low voice, then opened the door.

"Excuse me, sir," I heard a voice say. "But you left your credit card at the front desk."

"Oh, did we? Thanks," Peter said, accepting the card the man held out.

"You're welcome, sir. Have a good evening."

"Thanks, you too," Peter said. He took a half step toward me and looked down at the card. The door was slowly falling shut. There was a split second before it latched, and in that second someone pushed it open.

"There you are," a woman's voice said, with insincere warmth. "We were wondering when you two would get here."

And in walked my aunt Rosemary, closely followed by my uncle, Leonard.

The spiders had arrived.

chapter 18

As soon as Rosemary appeared in the doorway, Peter had moved to block her from entering—but the sight of the small, dully gleaming gun Leonard DiGregorio held made him stop and begin to back toward me instead. The door closed with a sickening thud, and Rosemary turned to quickly lock the bolt and chain before coming forward.

"Have a seat," she ordered, her face a smooth, expressionless mask.

We edged our way over to the low window seat and sat down, Peter taking my hand in his. It felt warm and clammy—but maybe it was mine that was clammy.

I didn't know how to react to this development. Part of my mind thought, *holy crap, it worked!*—*they traced us here*, while another part was absolutely terrified, and another regretted that they'd entered the trap before the police arrived, assuming they were going to arrive at all, which seemed unfortunate, and across it all I seemed to just be watching, waiting blankly for what came next.

Without touching anything, Rosemary sat down in one of the chairs beside the table, while Leonard stood stolidly at her shoulder. We all examined each other for a tense moment. They were older, I saw—the sun and time hadn't been especially kind to either of them. Leonard had lost of most of the top of his hair and shorn off the rest, leaving him bald. His clean-shaven face was lined, his eyes sharp and suspicious. He never once lowered the gun, pointed somewhere between the two of us. It had a silencer; at least, it had a long nose attached to the muzzle, so I dazedly assumed that it must be a silencer.

My aunt, who I'd vaguely known as a brunette like Marianne, was a fashionable redhead—though the color had begun to grow out, leaving a half-inch wide stripe of gray at her scalp. She wore heavy eye shadow and bright maroon lipstick, which I personally thought was a mistake. Her skin, too, was lined, and showed signs of sunspots in spite of an obvious attempt to hide them under makeup. Her eyes were sharp and subtle, giving nothing away.

Both of their teeth had grown brownish, and they smelled of stale cigarettes and cloying perfume and cologne. They wore plain clothing, khakis and light jackets and sensible shoes, carrying small canvas bags; clothing so plain you didn't notice what they had on. In a crowd of tourists in any city, they would blend in beautifully.

I didn't know what they saw when they looked at us, but whatever it was didn't seem to intimidate them.

"All too easy," Rosemary said coolly, echoing my thoughts. "You couldn't have been more obvious if you'd taken out an ad in the paper. Fortunately we were able to catch an early flight."

"A flight from where?" Peter inquired.

It was reassuring that his voice was so steady, even while his hand grasped mine tightly. Rosemary gave a short laugh and shook her head.

"Nice try, whoever you are. Your bad luck for getting mixed up in this." She sounded raspier than I remembered, less cultured. Probably they'd been putting on some kind of act when my parents were around. The humanitarian act. "So, Lola. We don't have a lot of time, and we don't want to spend it watching your boyfriend bleed out. What does Marianne have on us? And what the hell do you know about it?"

I swallowed, unsure of what to say. Nothing I'd thought or imagined had prepared me for this. For being face to face with them, eye to eye, questioned brutally and simply. I had no stratagems, no games, no glib answers.

"Is Marianne here?" I found myself asking—surprising all of us about equally.

"She's on her way," Leonard said, speaking for the first time. His accent wasn't American, but I couldn't bother to identify it just now.

"Yes, so there isn't any time to waste," Rosemary agreed, so much master of the situation that I felt a faint spark of annoyance. This was *our* trap. Whether or not they'd sprung it too soon, before the authorities had a chance to intervene, it was ours. They were *our* pawns, not the other way around.

Not that it really mattered. They had the gun.

"Marianne told us how to find evidence—against you," I said, sticking to the truth. "We got it to the authorities—and made a deal to get her immunity if she testified," I added. I'd been trying to think of a way to do that, so it didn't ring false to me. I didn't know if they'd believe it, but it would explain why Marianne had to be present.

A short, ominous pause followed.

"What evidence?" Rosemary asked lightly.

So Marianne hadn't shown it to them yet. Either she hadn't been able to access it, or she'd waited for us to make our move first...

"A bunch of stuff—I didn't see all of it," I said quickly. "Passports and names—it was about something in Brazil."

Leonard looked positively ugly with anger, but Rosemary took it in stride.

"So she was coming here to turn herself in? We guessed as much," she said, turning her head to briefly meet her partner's gaze. "We'll just have to make sure she doesn't have the chance."

"Should've done it ages ago," Leonard said darkly.

Australian, I guessed, unable to help myself.

"Maybe so," Rosemary shrugged. As if it didn't matter very much. She stared at me with narrowed eyes, which I met as unflinchingly as possible. "So this is how you turned out," she commented, not sounding impressed. "You look nothing like your mother."

I had no response. It was true: to a casual observer, I didn't look like either of my parents, though a more perceptive person could have told you that I had my mother's eyebrows and nose and my father's mouth. Now that I thought about it, Marianne looked a little like Rosemary; they had the same heart-shaped face. But the resemblance ended there.

"Better get on with it. Both of you, on your knees. Here." She pointed at the small area of carpet in front of her.

Peter, with a stricken glance at me, slowly stood up, pulling me with him. I knew what he meant to do. Before they had a chance to kill us outright, he was going to go for the gun. Leonard, while discernibly strong and wiry, was also at least thirty years older. Peter might just have a chance of taking Leonard down if he moved at the right moment.

Which meant I'd need to tackle Rosemary.

I couldn't tell if she was armed, but I could only assume she had some form of deadly weapon on her person and wouldn't be afraid to use it. I started to mentally psych myself up for it, knowing that my chances of success were slim at best. They were cagey and clever enough to watch for an attack. They would shoot before we got a chance to do more than try. We took a step forward, then another.

Rosemary stood, impatiently gesturing at the ground. My muscles tensed. I heard Peter take a quick breath.

Oh, God, this is it, I thought shakenly, even as I told myself to go for her eyes.

With the impact of a shot, a peremptory knock broke across the grim silence. I started as Rosemary involuntarily turned toward the sound and Leonard swung the gun directly into Peter's chest, staring at him with menacing intensity. After only the slightest hesitation, Rosemary walked cautiously to the door, just as Peter had done, and peered out through the peephole. Her breath came out in a quick, quiet huff.

A huff of triumph.

"Lo?" I heard a muffled voice say. "Are you in there?"

Marianne.

■ ■ ■

Rosemary reached to pull me roughly forward, her fingers digging into the flesh of my arm. Peter, frozen, the gun still pressed to his clavicle, stood back, watching me with a tight mouth and eyes. They didn't need to tell us to be quiet.

This close to her, the odors of tobacco and perfume were almost overpowering. I tried to hold my breath as the unpleasantly noxious combination hit my nose.

"Get her in here," she hissed in my ear.

Unlocking the door with shaking hands, I grasped the handle and opened it. Just outside, Marianne's eyes, wide and dark, met mine. Two men heavy with bulletproof gear stood some distance down the hall, out of sight of the peephole, staring at me. Holding guns.

The police.

"Marianne," I breathed, my eyes twitching to the men and back to her. "Come inside."

Marianne also glanced at her daunting companions, then back at me.

"I can't believe you were stupid enough to come here," she scolded audibly, then mouthed, "Are they in there?"

I nodded very slightly and swiveled my eyes to my right, behind the door. She looked around and nodded at the men I could see, who silently moved closer to the wall and gestured—presumably to others farther away.

I was too frightened to be reassured by their presence. Too frightened to be relieved to see my cousin or the reinforcements with her. Leonard had a gun pressed against Peter's heart.

I moved back a little, repeating nervously, "Come in."

Rosemary yanked me out of the way as Marianne stepped into the room, then set her shoulder against the door as it closed. Showing no surprise at the sight of her parents, Marianne gazed briefly at her mother before slipping a protective arm around my shoulders.

"Well, here we all are. Seems like old times, right?"

She never once looked at Leonard directly, with a dismissal that was an insult in itself. Through ringing ears, I heard him give a muted, vicious snarl. She kept a firm hold of me, maneuvering us so that our backs were to the open bathroom door.

"How fortunate," Rosemary said, with chilling satisfaction.

Marianne inclined her head. She wore black from head to toe: long black jacket buttoned to the neck, slacks and boots. Above the black, inches from mine, her face was drawn and bloodless. Her familiar scent surrounded me, and I took a deep breath, my eyes on Peter.

"Oh, I wouldn't have missed it for the world," Marianne was saying. "In fact, I ordered champagne—I didn't know you'd be here, of course, but it doesn't matter. You can toast with us."

"How civilized of you, Marianne. But I'm afraid we don't have time for that. One more body won't matter, will it? Everyone—down on your knees."

"Was that the plan? Hmm. Not an ideal place for a group execution, so messy..." Marianne murmured. "Three corpses *is* kind of a lot, you know."

"You may be right," Rosemary said, not at all thrown. "Just the two, then, as planned. The third person can, ah... take a little walk with us. Do you volunteer?"

"That could work," Marianne agreed, ignoring the question. "Though a bloodbath *and* a hostage—not quite your style, is it? 'Get out clean and fast,' isn't that what you always said? Not what you always did, though. Rio, for instance. This time you might not be so lucky."

Rosemary's icy façade showed a crack as she glared furiously at her daughter, quickly smoothed over. I wasn't sure which was more terrifying—the mask, or the glimpse of blinding rage.

"Well, all the more reason not to waste time. Step away from her—you two, down on your knees!"

"Oh, I don't think so," Marianne said sweetly.

The third knock shattered even Rosemary's calm—she barely moved, but visibly shook with rage and frustration. Marianne's hand tightened on my arm as my body gave a startled jolt. I looked anxiously at Peter, but thankfully for us, Leonard seemed to have nerves of steel. One finger twitch and Peter would be dead.

"Champagne," Marianne announced. "My treat."

Rosemary, after a long look through the door, stared suspiciously at her daughter. The knock came again, followed by a man's voice saying, "Room service."

"Don't try anything stupid," Rosemary warned softly.

She glanced at Leonard, who positioned himself behind Peter. I didn't have to see it to know the gun was now pressed into his spine.

"Oh, please," Marianne said impatiently, pushing me aside—off balance, I stumbled partway into the lighted bathroom—and reached to open the door.

I expected all hell to break loose—that the cops would come in, guns ablaze, shouting for everyone to put their hands up. But instead I heard the muted sound of a trolley being wheeled into the room. A correct-looking waiter was pulling a bottle out of an ice bucket, preparing to open it.

Marianne watched him, an ambivalent smile playing on her lips. Rosemary stood back, motionless, her face livid under the thick makeup, while Peter's expression was inscrutable. I saw a

glance pass between him and Marianne, but before I could guess
what it meant, the waiter had lifted the bottle slightly and, without
further ado, flung it directly at Peter and Leonard.

As it came flying, Peter dropped and hit the floor with a loud
thump. The bottle caught Leonard—still holding the gun—full in
the chest. He fired once as he staggered back, the bullet making
little sound as it left the chamber and lodged itself into a wall just
beyond Rosemary's head.

That's when hell broke loose. Somehow the door hadn't been
allowed to latch; it was flung open, the floodgate was released and
what seemed like dozens of armed and unyielding strangers filled
the small space, shouting commands. It was probably less than a
dozen, but all the noise and movement made everything more
frenzied.

I immediately put my hands in the air, as did Peter, still sitting
on the floor, in some danger of being trampled. I saw the waiter
and two other figures wrestling with Leonard, pushing him face
down across the window seat and seizing the gun from his
reluctant fist. Marianne and Rosemary stood surrounded,
Marianne with her hands up, Rosemary against the wall, rigid with
shock and fury.

She wasn't rigid for long, though.

In the chaos of the offensive, while more officers ran to help
subdue Leonard and others checked the room and covered the
rest of us, Rosemary collapsed into a wholly convincing faint,
caught just in time by two of the officers closest to her. Her body
went slack, drooping awkwardly as gravity pulled her full weight
downward. Just beyond her, I noticed Marianne move slightly,
opening her mouth as if to speak.

Before she could say anything, before the two would-be-
rescuers could do more than try to set the limp form down in the
limited floor space between boots and trolley, it came to sudden,
startling life in their arms. Taking advantage of the element of
surprise, Rosemary nimbly wriggled out of their now-slack hands
and threw herself toward the open doorway, twisting in mid-air to

viciously kick both of them in the knee. She twisted again and landed easily on her feet while the officers stumbled against each other with surprised grunts of pain, falling clumsily to block the exit behind her.

I'd never seen anything like it—the speed, the grace, and the violence of her movements.

She'd disappeared before they could do more than wheeze for backup, struggling to get up and give chase while more feet pounded down the hall.

■ ■ ■

There was no way to know if she'd managed to make it out. I couldn't think. I watched as Marianne, lowering her arms and hugging them to herself, talked to a woman who came in shortly after Rosemary's departure. Only five cops were left in the room now: two guarding the sullenly handcuffed Leonard, the one Marianne was talking to, one who was helping Peter up, and one who just finished checking the bathroom and closet.

"You can put your hands down," he said to me.

"Oh," I said, and did so.

Peter slowly walked over, nodding at the guard beside me. The man—I wasn't sure if he was an officer or an agent or what; his vest said FBI—patted each of us down, thoroughly if rapidly, and stepped away to talk to his colleagues. Marianne gestured for us to join her, reaching to hug me tightly as we approached.

"Was that what you expected?" she asked tartly, squeezing hard before letting go.

She gave me a little shake and looked from us to the official next to her—a woman of about forty, I now saw, who evidently held a position of authority. Like the others, she wore an FBI vest, hers over a severe white shirt and black slacks. Added to this were glasses and minimal makeup, dark hair pulled back in a tight ponytail. She held a phone in her hand, and seemed not to carry a gun.

"You're the people who sent the information to us," the official stated, her face giving nothing away.

"I did," I said quickly, before Peter could answer.

"Where did you get it?"

"On—from the darknet," I said steadily.

She nodded and looked at Marianne.

"Right. Well, we'll need to take your full statements about what happened tonight and leading up to this arrest."

"OK," I agreed, feeling like anything I said right now would be disjointed at best.

"For the time being, we're going to leave you here. We need to get the suspect processed and mobilize our teams. We'll have officers posted outside and in the lobby. Please don't try to leave."

"Did you get her?" Peter asked, speaking for the first time.

"Not yet," the official said stonily, and I wondered how many people would be held accountable for that. The idea of my aunt—who was even more dangerous than I'd ever imagined—having escaped, the threat she presented, hadn't sunk in yet. It was enough that Leonard was in custody.

That we were safe, at least for now.

We stood in the hallway—conveniently empty of other guests, lined with several more armed officers—while they brought Leonard out. Now that he was alone, unarmed and in restraints, he seemed less terrifying, more of a brutish bully than a cunning villain. It was a false impression; I'd seen in his eyes just how ruthless and calculating he was, but he'd been caught, and on top of that, abandoned by his helpmate. Not to say she'd given up on him, but you couldn't deny that she'd saved herself and left him to deal with his fate.

Sneering a little, Leonard marched down the hall under heavy guard, toward the nearest service elevator. Most of the rest of the officers followed, leaving one man in plainclothes—a secret-service-like suit—outside our door. He stood passively next to the abandoned champagne trolley, which had been wheeled outside to get it out of the way.

Pausing to speak to us before she left, the official in charge said, indicating the man, "There are more of them around. I doubt she'll come back—they lost her on Market—but if she does she won't make it up here. Stay in the room or we'll take you into custody."

We went inside and she shut the door firmly behind her, leaving us to look at one another. I went over and sat down on the bed, staring vacantly at the wall.

"How'd she do that?" Peter asked Marianne, coming to sit beside me. "Escape, I mean."

Marianne shrugged.

"Judo... and some other things," she said.

"But there were more police in the hall... downstairs..."

"She's fast—and thinks fast. I didn't think she'd manage a clean getaway, but you have to admit it was impressive."

She walked over to the hotel courtesy phone and picked up the receiver.

"I need a drink—or several," she muttered to no one in particular, then placed an order for three hamburgers with fries and a bottle of Johnny Walker Black.

"I can't afford that," I protested when she'd hung up, dollar signs dancing in front of my bleary eyes.

"It's fine," she waved it away. "I'll cover it." She threw herself into the nearest chair, which happened to be the one Rosemary had lately occupied, and gave a choke of laugher. "You wouldn't believe how excited they were to have a lead on such wanted criminals—on U.S. soil, no less. I think the Interpol people just about had kittens."

Without saying anything, Peter got up and handed each of us a cold bottle of water from the mini-bar, as well as taking one for himself. They were probably sixteen-dollar water bottles, but I heedlessly opened mine and drank deeply from it. Marianne did the same.

"Marianne, how did you get here? What happened?" I asked, suddenly wildly curious.

"I knew what you were planning from your email last night," she said. "It was what I'd hoped you'd do—I mean, not exactly *this*, but I hoped you send everything to the authorities. Thank God the evidence came through."

"We thought as much," Peter said. "Though I'm still curious as to why you didn't just turn it over to the authorities yourself."

"Chicken, I guess," she said, looking uncomfortable for the first time. "I… I'd seen what they did to people who crossed them. If I turned them in and they found out about it—they wouldn't just take me out, they'd take out Lo and anyone else connected to us. I mean, sure, ideally the Feds could protect us, but what if they didn't? And what if it didn't help—what if they never got arrested? I wasn't even convinced my contact hadn't cheated me and the proof wasn't there at all. If *you* got it to the powers that be, at least it couldn't be traced back to me and Lo, or not right away. And then I got Lo's email and saw what you meant to do, and that was even better. I'd be the best chance to pin them down—if I led them here it could only sweeten the temptation, so I let it be known I was on my way to San Francisco. They must have arrived not long before me. They were somewhere in Venezuela, working on a deal there, so it didn't take them long to get here."

"But how did you connect with the police—or whoever they were?" I asked.

"Mostly FBI, though the woman we were talking to was Interpol. They were in the service areas when I got here, just setting up their surveillance. Great timing, right? I asked at the front desk and was shown back, managed to talk my way to someone who'd listen and gave them a brief rundown on what was going on—with a few edits. I told them that as a family member and reformed associate of the DiGregorios, I'd been the source of the information which you'd sent on. As soon as they checked the register and hotel security cameras, they saw Rose and Leo heading to your room right on your heels, clear as day. I insisted that this was a trap and we were the bait, and they needed to act fast if they wanted to nab the bad guys. I don't think the rest of them would have listened, but the woman in charge— Nelson—had a lot of background on her targets and believed me when I said there was a hostage situation going on. You didn't mean to be sitting ducks, I told her, you just couldn't help it."

"I won't argue with you," Peter said with some bitterness. "We should have seen it coming."

Marianne shrugged.

"I don't know if you ever see them coming. At least help was nearby. Anyway, she held off arresting me long enough to check out my story and let me try the door first, with the whole champagne stunt. From something she said about 'not taking any chances this time,' it made me think she could have been part of the team who almost caught them in Rio. That was a huge clusterfuck, I wouldn't be surprised if it left some scars. Whatever happened, she wasn't willing to risk it happening again, and she's calling the shots—or at least she was. Seems like now the Feds are taking over." She gulped water and made a face. "I just hope none of them are ripe for corruption. Leonard's a master at bribing the un-bribable."

"It's crazy how fast everyone got here," I said, more to myself than anyone else.

"Hey, you get a hot tip like that, it's worth acting on. They didn't have a very big team, though, did you notice that? That's probably how she got away. I wonder if they even told SFPD they were coming here."

"Surely they have to?" Peter asked in surprise.

"Do they, though? At best it might be an FYI or something."

"I'm sure the hotel is thrilled," I said, thinking of what Brendan had said. Though really, wasn't that partly why I'd chosen it? The incongruity of a fancy hotel being the setting for a sting?

Marianne gave a short laugh.

"As long as they send up our food soon, I don't care. I'm starving. My last meal was airplane peanuts."

"Your parents must have gotten here before we did," Peter said pensively. "Waiting in the lobby, probably. I didn't even bother to look."

"Don't feel bad about it—they're masters at blending in. Probably hung around a big group and laid low until they could make a move. You wouldn't have seen them if you'd been looking. It worked out that you walked in without suspicion and the cops didn't have a big splashy presence, otherwise Rosemary would've sniffed the whole thing out. How did they get into your room, anyway?"

"With this," Peter said, leaning down to pick something up off the floor under the edge of the bed. It was a credit card, but not my credit card. The name was Jeremy Bristow. "One of the employees came to the room to return it to us. They pushed in as he left."

"An oldie, but a goodie. They probably stole the card, strolled by, pretended to pick it up and said, 'Oh, that nice young couple dropped this, someone should take it to their room immediately.'"

Her impression of her mother was uncannily accurate, if exaggerated. A shudder went up my spine.

"What if it hadn't worked?" Peter persisted.

"They'd have figured out something else. They always do."

■ ■ ■

A few minutes of silence followed this depressing remark. I finally got up and went to the bathroom, washed my hands and face, looked longingly at the shower but decided to wait. When I came back out, Marianne and Peter were still sitting on bed and chair, contemplating each other across the floor where he'd so recently fallen. Marianne had taken off her jacket and was fiddling with the long hem of her dark gray shirt. I sat down beside Peter and kicked off my shoes.

"I wish I'd known sooner," I said, sipping from my half-full bottle of water.

Marianne nodded.

"Well, I wish you didn't have to know at all," she said, meeting my eyes, "but I'm glad I don't have to lie anymore."

"What's going to happen—to you?"

She sighed and stretched out her legs.

"Oh, I'm turning myself in. What they want to do with me is up to them. I'm sort of surprised nobody's taken me into custody yet, given what I told them, but I guess I'm a small fish compared to Leonard. Anyway it isn't as though I'm going anywhere. Plenty of time to arrest me later." Her voice was breezy, but I wasn't fooled.

"It's… I can't believe how *brave* you are," I marveled. "Going through all of this alone, finding that evidence—"

"Me?" she interrupted. "You're the brave one, you idiot. All I did was keep my head down and cheat a bunch of people."

"You were protecting me—and my parents!"

"And me. Don't forget that," she pointed out sharply. "I could have reported them *years* ago and avoided all this. But you—Lo, when I showed up and told you to run, you *ran* and hid by yourself. I thought for sure you'd go to the police, knowing at least you'd be protected that way, but you didn't. And then you came *looking* for me—"

"That was Peter's idea," I objected, surprised by her vehemence.

"I only suggested it because of you," he said firmly, taking my hand. "Because of who you are. It was obvious that you didn't like the idea of hiding, especially when Marianne might be in trouble. I just gave you a reason to go." I stared at him uncomprehendingly, and he laughed. "You were the one who found *me*—that first night at the bar, when you came around the back, remember? You weren't afraid to take that step… to trust me without any rational reason to. Even though I felt such a strong attraction, I can't honestly say I would have followed up on it if you hadn't walked up to me that night. I agree with your cousin. You're incredibly brave. So is she," he added politely, and she grinned at him.

"But not *as* brave," she said.

"I don't see it," I said, moved and slightly overwhelmed by this unexpected tribute. "I feel like I'm afraid of everything. But thanks."

"It's not about not being afraid—that's where the *bravery* comes in. When push came to shove you were always tougher than me. Remember when you used your parents' computer to hack into that pizza place and get free pizzas delivered? That was the coolest thing I've ever seen, and you were, what, fourteen?"

"Oh, that…" I said, glancing sheepishly at Peter, who raised an eyebrow.

"As soon as you did it, I was positive we were going to get arrested and completely panicked, and you calmed me down and gritted your teeth and said at least we could eat all the pizza first. We ate every slice—and we never did get caught."

"I was probably too immature to know what I was doing. And I never hacked into anything again."

"That wasn't the only time. Far from it. You always just— *jumped*, even if you were scared. There's a reason you learned how to swim a year before I did—and why you were the one who finally convinced me to get into the pool. When Aunt Gina… She told me what you did for her the last time we talked. How strong you were. And, well… anyway." I blinked away sudden tears and swallowed the lump rising in my throat. Marianne gave her eyes a hasty rub, then continued briskly, "Given some of our exploits, I was kind of surprised you didn't offer to get the files off the darknet yourself."

"Ah," Peter said.

"Didn't know your new girlfriend was a certifiable genius, did you?"

"She kept that to herself."

"*Not* a genius," I said. "Far from it. But you're right—I could have done it. I just didn't know I could."

"A useful new skill," Marianne assured me. "Next time I need a hacker I know who to call."

A knock interrupted our conversation, the fourth and final knock that night. We opened the door to find our guard carefully examining a laden room service trolley, while the waiter—a real one this time—stood by, watching him interestedly. After finding nothing untoward in the three hamburgers and bottle of scotch, the guard politely wished us a good evening, nodded to the waiter to enter the room, and, once we'd finished our transaction, escorted him back out. I signed for the bill without even looking at the total, adding a hundred dollars as a tip. If we were going down, might as well go in a burst of fireworks.

We devoured that food—I didn't even remember eating it afterward, it was just a blur of greasy fries and meat and dripping sauce. As soon as we'd finished and were wiping sticky hands on white cloth napkins, Marianne poured the scotch. It went down beautifully, burning in the best way, immediately relaxing my taut nerves.

"So, what'd the parents say to you?" Marianne asked, already on her third glass.

I couldn't judge: I was also well into my third. Peter and I were lounging together on one side of the large bed, propped against the headboard, while she lay across the opposite corner.

"Not much, really," I said, feeling no pain at all. "She said I looked nothing like my mother. And made some threats... they were going to shoot Peter!"

"Both of us, actually," Peter said.

"Bastards," she said, and poured out another round.

"They wanted to know what the evidence was and how you were involved," Peter added, the soberest of the group. "Lola told them you were going to testify in exchange for immunity."

She began to laugh, giggling uncontrollably until she nearly fell off the bed. We watched her tolerantly while she writhed in mirth.

"Oh my God, they must have been wild!" she gasped, calming down at last. "I wish I'd seen it! That's basically their worst nightmare."

"They weren't happy about it," Peter said, then asked, "Would you do it?"

Wiping her eyes with her hands, Marianne took a long sip and swallowed before answering.

"I don't know if the Justice Department—or anybody—will want to make a deal with me," she said. "But yeah. I would. Even if they don't grant me immunity." She let out her breath in a long, shaky sigh. "I've done a lot of things I'm not proud of. Even if I didn't *want* to do them, I still did them. I convinced people the causes were legit. Good people. I lied and helped take their money. Maybe I don't… Maybe I don't *deserve* to be let off the hook."

"Don't sell yourself short," Peter said reasonably. "If it wasn't for you, they wouldn't have anyone to prosecute."

A short silence fell, and then I heard myself asking, "So what's the deal with Leonard—he's *Australian*?"

Marianne choked on another sip, laughing.

"I guess so," she said. "I only found out when they revealed their sordid life of crime. He's convincing in his roles, I'll give him that."

"I'd never have guessed," I said. "Is that his real name?"

"Who knows? They're on my birth certificate as Rosemary Brixton and Leonard DiGregorio, but it doesn't mean much." She hiccupped gently and continued, slurring only a little. "Y'know, I used to hope they weren't my real parents. Maybe they'd just— hic—picked me up somewhere. But I s'pose she gave birth to me. Unfortunately. Don't know if he's actually my dad, though. Hope—hic—lives on."

"Do you think it's strange that my mom never told me she and Rosemary weren't actually related?"

"I dunno. Maybe she wanted us to feel—hic—like real cousins. She was only about a year old when her dad got hitched to Rosemary's mom—looked it up a couple years ago. Rosemary was… twelve. Thirteen? Knowing her, you gotta think she hated a baby around. Bet she was up to no good for years 'fore she hooked up with Leonard and started their—hic—racket. Wherever that was."

"He might've had a record in Australia before coming here," Peter suggested lazily, his eyes half-shut.

"Wouldn't be surprised," Marianne drawled, sloshing another shot into her glass and draining it.

"I wonder whose idea it was," I thought aloud. "The family business."

"They've never shared the story, funny—fun'ly enough."

"It's kind of—fascinating, in a sick way," I said dreamily. The whiskey had made everything soft and blurred.

"Mm," she said, staring up at the ceiling. After a few minutes, her breathing became more regular. She was asleep.

I managed to take a shower without waking her, climbing into the bed as Peter took his turn showering. I was hazily aware of him turning off lights, checking the door, climbing in beside me. And then nothing more.

chapter 19

A loud banging on the door brought us wide awake at six: two sturdy SFPD officers had come to escort us to give our statements at one of the nearby stations. We hurried into clothes while Marianne, looking rumpled and definitely the worse for drink, splashed vigorously in the sink for a few minutes. Very soon after their arrival, the three of us, along with our plainclothes guard from the hall—who, I realized, was actually not the same man as the previous night—were following the officers down the hall to a service elevator, encountering only one surprised and curious pair of early risers leaving their room.

Downstairs, we were loaded into the back of a police SUV, the suited man melting away somewhere. The car windows were tinted a dark shade, so as we drove no one could see us inside, and traffic was light at just after six on a Sunday morning. It was a short trip down Market, turning south of the freeway. None of us spoke.

They pulled into a gated garage, parked and escorted us through a secure door through a network of hallways, asking that we check in our phones, complete with paperwork, before depositing each of us in a different room. I was first to be shown in, exchanging one last glance with Peter, seeing a glimpse of Marianne's pale face, before I was through the doorway and the door was shut behind me. I sat down in the nearest chair to wait.

It wasn't an interrogation room like you see on TV, no double-sided mirror or table with handcuffs. A table and three chairs stood on one side of the small space, while the other side held a scruffy padded bench without a back. The chairs were steel, and not uncomfortable.

After only about ten minutes, the woman in charge from the previous night came in, along with another woman. They introduced themselves as Supervisory Investigative Analyst Pam Nelson from Interpol Washington and Assistant Special Agent in Charge Gabriela Ramirez from the FBI San Francisco Division. Local police still had no place at the table, I noticed.

After they offered, and I accepted, a cup of coffee, which some lackey or other brought in, weak and stale but at least hot, we got down to it. They asked me to explain who I was, how I was involved and the events leading up to and of the previous night. Both jotted a few things down as I spoke, but if I was being recorded they didn't say so.

Peter, Marianne and I somewhat foolishly hadn't compared notes or prepared our stories, so I didn't know what the others were going to say. Figuring the truth—or most of the truth—was best, I told my story. I left out the details—how we tracked down Marianne in New York, for instance, and what we did there—and didn't mention Brendan's name, but otherwise I told them what I knew. I said that Marianne and I were cousins (we were by marriage if not blood) and the woman I knew as Rosemary DiGregorio was my mother's stepsister.

I described how Marianne and I grew up together, and lost touch as we got older, and how I'd never been in contact with my uncle and aunt. And then I said Marianne had told me to hide, that I'd gone to Half Moon Bay, staying at a family property there, until Peter and I had decided to go to New York and confront her.

When we'd found her, she'd told us about her parents' crimes—
not specific details, but generally how they defrauded people by
pretending to set up humanitarian causes, and said she had
evidence against them.

We went to Tucson, where Peter used to live and we figured
we'd be safe, and downloaded the information from the darknet
with Marianne's instructions. And then we'd sent it to the
authorities, along with where we'd be, in the hopes that the
DiGregorios would track us down and, doing so, give the
authorities a chance to catch them. It had worked better than we
expected—we'd never done anything like it before—and they
knew the result.

After hearing me out to this point, the investigators asked me
several questions. Who else knew about this? I said no one, having
already decided not to mention Brendan. What exactly had
Marianne told us?

That was more difficult, but I outlined it as best I could,
explaining that we hadn't had much time to talk. It came down to
the fact that they were using threats to me as leverage against her,
and she hoped to get leverage against them, in order to protect
both of us. They made no comment, but noted this and moved
on. When they asked me to describe the events of the previous
night, I quickly ran through everything that had happened from
the time that we arrived in the city to the moment armed officers
entered the room. It was a surprisingly short interlude in the
telling, though it had seemed to go on for endless, tortured hours
while we were facing the DiGregorios at gunpoint.

Finally, in response to their questions, I said I had no idea
where my aunt might go. We had never been in touch directly,
and both my parents were gone. They cleared up a few other
minor questions about the evidence and my role in obtaining and
sending that; it seemed like they were fishing a little to see if I
really knew what I was talking about. I threw out Tor browsers
and a few basic programming terms, and they seemed satisfied. I

said I'd used a borrowed computer, and they didn't ask whose it was.

Truth be told, I don't know that they really cared. This was all a formality—mine would be useful evidence to charge Leonard with attempted murder, but it was such small potatoes compared to everything else they wanted to get him on, that it seemed like kind of an aside. I did manage to ask them if Marianne was now in custody, but Special Agent Ramirez said they were "unable to discuss her position at this time," which seemed to definitively close that subject. They asked me for my contact information, and I gave it to them, agreeing not to leave the country. I said I'd be staying in Half Moon Bay for the foreseeable future, and then they said goodbye and walked out. I wasn't asked to sign a statement and didn't know if that was a good sign or a bad one, or if I'd be asked anything else.

After a tedious twenty minutes while I wished I could get another cup of terrible coffee and felt increasingly stifled and uneasy, the door opened and a new officer appeared. She handed back my phone, asked me to sign a receipt for it before ushering me out of the room. We walked down more hallways and through another security door, until we reached a sort of kitchen-lounge. The first thing I noticed was Peter, sitting at a table reading a magazine, and felt a powerful rush of relief and gladness.

"Hi," I said sedately, resisting the urge to throw my arms around him.

He smiled and stood.

"They're finished with both of you for today," the officer said simply, and showed us the way out.

We went quietly, following meekly in her wake until we were outside a side entrance to the building, and the door was firmly closed behind us. No ride was offered to take us back, adding even more to my impression of being dismissed as relatively negligible witnesses.

"OK with walking?" Peter asked, and I nodded my assent.

As soon as we'd started to approach nearest thoroughfare, I asked, "What about Marianne? Did they tell you anything?"

Somehow I hadn't wanted to bring it up while we were still within sight of the police building.

"I don't know," Peter said, putting an arm around me and hurrying me along. The morning was pearly gray and cool, the fresh air bracing on my cheeks. "I didn't feel like I could ask. I'm sorry."

"I asked, they said they couldn't discuss her status," I said. "They were polite about it, but I didn't press the issue. I hope she's OK."

"She's a valuable witness. That can only help."

It felt wrong to leave without her, but what choice did we have? Short of demanding information that they were unwilling to give us, and probably annoying them in the process, I didn't feel there was anything more we could do.

We paused to orient ourselves, crossing under the freeway, walking until we reached Harrison Street. Checking Peter's phone, we found the hotel was about a mile away, and once we got to Market it was a simple matter to get there. On the way we stopped at Starbucks and ordered coffees and bagels, eating as we walked.

The street was relatively quiet; we passed the occasional sleeping homeless person, bundled figures on the hard pavement, and scattered groups of early tourists. It was very different from the usual intense bustle and noise. Peaceful in an urban way.

"What did they ask you?" I asked between bites, and we found that both our stories and their questions aligned fairly well. Peter hadn't said anything about our activities in New York, either, nor had he mentioned Brendan.

"They didn't push very hard," he said. "I felt like they were just going through the motions."

"I did, too," I said. "Did they ask you about Hal?"

"No. Either it didn't come up when they checked on me, or they didn't care. It's not their patch, after all."

As we approached the Four Seasons, I said, "Peter—can we go home now?"

"I was hoping you'd say that," he said, opening the glass door for me. Inside, I went straight to the front desk, deserted at this hour but for one sleepy young woman, and said that we needed to check out early. She agreeably looked up our room, said that we were all paid up and just to drop our key cards off when we were on our way out.

We looked at each other in some confusion.

"We're—all paid up?" I asked. "You charged the card from the initial reservation?"

"No, it looks like it was paid in cash last night," she said, then grinned. "We get some of those—people like to throw cash around sometimes."

"And... the room service, too?"

"Yes, all the charges on the room. If any other charges arise, we'll charge the card on file, but all three nights and all room service charges were paid up front."

"Do you—is there any way to find out who paid it?" I asked, bewildered.

"I don't think so," she said doubtfully. "Is it a problem?"

"No," I said slowly. "I mean, of course not. Thanks so much for your help."

"You're welcome. We hope you enjoyed your stay," she recited, though her heart wasn't quite in it. As we turned away, she was surreptitiously yawning into her hand.

"Marianne?" I wondered, and Peter widened his eyes and shrugged. He hit the button to call the elevator as we pondered this new development. Could she have managed it after we fell asleep? Or did she pay when she arrived? She did say she would cover the food.

I couldn't imagine who else would hand over a large amount of cash for our expenses. I really doubted it was any of the agencies involved, no matter how grateful Interpol might be for our role in sharing the evidence. Maybe it would always remain a mystery—

one that I didn't intend to worry about solving. Not having to pay a few thousand for our stay was just fine by me.

We took BART south to the parking lot where we'd left my car. Just as we were stepping off the train, I wondered if it could really still be there, waiting for us. It seemed impossible that only seven days had passed. It felt like weeks—months, even. But my car was, in fact, where we left it, and it started right up. We paid the parking fee, pulled out of the lot, merged onto the nearest freeway entrance. In less than half an hour, we were already entering the outskirts of Half Moon Bay.

"We're home," Peter said, sounding more resigned than happy about it.

"Yeah," I said, echoing his tone.

Maybe it was the exhaustion, but I felt oddly deflated. As if everything had gone from overpowering Technicolor to a kind of drab sepia. Most of the last few weeks had been much more uncomfortable and upsetting than exciting, but all the same... The adventure was over.

For now, anyway.

"Do you mind if we stop by the bar first?"

I didn't mind. We pulled up in the nearly empty lot next to Peter's truck. From the puddles, I guessed it must have rained recently.

"That's Delia's car," he said, indicating a mud-spattered red Subaru Outback. We trudged around to the back entrance, Peter unlocking the door. Before we saw him, we heard the sound of madly scrabbling claws on linoleum, and as the door opened a large, furry form launched itself at Peter, yawping with ecstatic joy. "Get down, you crazy—Yes, buddy, I missed you too. So did Lola. Good boy, lick her instead."

I got my share of the greeting. As we patted the wriggling animal, Delia appeared in her office doorway.

"You're finally back," she said shortly, but there was relief in her eyes. "Did you have a nice trip?"

Peter gave me a quick, smiling glance before saying, "It was good. How's everything with you?"

■ ■ ■

Three afternoons later, I drove up to the bar and parked, grabbing several bags out of the trunk before walking inside through the front entrance. It was just after five on Wednesday and business was still thin, just a few regulars and random drinkers. Lyle was behind the bar, accepting his burger and fries with a drawled, "Thanks, doll." I went on into the back and found Delia and Peter sitting in his office. Delia occupied about a tenth of Osiris's love seat, while he took up the rest of it, his heavy head on her lap.

"Hey," I said, returning Peter's light kiss and handing around food. I told Delia not to get up and perched on the arm of the sofa, prompting Osiris to dig a pointed toe into my thigh. "Any news?"

"Nothing since this morning," Delia said, sounding worried.

Peter and I exchanged a brief, loaded look, then began to eat. Delia picked at her fries, much to Osiris's interest.

"*Down*, Oss," Peter ordered sternly, after the dog had managed to inhale three fries out of her hand. Reluctantly Osiris poured himself onto the floor, looking at his master with mournful brown eyes. I slid down to sit on the seat, ignoring the reproachful stare that came my way.

"What's the worst thing this indictment will do?" I asked. Delia had just heard from her lawyer that morning. The DEA had finally filed the indictment against Hal, and was seeking extradition from Mexico, where, according to her lawyer, he'd been holed up for a month.

"Freeze my assets," she said dully, her face ashen and drawn. "Probably including the bar accounts... Shut down the business."

"Not really," Peter said steadily. "Everything is in my name— even the business license, remember? You and Hal are listed as investors."

"When—did I know that?" Delia asked, bewildered.

"You did. I suggested it, and you both agreed. It gives you limited liability, but also means that technically Hal isn't an owner—neither are you."

"Oh." She stared blankly at him, and then her face crumpled in tears. "Could I... could I have a minute?" she sniffled from behind her hands.

After tactfully handing her a box of Kleenex, we took the rest of our meal and Osiris and left her snuffling quietly into the arm of the couch. As we walked out, Peter grabbed a large white envelope from the desk, handing it to me once we'd found seats at the back of the bar by the pool table. Nobody was playing, so we had the corner of the room to ourselves.

"What's this?" I asked, wiping my hands and taking it from him.

"No idea. It came this morning to your attention."

"To the bar?" He nodded. "That's odd," I said, looking at the return address. It meant nothing to me—an investment company in New York City. "Maybe an ad...? But how would anybody know my connection to the Hideout? My mail's going to your home address."

"Open it and find out."

I ripped the thick envelope and pulled out a stack of documents clipped together, finding a letter addressed to me on top. As I skimmed it, any idea of bizarrely omniscient marketing outreach faded. An electric shiver went up my spine. I choked on the fry I'd absently stuck in my mouth.

"What is it?" Peter asked, pushing his glass of water at me.

I cleared my throat and read him the letter. In summary, an investment firm in New York had been trying to reach me, and somehow—they didn't specify—had heard that I might be reachable at this address. They were the managers of an account started five years ago by my mother, with me listed as her primary legatee. The account had a considerable balance, and as they'd recently if somewhat belatedly been notified of my mother's death, it was now mine. If I would just sign the enclosed papers in the presence of a notary public and return at my earliest convenience, they would ensure my access to the account. If I chose to make any withdrawals, I would then be able to do so.

I flipped through the papers until I found an account statement. I gazed at the figure listed, holding it wordlessly out to Peter.

Nine hundred and sixty-eight thousand dollars and seventeen cents. Peter whistled and handed it back to me.

"Your cousin is really something," he said, with genuine admiration in his voice.

epilogue:
three months later

The bouquet of flowers had been delivered to the bar the previous afternoon, a Sunday, from a nationwide floral delivery service. It was now late Monday morning, overcast but mild with a fresh breeze from the sea. I sat, legs outstretched, in a weather-beaten chair outside the camper. Nearby, Osiris was investigating an interesting smell along the fence, while Peter tightened lug nuts on one of the camper's new tires. He'd suggested that we make it mobile again, and so long as he didn't mind squatting in the leafy dust and futzing with jacks and tools, I was willing to buy four of the right kind of tire and give him my blessing.

We were temporarily living in the camper now; it was too cramped to be a long-term solution, but allowed Peter to save his rent money for wherever we were going to live next. I'd heard from the lawyers that probate would be wound up soon, giving me the option of selling the property—I'd already had a casual offer from the people who owned the adjoining land—or, if permits and zoning could be worked out, building on it.

That was my first choice, and Peter had finally admitted it was his, too. He was reluctant to have me spend the money when he couldn't invest an equal amount. As much as I appreciated the thought, I wasn't about to let such a minor point stop me from going forward.

I still didn't know what I was going to do, but I had money to spare, and property, and a business to help run. Delia had been so distracted with Hal's legal problems, now that he'd been arrested and returned to the U.S. for prosecution, flying back and forth to Texas to deal with business there and see her son, that she hadn't been able to keep up her co-management of the bar. I was glad to help out, especially since the publicity of Hal's case had splashed their names and the Hideout all over the news and brought a rush of curious customers. It was dying down, but had meant a lot more work for everyone.

It was fun to work with Peter, an unexacting but attentive manager. He had a lot of ambitions for the Hideout, and though I wasn't convinced it was going to be my life's work as well as his, I was ready to support whatever he wanted to do.

I glanced over at him, focused and grunting slightly with exertion. The night we got back from San Francisco, we'd finally said out loud what we both felt. It wasn't too soon any longer, not after the agonizing minutes we'd spent with death so close by. Time was too precious to waste feeling bound by conventions.

My eyes moved to the small table next to me. On it sat the bouquet, a hefty, fragrant burst of bright freesias and greenery, clearly the work of an experienced florist. Osiris having knocked over and shattered the original small vase, they graced a plastic pitcher borrowed from the Hideout, looking no less cheerful or attractive for the pedestrian container. In my hand was a letter, which had come with the flowers, sealed tightly in an envelope within an envelope, the address printed on the outer paper.

I'd read it several times. Though I knew the contents by now, I wasn't ready to put it aside yet.

Dear Lo, it read.

I'm not really supposed to be contacting anyone, but I couldn't go any longer without reaching out and bargained for this chance. I'm all right, I promise. I'm in protective custody while they build the cases (there are dozens) against L. He's got extradition orders from about 15 countries and the charges keep piling up. Seems to be a large-scale coordinated investigation now, mostly through IP, and they tell me the information I'm giving is valuable. Though I meant what I said before—I probably don't deserve to go unpunished. Still, I'm not going to argue with them about it.

For now I'm content to sit tight and answer questions and make depositions, but I think I know what I want to do next. Remember when you asked me what I'd do if I got out? It seemed impossible at the time, but now that it's happened I'm getting clearer about who I want to be and what my purpose is. One way or another, I know I'm supposed to be working against people like R and L.

She's out there, Lo. God knows how she did it but she managed to disappear. One of my handlers heard she went down a laundry chute and/or that she had an accomplice. At least L is a consolation prize, but they're still furious about it. I think she's long gone, and it'll be a while before she risks coming to the U.S. again. They've traced a lot of the money to the Caymans and are watching to see if she'll show up (they tell me things like this sporadically) but nothing so far. I'm sure she's got plenty stashed elsewhere, and L's not giving her up, not even to save his own skin. If he wasn't such a creep, I could almost respect him for his loyalty. As bad as he is, she's even worse. And she won't forget easily.

Anyway, enough about that. I hope the flowers are pretty. Freesias always make me think of your mom, and how much she liked them. I don't know what would have happened to me if it wasn't for your parents and you. I thank my lucky stars every day that I got to grow up in your family. I wish mine had left me alone for good, but at least they gave me the gift of years without them and a wonderful, loving home.

I hope everything is good with you and Peter. I'm not sure when I'll be able to get in touch again, but it helps to think of you living a good life. Enjoy the money—it started with the first payout I got, which felt so dirty I just couldn't use it, along with the balance of what your parents saved for me over the years. Spend it on the things you want. (And don't feel like you have to donate it, I've already done that with the rest of what I earned.) Take care of yourself and stay out of trouble.

Love, M

I set the letter down on my knee and looked out across the wide, empty landscape. Marianne was going to be OK. I could only hope that whatever happened, we'd be a part of each other's lives, but even if that wasn't possible, she had the chance to start over and find a new purpose. Not only that, she'd done everything she could to make sure I was OK, too. Even to the point of investing in my future. Things looked much brighter now for all of us—thanks to her.

But she was right. Rosemary was still out there, no doubt plotting her next move. And loathing all of us for the trap we set. We took away the one person she trusted and cared about, forced her into hiding, made her more unpredictably lethal than ever.

The truth was, we might never be safe. Not completely. We'd never be able to forget what we knew about her, never stop being witnesses to her identity, and that was always going to be dangerous. But as much as I hated knowing, and the threat that knowledge was to people I cared about, I couldn't deny that it also gave us power, whether we wanted it or not.

She was out there. And we'd be watching for her.

ABOUT THE AUTHOR

Emily Senecal is the author of suspense novels and other fiction. Originally from Davis, California, and a UC Davis graduate, she continues to live in Northern California.

Made in the USA
Las Vegas, NV
09 June 2021